PIECE BY PIECE

EVERGREEN GROVE, BOOK FOUR

Elisabeth Staab

Publisher's Note: This is a work of fiction. Names, characters, places, and incidents are a product of the author's imagination or are used fictitiously.

Book Layout ©2013 BookDesignTemplates.com

Book Ordering Information:
Quantity sales and special discounts are available. For details, contact the publisher at the address above.

Piece by Piece/ Elisabeth Staab -- 1st ed.
ISBN 978-0-9971366-2-3

To my Tom for being the one who let me know it was safe to laugh out loud.

To Joan Swan, I couldn't have finished this book without you, and I totally owe you lunch. Like, a hundred times over.

To Jillian Stein and Carol Buswell for sharing your jokes, for being amazing ladies, and for more reasons than I could possibly ever list. Giggling with you has been one of my favorite things.

To that middle school art teacher who told me never to give up. I wish to God I could remember your name, but I will never forget your face, or your extremely kind, utterly inspiring words. I picture you when I think I've forgotten how to make art. <3

1. HAPPY FUCKING BIRTHDAY

Ethan

Lemme tell ya. Betrayal from the people you thought you trusted can be one motherfuck of a thwack to the nards.

Especially when the thwacker happens to be family.

Let's take a look at my dad, for example. He was a pretty decent guy when I was growing up. Not dad-like, so much. At least not the way I expected dads to be, based on television and whatnot, all bringing home the bacon and dishing out life lessons. Guess that's to be expected given the way I was suddenly thrust upon him unexpectedly after my biological mother passed away.

Still, he was a fun guy. More like an awesome older brother. Or an uncle. Taught me all sorts of cool stuff, from how to tie my shoes and drive a car, to how to fire a gun and juggle scarves (neither skill has ever come in handy, but I could still get held up by a circus performer someday...so I guess you never know).

Anyway. Magnetic personality, my dad. Nothing he didn't know, nothing he couldn't do. Nobody who didn't want to be around him.

Come to find out, on this bitch-ass freezing-cold Saturday morning, there really *is* nothing my dad can't do. Nobody who doesn't want to be with him. Including my girlfriend. Ex, actually. But still.

Still.

"What the fuck?"

I'm standing in the doorway to my girl's—ex-girl's—studio apartment. With a hot chocolate and a bag of muffins like the biggest tool on the face of the planet. Because fuck me,

5

but it's Valentine's Day weekend, and she said she didn't have any plans. She *said* she had to spend all day writing a paper.

Shana and I didn't actually go out long before we called it quits, but we've hung out as friends for goddamn ever. Seems like I'm the guy she trusts. The one she calls when she needs to talk. Guess I thought that meant we still had something. Or something that could turn into something? What. The. Fuck. Ev-aaar.

Clearly that was all bullshit. And *clearly* she did have plans this weekend.

"I get the distinct impression he's not here to help you with your aesthetics paper," I say to no one in particular. On account of nobody being dressed, I can't bring myself to make eye contact with anyone in this room.

Because straight across the neatly kept apartment is Shana sitting up in her bed, short blond hair freshly tousled with that world-just-got-rocked look, face flushed and lips puffy while my dad leans over her in a towel. Straightening up after kissing her.

Kissing her.

Did I mention the towel? It's baby blue cuz Shana's got a fetish for pastels and the whole damn place is an homage to pale, and extra fluffy (Cuz who doesn't love fluffy, I guess? Right now? This guy.).

Jesus, I've rubbed my face on those fucking towels. So gross.

Shana and I, we never went there. She always said she wasn't ready, and I wanted to be a good guy about it. A nice guy. Make sure she didn't feel pressured. Now, I know for damn sure what recently went down in this room. The room where I've stopped by to water Shana's ivy plants and help with homework and to hold her hair back when she's been sick. You know. To be *nice*.

Boy. I can't find a word for this situation right now.

Let's see... Fucked-up doesn't seem quite right.
Twisted...maybe. FUBAR? Insane? No.
That's the one. The word is nooo.

"Ethan, what in the hell are you doing here?"

I hold up my key ring. The one *she* gave me, with Buttercup from the *Powerpuff Girls* looking just as angry and big-eyed as I am. My cartoon keychain now seems extraordinarily lame. So does the fact that I came to feed her cat every day while she went skiing during winter break.

Holy shit. My dad went skiing over winter break.

A whirling tornado kicks up in my stomach.

Calico Picasso takes that moment to purr and rub against my leg, reminding me that he's the only one in the room currently showing me any loyalty.

Thanks, boy.

"I still have the key you gave me. Thought you might need help with your damn paper so I brought breakfast and— You know what? Never mind. What are *you* doing here?" I aim that last question at my dad, who's busy tightening his towel.

Thank God. Not like I've never been in a locker room with the old man before, but if I see his junk right now, they'll never get all my gray matter out of the cracks in the floor tile.

"E, calm down. This…wasn't supposed to happen." My dad has the same level tone I've heard him use when his students are having a conniption over their grades.

See, I know what he's doing. I've had some issues with anxiety. I manage it, but I can't as much as complain about a headache without my dad thinking I'm out on the ledge of the campus clock tower.

Frankly, I think I'm flipping out for a legit reason, here. "Which part? You guys fucking, or me finding out?"

They look at each other and then at me. Nobody answers, so I figure that tells me most of the answer lies behind door number two. Or both. Doesn't matter, actually. This is all so tangled up, I can't begin to pull the pieces apart.

"Ethan—" Dad lunges toward me and I take a huge step back before he even makes it halfway across the room.

In the moment before flinging that front door open, if asked, I'd have told you my dad was someone I trusted. He might not be the type for fixing up skinned knees and handing out sage life lessons, but he was somebody I believed I could count on. Same for Shana, frankly.

Knowing who has my back is a big damn deal to me. Right now, I wonder who I can count on.

"You know what, Dad? You can stop right there, because unless you're about to tell me you're dying, there's literally *no* explanation you can give me for this that's going to make me want to go piss on your paintings and egg your car any less."

My dad's restored GTO is his pride and joy. He got it when he and my mom split. About now, I'm wishing I hadn't come up the back stairs or I might have seen it parked out in the front lot and gotten an early warning for this little surprise party.

The pissing thing I wouldn't really do, because I would never want to see another person's creative work destroyed. Still, I said it for giggles, because I'm bleeding out emotionally and feeling real fucking mature.

"Eth—"

"You're not, are you? Dying? Because this would still be shitty, but I might not egg your car."

Unlikely, right? He's only twenty years older than I am.

Nah. I can see it, when I look at her and she looks at him. The way *they* keep looking at each other. The way he grabs his pants from over the back of the reading chair by her bed without looking and pulls them on. This isn't some "oops" kind of thing. He knows this place. He's been here. Probably lots of times.

Shana swipes her hand over a wet cheek. "Ethan, I'm sorry."

"Yeah?" Suddenly I don't recognize her anymore. What in the hell made me think I should wait for her to want me? "That's just great. *Sorry* is for when you accidentally bump someone in the hallway, Shana. Not when you bump uglies with their dad."

My dad looks twitchy and then pulls a clean shirt from her flower-painted chest of drawers (also pastels). I've known Shana since my senior year in high school, and I never got to put shit in her drawers. Maybe because they were already taken.

I put my arms out to the sides. "How the hell long has this been happening?"

"Ethan...I don't think now's the time." Shana pulls up the sheet she's been holding higher against her chest. I realize the only time I've ever seen her fully nude is when she was modeling for an art class.

For my dad's art class.

For serious? Now would be an excellent time for a mountain lion to come out of nowhere and swallow me whole. I'd appreciate the diversion.

Man, I didn't think a thing of it at the time. Lots of art classes use nude models, after all. Dad has used Shana as a model in his classes off and on. Shana wanted to be "just friends" after only a few dates. We never did get past kissing. Since she was a year ahead in school, I wondered if she might want someone more mature.

Who knew my concerns could be so disturbingly founded?

How long has this thing with my dad and Shana been right in front of me? How stupid am I?

I've got nothing. There's a giant piece of glass I carry around inside me. It gets bigger and smaller, depending on the DEFCON level of my anxiousness that day. Right now it makes its presence known, twisting and digging into my gut, driving home with each cut just how stupid I'm feeling.

If I was wrong about this, what other fuck-ups have I made without knowing?

"You know what? You're right. Now is not the time." Never would be good. I take another step back, pulling the door to Shana's apartment wider and stepping out into the chilly air. "You guys enjoy your morning. This is a nightmare, so I'm going to go bleach my brain now."

With a shit-ton of beer.

I thought I still loved Shana. Seeing her in that tiny, one-room apartment with its sex smells and with my dad right there? Damn. I wonder what the hell I was ever thinking.

"Ethan. What's up, man?" Shana's neighbor, a friendly hipster-type named Zeb, is coming out of his place one flight up. When he stops on the landing outside Shana's door and looks at me like *I'm* the one who's dying, I realize I'm still standing there with the door open. Gripping the knob so tight my fingers have gone white.

Sweat beads on my forehead in spite of the cold. My glasses slip down my nose, but I'm short on free fingers to push them up.

"You know, fuck this. I don't know what I was thinking coming here. Happy fucking birthday to me, huh?"

My birthday is actually tomorrow, but I guess I'd had it in my head that if I could help Shana finish her paper, maybe tomorrow she and I could hang out to celebrate. Wow. D-U-M-B-A-S-S spells "Ethan."

I toss the muffins in Shana's trash can and pull the door toward me while her and my dad are still staring as if they saw an alien. I want to slam it fast so nobody, not Zeb or anyone else, can bear witness to my humiliation. It's a windy day though, and gust after gust makes sure the door is buffered on a nice cushion of air as it closes. Quietly and gently. So nicely and politely.

Super.

"Uh, uh. Hey there, Professor Kinney." Zeb waves before I get the door all the way closed. Cuz yeah, Zeb's a photography major so of course he recognizes my dad from the department. He's suddenly shifty and awkward when he looks at me. Eyes wide, he shoves his hands in his pockets, sidling between me and the stairs to get off to wherever it is he's heading.

I wonder if he knows. How many people do? My dad's been here before, so surely Zeb's seen him. Maybe I was the last to find out.

With that awesome cherry on my embarrassing-as-shit sundae, I mumble, "I'm outta here," and pull the door the rest of the way shut. There's no satisfying slam like I wanted, but I guess the morning's gonna be a bust all the way around.

I realize, as I race down the stairs, I'm still gripping the cocoa I'd brought for Shana. A massive anger swig burns the inside of my mouth. "Come *on*. Are you kidding me? What do they do, heat the water with a nuclear reactor first?" After carrying that stuff all the way from the campus coffee shop, it should be cooled off by now.

Out of stubbornness, I swallow the hot gulp and try to be a man about it.

Heading for the bus, I dial my friend Michelle to vent so I'm not shouting my frustration into thin air. She's usually up early and she hardly ever flinches at my crazy. Believe me, I've got plenty.

Even on a Saturday morning, it takes only two rings for her to pick up. "Hey, I was actually about to call you. Something's come up. We're not going to be able to get together tonight for your birthday. I'm so sorry."

Well, the hits just keep on coming, don't they? "Hey, I get it. If you and Dante would rather do something romantic, I can understand."

Michelle's boyfriend, Dante, looks like an underwear model and used to box professionally. Frankly, the way they make goo-goo eyes at each other, I'm amazed they ever make it out in public.

"Actually, it's got nothing to do with romance. Dante's trying to sue his old boxing coach, this guy Arlo Specter. He found another boxer who could maybe testify or even also file charges, so we're heading out of town right away to talk to him. It's more about getting what he did into the light of day than making money, so we're looking for as many people as possible, but a lot of his former clients still fight professionally and refuse to say anything on record."

It sucks to suddenly be on my own, but I can't ignore the tension in Michelle's voice. She's not looking forward to dealing with this, and I don't need to go making that worse.

So I keep my mouth shut about Shana and my dad. "Yeah, it's all good. Safe travels and everything."

"Sure. I'll stop by after we get back."

I say goodbye and hang up, deciding to head to the gym so I can pound on a heavy bag until the urge to beat my head on a rock slowly fades. Dante's taught me a few moves in the ring, and I've found it really does help to loosen up that imaginary piece of glass when I feel like it's lodged deep inside my stomach. The way it is now. If that shit doesn't work, Lord knows there'll be a house party on this campus somewhere.

The pointy end of that glass pokes my soft underbelly. Paranoid whispers in my head tell me I just lost my tribe in one hammer fall, and what's wrong with me to make that happen? Maybe everyone else has other shit going on, or maybe nobody cares enough to have my back. A white-hot flare of pain bursts in my chest, but I beat it back. For now.

I tell myself none of it matters, toss the cocoa in the trash by the bus stop, and keep walking.

#

LeeAnne

Joe's Bar doesn't open until eleven, I've been here since nine in the morning, because that's as early as I can get away with showing up to clean and do inventory. Any earlier and Joe asks questions.

If I stack and restack the glasses and vacuum the decades-old checkered carpet enough, I can kill an amazing amount of time. It's almost like a meditation. Or so I tell myself.

It's not that I don't have anywhere else I can be. It's that lately, being in one spot for too long makes me itchy. And by lately, I mean the past year or so. I'm used to being lonely, but I'm not used to relaxing.

I've been on high alert since my mom died. Waiting for the other shoe to drop. When I was a kid, it was waiting for my dad to come home and shout the house down for some infraction. Later, after I got married, waiting for my husband to blame me for his life turning out wrong. Waiting for a glass to shatter against the wall. For someone to tell me that even though I cleaned, even though I tried to get things right, I did it all wrong.

All that waiting...God, I'm tired.

Somehow, in finally getting up the gumption to leave my husband last year, I screwed myself. Turned out the devil I knew at least didn't keep me wondering. With him, I knew messing up was inevitable. The only question was when.

Now? Now...

"Doing okay in here, girlie?" Joe, a large man in his upper sixties, pokes his head in from the kitchen area.

It's tough to look guilty when you're in the middle of cleaning beer taps, but I manage. "Hey, Joe. Doing fine. Thought I'd get a jump on the day."

"You jump the day any harder, it's gonna file a complaint, sweetheart. You need to give yourself a break."

There's no way to explain it to him. Or to anyone who's never had the sound of their own thoughts keep them awake at night.

If I relax, that might be when the next thing comes flying at my head.

I fold the bar rag in my hand and lay it down. Carefully, to give myself a moment. "I'm only trying to get my head together, Joe."

I feel like all of me is scattered in a million pieces lately. I don't know how to put all of me back together. I don't know how to see the picture, only the little bits of torn paper strewn around. Most of all, I don't know if I'll ever go back together again, or if I ever was, and I don't know how to explain that to Joe.

"Sure, sweetheart. And you know I don't mind you coming in early. But you gotta figure that this isn't good for you. It's been a year now, and you're still moping around here the same way you have been. Hoped getting free of that man would put more spring in your step."

"It did. Really." It's just that now I see ghosts and demons in the shadows. Sometimes the spring is me jumping at them like a fraidy-cat.

"Well…" He pauses behind me. I've turned to fiddle with the alignment of the bottles behind the bar, but I know darn well all I'm really doing is avoiding eye contact. "If there's anything I can do, LeeAnne. You let me know."

"I know. Thank you." I force myself to look back into his eyes, because Joe really has been decent to me. He gave me a waitress job after Charles and I first married. I was eighteen, just out of high school, and wasn't even old enough to serve hard liquor in his bar. Had to have someone else bring out the mixed drinks, thanks to stupid North Carolina laws. I've always appreciated Joe's help, even though it felt like a pity job.

"Honestly, Joe. Thank you."

He nods. "Hate to see you in such a funk, child."

He's making his way toward the back when the front door opens. Before I can say anything, Joe's barked out a curt, "we're closed," at the huddled figure coming through the front entrance.

Me, I don't say a word—because I recognize the person walking in.

It's Charles. My ex. His walk, the heavy, uneven shuffle, is the thing that used to wake me in the middle of the night when he'd arrive home from driving a load. I heard he lost his job, so I don't know where he's been living or what he's been up to. We haven't talked in a year.

A year. His eyes still hold the same hurt as when they stared me down from across the county courtroom.

"Sorry, Joe. Thought I locked it when I came in."

"Don't trouble yourself, sweetheart." To Charles, he says, "You're not welcome here, young man."

Charles is older than I am, by a year and a half. When I look into his eyes, I see a man so haunted, he's never been young. Neither of us ever were, I don't think. It's hard to remember the fumbling teenagers we were when he got me pregnant. But to Joe, everyone's young I suppose.

"It's all right, Joe." Charles appears to be sober right now. He's calm. Joe turning him away might rile him up, and that's the last thing any of us need.

Charles pushes the hood of his sweatshirt off his buzzed head. "I won't stay long. Promise." He turns to me. "You look good. Uh... Here."

A single rosebud appears from inside his coat. Slightly tired looking, its length is wrapped in the cloudy plastic they use over at the Gas Stop on the edge of Evergreen Grove. The ones you just know are there by the door for the poor saps who forgot about Valentine's Day and either didn't have time to hit the grocery store before they cleared out or go to the fancy florist one town over.

My heart hurts, seeing that sad rose. "That's sweet, Charles. But I can't accept."

His gaze jumps around the bar, maybe looking for some place to put the wilted flower. "Oh. Well... Uh... Okay. So... The protective order expired last week. Thought I'd ask if you planned on getting it renewed, you know. My aunt doesn't really have room for me to stay long term, and if you ain't using the house, I could move back here to Evergreen Grove, maybe..."

I sigh. "Kinda hoped I wouldn't have to renew the protective order, Charles. I don't want you and me to have any trouble."

His smile dredges up all my sadness. All the guilt. It's a ghost of the smile that got me into bed one night when I was seventeen and he had stolen a case of his daddy's beer. When I thought maybe he could rescue me from my own father, and lying under the moon with him in a flatbed made us both invincible.

"I haven't been drinking. Things are better. Promise." He leans his hip against a square table with its chairs still stacked up top, and I can see the question before he asks. The hopeful smile. "Hey, do you think maybe sometime we could—?"

"Charles, no. We can't. No trying again. No getting back together. Too much has happened." He'd asked before. I'd felt bad and let him come back. Fool me once, you know?

Part of me wants to say yes, if only because I hate for my father to be right. I hate to have failed. Something in my life has got to finally go right. Whatever I felt for Charles is long gone, though. It's time we both understood.

He comes over to the bar, leaning across to touch my cheek. I brush him away. There's a small scar there by my ear from one of the last times he hit me that I keep covered with makeup. "God, I'm sorry, LeeAnne. You know I'd do anything to take it back. And you know I'm no good on my own."

I don't know what troubles me more. The hot, heavy wave of guilt that makes me want to apologize for *his* hurt or the fact that he isn't saying he misses or loves me. Only that he thinks he needs me to take care of him.

"I know you're sorry. But we've tried. It always ends up the same way. And I can't be the one you lean on. I've been talking to this therapist, and she's helped me see that I'm part of your problem."

His fingers tighten around the leg of an upended bar stool that I hadn't yet put down on the floor. "And just how in the hell does that figure?"

I straighten my spine in spite of the way his stormy gray eyes flash with anger. "You need help I'm not qualified to give, Charles. And I need... I need not to be around you. I don't like who I am when we're together."

Even after so much time apart and with Joe in the next room, it's scary to say this to him.

"It's just..." He taps his fist against the bar and shakes his head. "Never mind. I know." At first he turns partway around, but then he brings his fist down, knocking one of the stools to the floor. "Dammit, LeeAnne!"

It's not the worst I've seen him, but I take a few steps back, reaching for my phone under the back shelves behind the bar. "Charles, Joe's going to come up here and kick you out. Now you can either leave nicely or I'll have to call the sheriff. And I don't want to make things more difficult for either of us, but if you can't keep your distance then I'll go ahead and re-new the protective order."

For a flash, his face twists into a pained mask. Then it's gone. "Distance. Right. You got it, LeeAnne."

There's a look I've never seen before in Charles's eyes when he turns to walk away. Something chilly and blank, and I'm honestly not sure what to think. I'm only hoping he doesn't come back.

2. SHUT YOUR FACE

Ethan

I'm not even sure when we got to Joe's Bar. How is also somewhat blurry.

What I do know is that we've been here for far too long. My "friends" are getting obnoxious, and I'm fucking sobering up. Sadly, I only turn twenty whenever the clock strikes midnight so I can't drink here.

My pity bender ended like a few hours ago when we left this guy Alonzo's place. Real shame. At least I've got nachos.

Alonzo's in my poetry class (Rumors of this class being the easiest A you can get for an English requirement have been grossly exaggerated). I remember going to the gym and running into him there. His roommate was with him and mentioned some Anti-Valentine's party they were having. What the hell, right? Going home had been a nonstarter after Michelle and Dante had to cancel on me, since I currently live with my dad and I was *not* ready to run into him in the kitchen.

So, how was your morning? Mine was pretty heinous. Yours?

Heeell no.

Today hasn't been a good-decision day. The last clear thing I recall is being so desperate to get unstuck from my own head, I literally drank enough at Alonzo's place to topple into a life-size cardboard cutout of Ryan Gosling while accepting a dare to make out with it (Which Alonzo was pretty attached to. Says I owe him a new Ryan).

I think we also played avalanche or pennies or some equally ill-advised drinking games. Vaguely, I recall someone busting out a bottle of illegally acquired grain alcohol. I'd count up all the things today that I wouldn't have been caught dead doing yesterday, but my brain's still too fried for basic math.

Winding up here at Joe's Bar in Evergreen Grove, though, that's a little more fuzzy. Fuzzier? More fuzzier? *Definitely.*

All's I know is, I'm in a townie bar surrounded by drunk college students, drunker folks in boots and flannel, and I'm pretty sure if we're not careful, Alonzo's gonna pull down the decorative Christmas lights running around the walls with all his intoxicated gesturing. Is... Is he trying to give Jesse a lap dance? I don't even know.

Turns out Alonzo has a *lot* of friends, or at least a ton of people who show up to hang out at his house on the edge of Evergreen Grove. When day turned to night, we all surged from the town border down to Main Street, the lamest drunken parade ever. I'm pretty sure I let one of the guys in our group drive my car, which is kind of fucked because my CRX is my baby and I never let anyone drive her. Plus, I don't have a clue how we made everybody fit. Or where my car's been parked.

Since I can't actually drink at Joe's, I ate nachos instead and finally sobered up some. Now the hazy weirdness is coming back, and it isn't pretty. Things like spilling my guts out about my lame love life in a cloud of pot smoke. Then someone suggesting a trip here because Alonzo was out of snacks, and Joe's has the best food for munchies. Crazy, yet it doesn't even compare to how my day started.

"Can I get you guys anything else?" The bartender/waitress shows up at our table, swinging her sandy-blond ponytail and flashing her smile like a girl-next-door movie heroine. She asks this after bringing me a Cherry Coke and a new basket of fries, which makes me literally want to marry her.

Maybe I *am* stoned. However...

True confession: I like this girl. I have since before I met Shana. Back before I started as a student at Pender Tech, dad brought me here for lunch on the weekends because he liked the wings. LeeAnne's always sweet to me. Guess she's that way with everyone, but still.

Her body's amazing. Curvy and soft and real, like a woman in a Dali painting. Even though photorealism isn't my bag, I'd kill to sit her down and draw her. Paint her. I have, actually, but from memory. Might sound pervy to some, perhaps, but it was only because the curve of her lips and that dusting of freckles were impossible to ignore. The sexy "S" formed by the sway of her lower back and the curve of her ass make my brain go haywire.

All of that is nothing compared to her eyes, which are the duskiest green ever. For all her warmth with the customers, they're frozen, glittery-pond-at-night dark. Abandoned-asylum dark. Just as pulse quickening and intriguing. You just know there are secrets buried in the shadows. Sure, something might tell you it's dangerous territory, but that only makes you wonder.

What would happen if I stepped on the ice? If I picked up a camera and some spray paint and walked into that strange-ass empty building? What if I walked up to LeeAnne, the sunny waitress with the dark emerald eyes, and tried to see why she's so closed off inside?

LeeAnne used to wear a wedding ring, so I never tried. It's gone now. There was a rumor about her and one of the other dudes who works here at some point, too. But *that* guy is dating Cassie, the girl who sometimes plays guitar here, so I think that's nothing to worry about at this point.

Before, even if LeeAnne had been available, I still had Shana asking me to hang out and make mac and cheese while we watched *Fushigi Yûgi*. Idiot that I was, somehow I took that as a sign that she still might want me as more than a friend. That she simply wasn't there yet, or whatever stupid excuse I let her feed me. If I was a nice guy and waited…

"What the *fuck* ever, dude." Alonzo's not talking to me, he's arguing with his roommate, Jesse, about the philosophical possibility that we're all living in a computer unaware vs. the idea that we're all puppets to hidden alien masters, but his comment nevertheless fits the moment.

I kinda wonder if these guys are major nerds, or just too smashed to realize they're arguing human existence in the form of two fictional movie plots? I only sort of care, because LeeAnne's wearing a more distant smile than usual this evening.

She sort of looks the way I feel, and I want to know why.

One of the guys in our motley crew asks for another pitcher. When she turns back toward the bar, I'm out of my seat without thinking.

"Actually," I say in a voice that's too rough and too low to actually be mine. Maybe I did smoke something. "There's something I'd really like."

"Oh?"

This is so unbelievably cliché. When she turns toward me with her tired smile and her order pad raised, I wonder how many guys have come on to her this way, and how fast she'll shoot me down.

"What can I get for you, sir?"

And here we go in three...two...one...

"Sir." I snort. Maybe I'm still a little drunk after all. "I'm not a sir. I'm just... Whatever. You know me, LeeAnne. I come in here all the time. I'm Ethan. My best friend Michelle is friends with Cassie, who lives with that guy Jake who works here sometimes, who also, I don't know, probably sat at a boxing match next to Kevin Bacon once or something. I'm Ethan."

"You said that already."

God, I want to beat my head into the jukebox for being a raging moron. Except I think, maybe, her smile warms up a

little. Maybe dumbassery is working in my favor at this particular moment.

"So, yeah. I'm repeating myself. I do that. Anyway,
you look sort of sad and I've been having a crap day myself,
you know? Maybe we could go out sometime. Coffee or whatever. Nothing fancy. Unless you like fancy. I'm open."

Dear Ethan: Shut your face before she slaps you in it.
—Your Last Remaining Shred of Dignity

For hardly a second, her smile slips. Like the professional she is, she puts it back fast, only her eyes dim another
notch.

She sticks her pen behind one ear. "You think I look
sad, so you're inviting me out for coffee?"

Yeah, I guess the logic fell a little short. "I know some
good jokes."

Now her smile takes on more of an I'm-humoring-you
sort of expression. "That's a sweet offer, Ethan, but I'm afraid I
don't date customers."

Uh-huh. She's shut me down in a super kind but firm
way, and my first instinct is to leave her alone and walk away.
Not do anything that might rock the boat or be bothersome.

Yesterday, I might have.

Well, yesterday I wouldn't have even asked her out.
After all, I was still pining for the girl I stupidly thought was
my soul mate. My soul mate who was sleeping with my dad.
Can I get a *yeesh* with a side of *gaaah?!?*

Yesterday was yesterday. Or maybe it's already after
midnight and yesterday was actually two days ago. Not so sure.
Point is, today is a new day and a new Ethan. *Today,* I have to
give it one more try. Especially since she called me "sweet"
and that's just fucking unacceptable.

"Right. I hear you. It's an understandable policy.
Makes total sense. Can I just ask one favor?"

She shifts her weight to one leg, popping out one of
those gorgeous hips and pursing her lips like she knows I'm

about to try to feed her some horseshit. I guess she's not wrong. I'm not trying to be an asshole, I'm just done being the nice guy.

The nice guy gets nowhere. I'm *so* fucking done being the nice guy.

I mean, I've got no problem with being kind. You know, being considerate. My mom taught me to treat others with respect, and I'm still sure that's a good thing. I *do* have a problem with being kept on the line as the affable idiot who's always around, knowing damn well he'll do whatever because he's hoping for more.

I have a problem with people thinking *nice* equals *doormat.*

Being nice got me nothing but kicked around. More than once. Fuck that business.

Sure, I'm channeling a little anger right now. It'll die down. Pinkie swear.

I grab LeeAnne's order pad, swiping the pen from behind her ear. I like the way her eyes widen and her cheeks stain when my hand brushes her hair. She doesn't look mad, but she looks surprised and maybe sort of amused. It's cool to see some light in those dark eyes.

"You know," I say. "There's this kickass kebab place over in Pender. Sometimes I'm like seriously craving food from there, but then I ask around and nobody else wants savory meat on a stick. So I don't go because eating alone is no fun, you get what I'm saying?"

"I don't really—No."

Yeah. I ramble. A lot. Especially if I'm nervous. Which is almost always. "So all I'm saying is, I'm really good company if you're ever in need of some. Company. You can ask around. People like me, and I'm not at all creepy. Zero spree-killings so far this year."

"It's February."

"I stand by my track record."

I'm gratified by a small laugh but it doesn't last nearly long enough, because she looks over my shoulder with a deep crease in her forehead. "Uh, you'd better go get your friends out of here. One looks sick and the others look ready for a fight."

"They're not actually my... Aww, damn." Some guy I don't know is listing sideways on the chair I recently vacated. The green cast of his face says he may be putting my leather jacket in peril. Alonzo's got Jesse by the collar, and I can't tell if they're about to throw down or make out. Considering all the flannel and trucker hats around the bar, this probably isn't a good place for either.

I'm tempted to say it isn't my problem, but if a fight breaks out in the bar, it *will* be LeeAnne's. That probably won't help my chances of getting a date.

Fuck.

I turn back to the table. "All right, party people, let's GTFO."

I grab my jacket and pull the skinny one who's about to puke back by his T-shirt, so I can march him toward the door. Dude struggles more than I expect, considering how hammered he is, but after a couple of good stumbles, I've got him under control. Jesse and Alonzo follow with surprising ease, and we're on our way to the bus stop looking like one big happy gang of "I love you man!"

I love you, man. No, really! I love you! No, man, I love YOU! You're the best, dude. No, you are!

Except really, I've got my arms around Jesse and skinny drunk dude to keep them from scampering off like puppies or falling down like, well, you know. It's not easy, but they're both your average lazy college nerd, and I've been working out almost daily for the past few years.

Everyone's got their demons, and running or doing pushups until I can't think helps keep mine at bay. Mostly. Sometimes.

I finally pour everyone onto the local connector bus and wander to my car, feeling in my jacket pocket for my phone so I can surf Instagram or read until I'm a hundred percent sure I'm not going to get pulled over on my drive home. Set an alarm perhaps, in case I fall asleep.

Except...fuck. My phone isn't in my jacket pocket.

It's always in my jacket pocket.

Jesus. When do I get to go to bed and forget the last twenty-four hours ever happened?

#

When I finally make my way back up to Joe's Bar, it's later than I thought. Only people I see left are a couple of townies on stools, and LeeAnne, who's already hard at work vacuuming what must be one hell of a nasty floor. The lights are turned up brighter, showing yellowing walls scattered with pictures and memorabilia, and a dining room crammed with little rectangular tables. Not exactly a place made for lingering after last call.

Joe's is upstairs from a coffee shop/bakery kinda place, and damned if I wouldn't kill for a powdered sugar donut to wash down this shit-tastic night. Unfortunately, Joe's doesn't serve desserts and, anyway, I'm betting the kitchen is closed.

"Can I help you?" LeeAnne asks me the same question as before with the same neutral smile pasted on. This time her foot taps to show how little patience she has left. Guess I can't blame her. She's trying to fend me off before I make another move.

"Oh. Uh...I thought maybe I left my phone up here."

"Hmm." She glances around. "I don't think I saw it when I cleared your table. Let me see if it fell underneath."

She's over there before I can process, stooped down with her hands on her thighs, curvaceous butt sticking right out at me. She's wearing a pair of leggings under her skirt so it's not like she's flashing all the cash and prizes, but man...it's hard to miss those legs and…well, my imagination *is* pretty damn vivid.

I maneuver around, trying to help her look under the chairs and everything, but it seems like each time I move left, so does she, and same when I move right. It all gets even more awkward when suddenly I realize my butt is vibrating.

My. Butt. Is. Vibrating.

As in…

I reach back and slap my pocket, tracing over the rectangle of my phone. Which has been with me the whole time, and now it's WAY uncomfortable because I've got LeeAnne's backside right in my face as she pats the floor under the heating unit that runs along the wall to check for my smartphone. The one that's buzzing away in my not-so-smart pants. This is not a particularly convenient time to tap her on the shoulder and be all, "Hey, false alarm. I had it the whole time. Crazy, right?"

I mean, what if I tap her and she bangs her head on the underside of the table? Or I accidentally tap other parts of her? Or she thinks I'm some perv who made up the phone story only so I could watch her bend over?

Which, being honest? Not a terrible side effect of this entire mishap. Except now I'm thinking all sorts of super inappropriate thoughts. Shit.

I push my glasses up and clear my throat, ready to come clean, when I hear a noise behind me.

"Not sure what you're looking for, buddy, but you'd best keep your hands to yourself if you know what's good for ya."

LeeAnne shoots up, missing the edge of the table with no trouble at all, as it turns out. "Randy." She gives him a half smile and a stern look. Those dark eyes are distant again. "This is not your concern. And it's past time for you to go."

"I'm only keepin' an eye on things. Whad'you think Charles would do if he knew you was in here bending over for all the customers?"

Oh, fuck. She's got a boyfriend? Fantastic.

LeeAnne throws an anxious glance towards what I assume is the door to the kitchen. There was a big guy up here earlier, but I'm not sure where he is now.

I clear my throat and nudge my glasses up again. "Hey, now. Say what you want about me, cuz I'll definitely bend over for anyone. But let's be respectful to the lady."

Maybe I'm feeling like being a nice guy has gotten me beaten with the butt end of the fairness stick a few times, but regardless, I don't believe in disrespecting women. My mom told me once that a bastard might get his way for a time, but eventually he'd anger the wrong person and wind up with an angry lady standing over him with a sharp knife in one hand and his willie in the other. Some theories you don't wanna test.

Not to mention, I *do* have a mom and a little sister. It wouldn't be cool to have anybody talking to them all shitty like that.

LeeAnne's face reddens. It's not embarrassment though. Uh-uh. I can see from the slash of her eyebrows and the tight balls she's made out of her hands, she's pissed at this other guy. At least, I hope that's who she's pissed at.

"Charles lost that right when we got divorced. Now leave, before I call the police and tell Joe to have you banned."

The man spits on the floor and adjusts his hat, still looking like he's got more to say. I glance over at the bar to realize the other dude who was in here slipped out while I was distracted by LeeAnne's charming assets. All that's left is a smoke trail and some cash pinned under an empty glass.

I grab my phone from my back pocket and step in front of a shaky looking LeeAnne. "Come on, man. You heard her. Let's drop this peacefully."

"You gonna do something about it, kid?"

He pushes up his sleeves and flexes his muscles. Oh hell, I'd rather not. Am I going to get into a damn bar fight on my birthday? Talk about things that weren't on my to-do list.

Catching my dad in bed with my ex?
Drunk fumble with paper Ryan Gosling?
Alonzo groping my ass when I tried to get him into the
bus?

Seriously, I just wanted to hang out with Michelle and play some darts. Was that too much to ask?

I give Trucker Hat Guy the stare-down. "I'm telling you, dude. You don't want to start something here." Pretty sure it's the glasses, but nobody sees me as a threat. Ever. I'm stronger than I look, though. Also, I think way more sober than my opponent. "Now, come on and listen to the lady. Get out of here."

He rocks back on his feet. Takes one step and then another. Behind me, LeeAnne lets out a breath of relief. Looks like the guy got smart enough to listen.

Until he blows out a wall-shaking bellow and throws a sloppy right hook at me. Dammit.

The first shot I dodge easily. He's sloppy drunk, and I'm down to a mellow buzz and the beginnings of a pesky headache that'll have me pissed-off tomorrow.

After that? Yeah well, after that, he's angry. When he runs at me, I suppose I could dodge again. I *should* dodge him. Then his stupid ass would run into the wall and I'd be on my way home. That'd be the smart thing. The reasonable thing.

I don't do the reasonable thing.

No, what I do is drop my shoulder and meet him halfway, shoving us both into a table. Him on his back, and me sprawled on top with my hands on his chest like we're having a clumsy grope-off. I can't understand much of what he says until he lifts his head and calls me a fag.

Oh, that's *so* not okay. Really it's the slur that makes me mad. I full-on kissed my best friend, Lucas, back in high school. Albeit in the privacy of his room, and more because I thought he needed to be kissed than from me wanting to bone him or anything. But that word's fucking ugly and it stirs up a lot of unpleasant shit.

"I think you want to shut up and walk away." This is Ethan, the rule follower, trying to fight through my lingering liquor buzz before we wind up spending my/our birthday with the county sheriff.

Dude spits and calls me that damned word again.

I see red.

The next thing I know, my knuckles are bloody, and so is his face.

#

LeeAnne

"Ethan!" I'm pulling at his arm, trying to get him to stop. He doesn't seem to hear me. Neither of them do.

I look to the kitchen door for maybe the fiftieth time. The cook's gone home. Joe's down in the back alley rounding up the trash and breaking down boxes for recycling. While down there, he'll probably also have a smoke and call to check on his wife, who recently had surgery on a torn rotator cuff. I think. With only a couple of customers left, I'd assured him I was fine alone for a few minutes. Who knew this would happen?

"Ethan, you have to stop. You're going to break his— Ow."

I jump from the pain of my thumb getting squeezed in someone's clenching hand, and yank back. My dad used to say never get between two fighting dogs. At the moment, I'm thinking the rule doesn't apply only to canines. These guys are liquored up, riled up, and looking to be stupid. Or *being* stupid, actually.

One defending the honor of a friend. The other, unbelievably, seems to be defending mine.

That insane idea makes a flock of birds take off in my chest.

It's not like I haven't seen a bar fight. In my years of working at Joe's, I've seen plenty. Usually it's a matter of grabbing one of the two parties by the scruff of their neck, getting them out into the fresh air, and threatening to call their wives or the cops.

These two guys in front of me are hip-deep in the middle of a snarling, testosterone-fueled affair that I worry will only end when someone's not moving.

Or when someone shocks them out of it. Which is what I intend to do.

With record speed, I run to the bar, jumping across to grab the soda dispenser. I turn to aim as Ethan jumps off the table—I hate to think why, but the wicked gleam in his eye says he might have body slam on the brain—so I unleash my fury.

Well, it's not fury so much as a face full of frosty diet cola, but the results are the same.

"Holy— What the—" Ethan and Randy cough and choke with their faces full of cola. Ethan whips his glasses off to try to save them from sticky destruction.

Randy—Charles's friend—seems to think this is all hysterical. I walk over and swat him with a bar towel. "I don't know what *you're* laughing at, with your bloody nose and your fat lip. Now, you get out of here before I call the sheriff."

"What the hell? He's the one who—"

"Don't start. You attacked first. Before that, you poked your nose into my business where it didn't belong. So get!"

I glare firmly as he lumbers out the door, but inside I'm shaking. Standing my ground with the bar customers is something I'm used to. Something my boss made it clear was required of me, and I forced myself to do it no matter what things were like at home. But it all feels different now. Scarier, and less like playacting. Especially with someone who knows my ex. I fear consequences, even if it might be irrational.

"Here." I hand Ethan another towel and then walk to the door to throw the bolt so Randy can't come back in, doing the same at the back door before I return to where he's standing.

A frown mars his handsome face as he tries to shove his glasses back on the right way. Removing them again, he tugs his jacket and damp shirt off entirely so he can wipe the caramel-colored droplets from his cheeks and forehead. A quiet gasp escapes my mouth. I'm struck for a moment by this transformation. With his hair wet, his face and upper body visible, I can see much more clearly how physically attractive Ethan is.

I try never to look at the bar patrons that way; I wasn't simply blowing smoke when I said I don't date customers. But I'd be lying if I said I hadn't noticed Ethan, because he's not all rowdy and obnoxious like the other college kids that come in. Now that we're alone, it's hard to ignore how his chest and abs are awfully ripped for a guy I would've assumed was too busy with his nose in a book to ever go for a run or set foot in a gym.

Of all people, I should know not to make assumptions. "Umm, I gave you the cloth so you could dry off. You didn't need to remove your shirt."

My stomach is tight and fluttery and it's getting a little difficult to breathe in here. In spite of my reasonable certainty that Ethan is a decent guy—and I've known enough of the not-so-decent ones that I believe I can tell the difference—his presence is making me all flustered. Particularly his shirtless presence. This reaction isn't familiar, and the sensations have me all jumbled.

He holds up the tiny towel I'd given him. "This little thing's gonna mop up all the soda you blasted me with?"

On the one hand, I think I was totally justified in stopping that scuffle before it got out of control. On the other, he's sort of grinning at me with this look that makes my face hot.

"Right. I think we have some spare shirts in the back." I spin around, rushing towards the kitchen to hide the blush I know is spreading across my cheeks. It's funny how I used to have such a good poker face, but lately I'm too tired to keep everything to myself.

I'm not solid like I used to be. Things don't bounce off. They land. They stick. I cry. I blush. Sometimes I can't even figure out the reason.

"Listen, you don't have to—"

"Oh my God!" I didn't realize he'd followed me. The tumble of his voice in my ear sends me right into the air.

When I stop short, his front presses against my back. *God, LeeAnne. Pay attention.*

"Hey. Sorry. I didn't mean to freak you out. You okay?" He touches me down by the waist, like he's soothing a skittish horse. His other hand cups my shoulder, his fingers squeezing and stroking like he's trying to ground me.

It's weird, but his touch actually feels kind of nice. Kind of…comforting. His fingers are strong and his body is sort of perfect against mine. Solid and warm. And his chin comes to the top of my head, which tells me I could turn around and look him right in the eye if I wanted, without having to crane my neck.

Charles was such a big guy, and when he got mean, it wasn't sexy.

"Didn't expect you to be right on my tail, that's all." To test my theory, I turn around and yes, in fact, I can look him right in the eye. They're brown and liquidy and sweet looking. Like a cool glass of sweet tea at the end of a long day.

Speaking of which, I could totally go for one of those right now. It's crazy hot in here. My heart is thumping extra fast, and I tell myself it's only because Ethan surprised me. The tingles on my skin tell me something else.

When I breathe deep, I smell the lingering sweetness of soda on his skin and the spice of his cologne or aftershave or something. He puffs a hot breath of air when he laughs, and the rush of it against my cheek makes me tingle all over again. It makes me tingle in places I thought I didn't tingle anymore.

"Guess I felt strange, standing out there in the middle of an empty bar with my shirt off. Like I was there for *Magic Mike* tryouts or something." He chuckles again, and another shiver races over my throat. Down my chest. My arms. Down to…other places.

Part of me feels like I should ignore that sensation. The way his breath on my neck tightens my nipples and raises the hairs on my arms. I'm not supposed to feel these sorts of things. Not now. Not ever.

Every time I've tried, the universe has punished me. My father would probably say it's God who punished me.

Then again, thinking of my dad makes me want to do exactly the thing I shouldn't. It always has.

It feels nice, the way Ethan's hand squeezes my shoulder. His touch is gentle but confident, and so deliciously firm. I try to tell myself I should make him stop—Joe won't be down in the back alley forever—but it's such a rare thing that I actually *like* being touched.

And his hands… Oh no. His hands.

I look up with a gasp. "I need to get you some ice. Your hand is swelling."

Angling my face toward his certainly seemed like a wise idea a moment ago. After all, I had an urgent message for him. His hand, still split and bleeding from punching Charles's asshole buddy, is a mess and a half and will only look worse the longer it sits.

Except now we're nose to nose. Or, well, sort of forehead to chin, but then when I look up and he looks down, it lines our faces up nicely. Everything suddenly seems like it's in slow motion.

It all seems very…right.

"Hey, LeeAnne?"

"Uh-huh?" I think I might literally be breathing his oxygen. Or his carbon dioxide? Maybe that's why I'm lightheaded.

He licks his lips. "So, yeah. I know you said you don't date customers. I don't want to be a dick about that or anything. I also don't want to leave here without telling you that I've thought about you since the first time my dad brought me in here for suicide wings and potato skins when I was eighteen. You had a wedding ring then and I was trying to be nice, so I kept my mouth shut. I'm saying something now. Maybe we could make those eyes of yours a little less sad."

Oh. Wow.

Somewhere deep in the back of my brain, I'm thinking no, no of course he can't, because I already turned him down for coffee so why on earth would I change my mind now? That would be crazy. My life has been a cascade of stupid decisions and ugly consequences. I've sworn to myself I would be smarter in the future.

I think kissing some shirtless guy—shirtless with a suspicious bandage the size of my hand on his chest, by the way, *and* with bloody knuckles—in the kitchen might not be exactly smart. Then I think...

He defended me.

Of all the people in this town. Since my mom died. Since my dad sent me packing. Both before I left Charles and after. Nobody's ever stood up and tried to be my hero. They've either called me names or refused to look me in the eyes. I don't think I expected anyone ever would. I don't know if I even believed I deserved defending, but it means something that Ethan did.

It means an awful lot.

I take in his glasses and his messy curls and think how he's exactly the kind of guy my father would write off as weak. The kind of guy Charles would've made fun of back when we were in high school. Like an idiot, I'd have stood by and stayed silent, because I would've been too worried about opinions to act.

I don't know why Ethan did what he did, but I liked it. I like how his presence and his touch are making me feel. That's not something I've been able to say about almost anyone or anything. And I've had enough of holding myself in. Of holding myself up. After seeing Charles, and after his friend calling me names, I would love not to feel so alone. Just this once, I'd like to lean on someone a tiny little bit.

So I listen for a second to hear for signs of Joe's return. When I detect none, I push my hands into Ethan's messy hair and press my lips against his. Kissing him before he can see the tears forming in my eyes.

3. HERE BE DRAGONS

Ethan

Holy fuck. A beautiful girl is kissing me. *LeeAnne* is kissing me. She honestly is, with her full, pink lips and her tongue that tastes like club soda with lemon. I might pass out.

I can't even believe this. I can't process. Sensation comes at me from everywhere, and all I can do is focus on the taste of her and the strands of her hair slipping through my fingers, otherwise I'll get overrun by the way my head is starting to ache or how my hand and chest and back are throbbing from that idiotic fight.

Screw it. Screw everything else. LeeAnne *actually* kissed me. I spoke up about what was on my fucking mind, and she did. This seems like a lesson I should've learned maybe ten damn years ago, but I guess now's a hell of a time to catch a clue.

I'm kind of wondering if I hit my head back there on that table. Things like this don't happen to me. Ever. Or maybe they didn't happen to Nice Ethan. Maybe she didn't like me until I made it super clear I was into her. Or until I smashed some guy's face in.

Which I totally didn't mean to do, by the way. I meant to stop him from talking smack. Give him one good pop to show him I wasn't some loser he could push around. My anger at my dad and about twelve years of school assholes took control of my body. Next thing I knew, my mind was blank and LeeAnne was spraying me with a hose full of cola.

My mind is far from blank right now. It's full of LeeAnne and, *oh God*, her teeth. Her teeth are scraping my lip. Her nose is nuzzling mine and she's breathing these short, rapid sighs. I'm wishing I knew how to be all suave right here the way I'm betting most guys would be, except I'm coming off an

all-night buzz made of cheap beer and secondhand pot smoke.
(Really hoping it was only secondhand. My mom would kill
me.)
        Also, let's be honest. I'm not that experienced with
women. Shana never let me touch her much, and I guess now I
get why. Since I don't want to get pissed off again, I don't
think about it long. There was Maria Poindexter who let me get
to…third base? At a party junior year of high school. Fuck, this
is not the time to be thinking about bases.
        "Ow! Fuck me."
        "Sorry!"
        I'd completely forgotten about the bandage on my
chest. In our haze of exploring mouths and roaming hands,
LeeAnne's palm pressed against my chest and it hurt like a
mother. My recollection is vague, but I kind of think I was stupid enough to let Alonzo and Jesse talk me into letting this guy
they know, who's apprenticing at a tattoo parlor, use me for
practice.
        With a wince, I pull down the bandage to reveal a
tribal serpent-type design covering… wow. My entire right
pec. "Oh, hey. Sucker's big. Kinda hoped maybe the dressing
was overstating things. Not as bad as I thought it might be, but
still probably one of my stupider ideas."
        Her lip twitches into a smile though, which is nice.
"You got a tattoo? While drunk?"
        "I guess I did." I lean back and clunk my head against
a row of stainless steel cabinets. "Man, why the fuck did I get a
tattoo?"
        "You don't remember?"
        "It's been a long night, honey." I rub the back of my
head. "I kinda remember… Telling the tattoo guy I thought
snakes were badass. Seemed like a good idea at the time. My
ex thought tattoos were on par with self-mutilation or whatever, and I guess I was feeling extra rebellious."

A tickle at the edge of the bandage as she pulls it away so she can get a look. A quiet giggle escapes her lips. "At least you didn't get it in prison." I think it looks pretty good on you." "Came down to the wire on the prison thing, I think. I had a seriously awful day. There was lots of alcohol. As in...lots." I press forward, sliding my hands up and down the curves of her hips. The last thing I want to talk about is my dad, or why I got so shitfaced stupid.

So instead I kiss her again. And again. Right then, licking the corner of her mouth and the edge of her jaw is the absolute, most energizing moment of my life. The softness of her against my tongue and the way her body melts into mine is more intoxicating than all the collective drinks I consumed before stumbling into this bar tonight.

My fingers trace the lines of her collarbone as I inhale, greedy for the citrus and evergreen scent of her that fills my nose.

"So good," I say as I kiss over the tops of her shoulders. "You smell so good. You taste amazing. You're..."

I don't even know. My brain is too fuzzy and my tongue is too frantic. Usually I'm one long stream of nervous chatter, but at the moment I've lost my voice. I've got no idea what to do here, and I just realized I'm heading towards her neckline, suspiciously close to nipple territory, and nipple territory is still a vastly unexplored land to me.

Sure, I've *seen* them. Girl ones. Guy ones. I've sketched them from a neutral distance, carefully evaluating a model's parts and ratios the same as I would a vase of flowers or a bowl of fruit. It's not a lot in the way of practice. Aside from that one time with Maria Poindexter, you might as well write "HERE BE DRAGONS" across most parts of a naked woman.

For a moment, I freeze.

Fuck. No. Move, dammit. Nice Guy Ethan would freeze. He'd fall prey to his anxiety and let that jabbing piece of

glass get him so freaked about doing the right thing that he'd
do nothing at all.

So what if I ignored all that shit and just plowed ahead
(so to speak)? What if I acted like I knew what the fuck I was
doing and felt my way through (as it were), instead of holding
up a ginormous sign that says "Ethan has no game whatsoever!"

*Come on, dumbasss. Pretend it's a learning lab or
something. Hands on education. Yeah.*

The rise and fall of LeeAnne's chest is choppy and
harsh. Her fingers dig into my back as she squeezes herself
closer to me, and my want for her is so heavy and loud that I
think I'd rather drink paint thinner than walk away without giving everything I have to this moment.

So I dig inside for some confidence. "Lift your legs."
God, listen to me.

Except, amazingly, that piece of glass doesn't feel so
sharp and heavy inside when I touch her. I'm too busy feeling
other things. Feeling *for* other things.

Amazing things.

"What? Geez, Ethan, Joe could come back any minute.
This is not the place for..."

Except she lifts her legs anyway. Whatever protest she
was working up dies on her lips as I hook my arms under that
amazing ass of hers, and set her on some stainless steel counter
that's probably used for preparing food or drinks.

Guess I'd better work fast. Strangely, knowing the
owner is coming back soon only heightens the adrenaline buzzing in my brain.

Her lips part, eyes looking a little frantic. She's not the
only one.

"Listen, honey. I want to please you and it sounds like
I need to do it super quick so you gotta help me out."

God, she's breathing so hard. "We really shouldn't be
doing this back here."

Her thighs are squeezing around my waist and her cheeks are stained the color of a really brilliant sunset, so I feel pretty confident about my odds when I ask, "So do you want me to stop?"

She digs her fingers into me. A strangled sound squeaks out of her throat. "God, not yet. One second. It's just... I like this. I like *you.*"

"I can promise you the feeling is extremely mutual."

I keep kissing her. Short bursts of kissing where I tease her with the tip of my tongue. Or maybe I'm teasing myself. I've never kissed like this before. Like I'm having a really delicious appetizer and I don't mind if I never get to the main course.

Yes! New, bold Ethan's hand has made contact with those skin-tight leggings under her skirt. "Oh man. Oh man, you know, you should tell me to stop. You should tell me to now, because I don't want to be a jerk but if I get my hands under these things I might combust."

Seriously. Did someone leave something on in this kitchen? It's like three thousand degrees.

LeeAnne wraps her legs around me tighter, drawing me and my aching erection into the heat between her legs. "The thing is, I want to. We shouldn't, but...I never do this, and I want to. Whatever you might've heard, I don't do hookups. It's hard to be that into sex when you never even...you know."

Whatever she's trying to say stains her cheeks an even deeper pink. Pretty sure I got the memo, though.

"I think I get it. You, uh, have trouble getting off?"

Oh yeah. I know a little something about that. She doesn't answer, but she doesn't have to. The way she glances away and her blush climbs into her hair, I can totally tell I've hit the orgasm on the head. Or... Well, anyway.

"Hey, no. *No,* all right? Believe me, I was on these meds for a while that gave me so many boner problems it wasn't even worth *trying* to jerk off. So don't you go getting embarrassed, okay?"

This moment is supposed to be about me proving to myself I can make a girl feel good. This particular girl. That is, if she doesn't laugh me out of this kitchen for my TMI-infused boner comment.

She does laugh, only a little. I guess she didn't mind the story though, because then she's biting her lip and sliding her hand around my side again.

I touch her cheek to get her eyes back on mine. "Hey, sorry. I don't have a filter sometimes. A lot of the times. Let's just have a little fun. You tell me if what I'm doing feels good. If it doesn't, you tell me and we'll stop."

I might also be way out of my league here, but at least I can give it a shot. Making LeeAnne feel good, after the day I've had? *God, please.*

The red in her face has dialed itself back to a nicely-done dusty rose. "Um, what did you have in mind?"

That's the question, isn't it? "All right. So is it okay if I remove these?" I slide my hands up her thighs and under her skirt, arriving with greedy fingers, ready to pull at the band of her stretchy leggings.

I love the way her teeth sink into her lip when she nods. I reach up to the back of her ponytail, pulling out the band that keeps it all bound up. "That's been driving me crazy. And I always thought you'd look good with your hair down."

She shakes her hair. "I don't mind. It's just, uh, for work. I have to keep it pulled back."

I gesture to the surface beneath her. Marred with my handprints and overturned salt and pepper shakers, it needs a definite once-over. "I think we're done worrying about work stuff for the moment." With that, I slide off her sneakers and her stretchy black pants.

Oh, mother of… "You're not wearing anything underneath."

"Laundry day."

God bless laundry day.

For all the fucked-up-ness of my past twenty-four hours, if this is my reward…I'll take it.

As I'm kissing my way up her inner thigh, she stops me with a hand to my head. "This is completely crazy."

She looks so amazing and beautiful with her legs spread and her hair flowing over her shoulders. "It's been a crazy night. You want me to stop?"

LeeAnne's lip trembles. "I don't want you to be disappointed."

I'm smiling at her while I draw shapes on her thigh with my fingers. A heart…a cube…a bear. God, I could do that alone all damn day. "Not possible. This is already the best thing that's happened to me all year."

Fingers are in my hair, massaging my scalp. Everything's all a little blurry because I've managed to smudge my glasses, and now isn't the time to stop and give them a nice cleaning.

"The way you touch me feels good," she whispers. "Don't stop."

I command my addled brain never to forget those words. The way she's saying them. The way she's brushing her fingertips over me. I want to remember everything.

Her gasp when I put my mouth on her is the best sound I've ever heard. It's eerie silent in here, except for the *swish* of her legs brushing my shoulder and my cheek, and a distant thumping outside in the alley.

I focus on my lips and tongue. The one girl who ever let me give her oral, she went both ways. You'd better believe I listened closer than I've listened to any lesson in my life when she explained her approved technique.

When I look up, there's some major manly gratification in the way LeeAnne's got her head back and her chest going in and out like it's hard to catch her breath.

"LeeAnne. Still with me?"

"Huh? Yeah. Here."

"Cool, so I need you to do one thing for me. Can you do one thing? If what I do is good, tell me. Tell me you want more. If it doesn't feel good, say that, too. I need to know what you like, all right?"

She nods, lips parted and cheeks flaming up again. "O...kay."

"Good."

With my eyes on her, I slip one finger inside, then another, curling gently the way I was taught. She gasps and nods her head, which I take as a sign to keep going. When she leans back and I go to brush my lips across her stomach, though, she makes a noise and pushes my head back down with her hand.

"Message received." My whisper echoes loud and harsh in the silent steel room. Dragging the flat of my tongue over her, I murmur, "You have such a gorgeous body. If I could, I'd do this to you for hours."

I think it's the coolest thing how everyone looks completely unique naked. Their lines and curves, the shapes of their anatomy, are like individual works of art. Sensual, tactile works of art. LeeAnne's body is rounded and smooth and more perfect than any sheet-draped vision lounging in a chaise.

LeeAnne's answering gasp swells my chest. So does the sight of her eyes going glassy and her legs sliding a little...bit...wider.

I refocus my efforts between her thighs. On licking, on sucking gently to coax the pleasure out of her. In a moment of what is either pure genius or pure insanity, I try humming a little tuneless something while I'm doing my thing, vibrating my fingers inside her a little to really get the full effect.

"Ethan..."

"Hmmm...?" Since she's grabbing at my hair and kind of, you know. Squeezing me? I don't want to have to ask her for more information.

"Yes," she whispers. "More."

Sheeyah! Right on. More it is. I suck harder. I hum louder. I pump my fingers in and out of her, careful and steady as if I might win a prize if I get her off tonight.

Considering the way she's sounding right now, getting her off would actually be the best prize of all.

"More…more…" She's chanting it now. My face is pressed so tight to her body I can't move much, not that I'm complaining.

So I curl my tongue around that magic bundle of nerves between my lips, and I work it with every bit of mojo I've got, plus other mojo I faked or mustered up or borrowed from the mojo gods by some miracle. More humming. More suction. I keep going, even when my jaw feels tired. Even after I've thrown my glasses on the counter because they're plain old in the way.

For a little while, I worry maybe the entire effort has stalled. She's moaning and panting above me, but I need to make some magic happen. I want to put a satisfied flush on this girl's face. Yeah, I also want the pride of knowing I can get her there.

With my free hand, I reach up, brushing across her chest with my palm. Stroking over hard nipples through her shirt. I try to ask her if it feels good but since my mouth is busy, it comes out sounding like, "Gmmph?"

My answer is a painful tug on my hair, followed by a breathy "yes" and the clang of someone's head bumping the cabinet behind them. Not me.

"Jesus. You all right?"

Her arm gestures are sharp and wild. "Good. Fine. Don't stop."

I breathe deep and bring the little song back, working my fingers in time to my notes. Soon she's rocking against me, her fingers curling in my hair.

Then the dam breaks.

She bucks and grinds against me, pushing against my mouth, moaning high and loud into the air over our heads. Her pleasured screams echo off stainless steel walls.

I'm still horny when I stand but too pleased to care.

She, on the other hand, doesn't look so thrilled in spite of what sounded like a pretty rockin' orgasm. Her look of panic only lasts a few seconds before she jumps down and sets about righting all the condiments and napkin holders that got knocked out of place by our fooling around.

"Oh my god, oh my god, oh my *god.* I can't believe we did that. Joe's going to be back any second," she groans as she fixes her clothes and hurriedly swipes over the counter with a dishrag.

I'm torn between arguing and offering up some cleaning help when a shout comes from the bottom of the service stairs at the back of the kitchen. "LeeAnne? Everything okay up here, girl?"

"Shit! That's Joe. You need to get out of here." Green eyes that had earlier glittered with heat now widen with panic.

Joe of Joe's Bar is in the house. Oh, crudpeppers. I gesture to the messy counter. "I was gonna help with clean up."

"I'll handle it. Just go."

"Right." I lean in to kiss her, and she lets me. Given how she was all freaked, it's almost a pleasant surprise. "Hey. So, it's my birthday tomorrow. Or…I guess it's today? Thing is, the whole thing was shaping up to be kind of awful until just now. Wanted to say so."

Her boss's footsteps approach from the exit door at the back of the kitchen, so all I get in reply are parted lips, wide eyes, and then a frantic shove that sends me back into the bar area. Guess I didn't expect an answer. Had to say what was on my mind, though. Nice Ethan woulda been too afraid of rejection to speak, and we're not doing that anymore.

Still… I'm suddenly a hell of a lot more sober, and feeling the pain of the night's previous activities in brand new parts of my body. I make sure I've got my phone this time before heading out into the cold, with a wet shirt and a whole lot of questions.

#

LeeAnne

Ever since Charles and I got married, I've attended church on Sunday mornings. We said our vows right here in Evergreen Grove while my father all but jammed a shotgun in my ribs, at the same little church on the edge of town where my parents got married. Same one I'm sitting in the back of now, listening as the reverend tells a story about parenthood that I only half understand and that seems odd for a Valentine's Day sermon.

Then again, what do I know?

I'm sure I'm the exact opposite of a good churchgoer. Sometimes—most of the time—I'm not entirely sure why I come here. Especially today, when I'm exhausted from closing the bar and, well…Ethan.

Reverend Meyer walks the aisles as he talks with a little wireless headset thingy. Pretty cutting edge for our tiny church that doesn't seem to have updated its heating in a hundred years. Or maybe I'm overheated because I'm thinking again of the things I did, the things I let Ethan do to me, and the fact that we came so close to getting caught.

I squirm with awareness, sore from the places Ethan's fingers gripped my hips and dug into the flesh of my legs. I'm still humming from the best orgasm I can remember having, ever. At the moment when I'm uncrossing and re-crossing my legs, I look up to find Reverend Meyer looking right at me. *Right* at me.

Oh God. Can I burst into flames now? Please? Pretty please.

But God doesn't answer, maybe because he knows I'm only here for guilty reasons. I'm not sure what else to do with myself on Sunday mornings when the rest of Evergreen Grove is sleeping. Moments when I'm at loose ends are trouble. So I come here, and I pray for magic or inspiration, but none comes. None has.

Not when I lost the baby. Not when word came of Charles's injury. Not now.

When the service is over, I slip out into the front hall, making my way to the outer doors while everyone else is still chatting and catching up on the latest town gossip. No need for me to stay. Too often, I *am* the town's latest gossip.

"LeeAnne, how are you?"

Wow, how did he even catch me? I must really be in trouble with the man upstairs. "Reverend Meyer. Lovely service. How are you?"

I didn't get it. I never have. But that's the right thing to say, isn't it?

The way he tips his head and smiles makes me wonder if he can tell I've been faking my piousness. My religiosity?

"I'm just fine. And how are you? You look tired today."

What a bad moment for my brain to supply an image of Ethan with his mouth between my legs. But that's what happens.

Tell me you want more.

For only a second, my knees lose their strength. "Fine. Good. Late shift last night. You know how exhausting wrangling drunks all night can be."

The reverend smiles patiently.

"All right, maybe you don't. But yeah. Just…a long night."

You have such a gorgeous body.

God, it really is hot in here. Reverend Meyer is a nice man, but I'm trying hard not to look longingly at the door. The people are wandering out in their nice outfits, stopping to congratulate the reverend on his service, and I'm feeling frumpy and all wrong in my sweater dress and tights that I got from the thrift shop.

"Of course." In spite of the throng, Reverend Meyer is still focused on me. "How is your father?"

My gut clenches. Anger. Guilt. Hurt. It's a powerful combination. "He's hanging in there. I was on my way to see him, in fact."

I wasn't. My father and I hardly speak. Not that I enjoy lying, but I need some air and I need it now.

The reverend pats my hand. It strikes me as an oddly grandfatherly gesture for a man who looks under thirty himself. Hard to tell with the beard. "Of course. I do hope you get some rest. It must be a challenge, working such odd hours."

Yes, the bar. That's why I look like a zombie.

If I could, I'd do this to you for hours.

"Oh. Absolutely. I will definitely get in bed as soon as I can. Thank you, Reverend."

Nice one, LeeAnne. You've lied to a pastor and thought sex things in his presence. You are most definitely going to hell.

I dodge Mrs. Kimball, who used to teach third grade, and I race out the door. By the time I've made it down the block and to the bus stop, I'm gnawing on all kinds of guilt. Guilt for what happened last night with Ethan (which was impulsive. Stupid. Wrong. Soooo good. But wrong.). Guilt for lying to Reverend Meyer. For neglecting my father, even though he neglected me first.

While I wait for the bus, I call.

"'lo?" Not too surprising that my father sounds mumbly and slurred at ten in the morning.

"Daddy?" Nothing. "Daddy, it's LeeAnne. Are you there?"

"Course I am. Where else would I be?"

"Oh. Well, I just wanted to call and say hi. See how you're doing."

"Coulda done that at a more decent hour."

I sigh and lean back against the chilly plastic of the bus shelter, trying not to be hurt by his words. Not that I didn't expect them, but they still burn. "Sorry, Dad. I was at church and the reverend asked how you were—"

"Waste of time. Disloyal ingrate like you? God's not gonna give a shit if you show up."

At least, I think that's what he said. Even after all these years, I have trouble understanding when he slurs. "Daddy, have you been drinking?"

He grumbles into the phone. "Been sleepin'. You called way too fucking early."

Again, none of this is unexpected. So why does it hurt? At least I called. He's alive. He's fine—or his own version, anyhow.

The bus approaches. "All right, Daddy. I'm gonna let you go." I pull a tissue from my pocket to wipe a tear that's because of the cold, dammit, not because my dad's only response to me is annoyance.

"Fine. Don't call so early." The line goes quiet.

"Love you, Daddy," I whisper into the dead phone. Because he may be a lot of things, but for years he was all I had. He's still my father.

Then I blow my nose, blame the dry air, and step onto the bus.

4. TRAIN WRECK

Ethan

A harsh burst of sunlight hammers me between the eyes. My head and bladder immediately express their rage, and when I try to cover my face with a pillow, someone pulls it off. I groan and roll over to find my friend Michelle, staring down at me with intense disapproval.

"Missed you in class this morning."

That's right, it's Monday. Or is it Tuesday?

Last few days kinda got away from me. I'd spotted LeeAnne's cell phone sitting on the bar in the middle of my speed walk of shame the other night, and tried to pull off this slick maneuver where I texted a "Let's do that again sometime" message from her phone to mine. You know, like it was her idea? Then replied suggesting a date and time.

Never heard from her. So. Not such a cute trick after all.

After that, let's say I got bummed out and anxious. Used a lot of party punch to take the edge of that piece of glass poking at my insides. A whole lot.

"Class? I heard there might be people there. Didn't wanna see any." What can I say? I get antisocial when I'm feeling unwanted.

Usually when I'm feeling shitty, I work out. Making sure I'm taking care of myself physically is the best way to make sure I'm in good shape mentally. Trouble is, we all drop the ball now and again. Or in my current case, a whole lot of balls.

Michelle's scowl could chase Degas's dancers offstage. I try to tug my pillow back from her hands but the motion makes my stomach slosh. It, too, has to prove its anger.

"Come on. Since when are you my keeper? What are you even doing here?"

It's not like I'm pissed at her for bailing on my birthday. She had good reasons. Still, between this thing with my dad and not hearing from LeeAnne, I'm much happier partying 'til I don't wonder what's wrong with me. Michelle doesn't party and doesn't seem to like people who do, so God knows what she's thinking of me right now.

She tips her head to the side. Less angry now, and more *You poor, stupid, idiot.* I think I liked her first expression better. "The cleaning lady let me in. I tried calling last night to see about rescheduling your birthday celebration, but the one time I got an answer it was some dudebro shouting that 'my main-man Ethan can't talk right now because he has to go pound some more Goldschläger." She slaps my leg with the force that backs up her clear disapproval. "What's going on, Ethan? This isn't like you. Did you accidentally drop all your IQ points inside of a beer trough?"

Michelle's a sweet girl. Emphasis on "sweet." It boggles my mind that her boyfriend is a massive, tatted-up boxer dude because she hates drinking, smoking, swearing and, as far as I can tell, pretty much any vice whatsoever.

I'll save the showing my new tattoo for a special occasion when I really want to flip her out.

Then again, with the way my stomach is churning right now, I can honestly appreciate the alcohol aversion. "Nothing the hell is wrong with me. Situation normal, all fucked up."

She gives me another look. "Since when do you go to frat parties?"

Since never. It actually wasn't my intention to go hit up the crazy tequila pong tournament on Greek Row last night. I let Alonzo and his squad drag me out. "It's been a rocky week. The need to let off steam was real."

"Looks to me like you let off the whole damn smokestack." A pair of sweats hits me in the head. "Now put these on, will you? Aside from the pain of looking at your hairy chicken legs, it looks like someone drew penises all over your calves with magic marker after you passed out. You're going to want to cover those up."

I look down at my legs, one of which was exposed by the tangled-up covers. Sure enough, someone had gone to the (probably drunken) trouble of decorating my legs with some crude phallic symbols. Some writing accompanied the X-rated hieroglyphics but I couldn't tell what it was supposed to say.

Only one word stood out: Virgin.

Yep. That'd be me.

Sort of, anyway. Mostly.

LeeAnne and I the other night, well…I don't think that counts. Does it? Shana and I definitely didn't. God, now that I think of it, I'm awfully fucking relieved.

Fuck, now my head is pounding harder.

With another muttered, "Fuck," I climb out of bed and yank on my sweats. "You didn't see my dad out there, did you?"

Michelle shrugged. "No, but I wouldn't have expected to. Doesn't he teach Composition and Color Theory right now?"

So it *is* Tuesday. "Ugh. Yeah." My tortured agreement can't be contained thanks to how shitty I feel. Maybe Michelle will assume it's the hangover and not ask—

"Ethan, seriously. What's going on?"

I shake my head. Boy, talk about a mistake. "Nothing. Tell me how things are going with you."

A distraction from my humiliation would be great right now.

"Things with me are fine. Dante thought he had a line on someone who might be able to testify against Arlo, his abusive ex-coach. The trip wasn't as productive as we'd hoped but it was what it was. Now," she grabs my hand, "What would cheer you up tonight? We could hit up Joe's Bar for darts and wings, or we could go dancing, or out for a nice dinner, or oh! I heard that they have that psychedelic midnight bowling thing over at the student center."

Staggering to the bathroom, I give Michelle a "wait a minute" signal while I take care of business and make sure my breath isn't heinous.

Honestly, I don't want to do anything. I want to lie in bed and suck my thumb and feel shitty about the fact that my forty-year-old dad has some kind of mojo I don't, and girls actually call *him* back apparently.

"Oh, hell. Just remembered. I think I'm supposed to tutor this afternoon." Twenty-five elementary school kids, and I've got a hangover. Brilliant.

Thank God I'm only the assistant. There's a licensed teacher who oversees the program, so I'm not officially in charge. Still though.

I squint at Michelle. "Look, it's really cool of you to come here and make sure I'm not dead and all, but even if I'm not, I kind of wish I was. My birthday wasn't the worst thing in the world. I got an ill-advised tattoo, committed some arrest-worthy offenses, and I learned I'm as bad at beer pong as I thought. Not in that order."

Keg stands, on the other hand? That was a *real* train wreck.

Michelle tugs a strand of her hair. "So we need to do something to wipe the slate clean."

Without my permission, a mental picture of LeeAnne appears, with her chest heaving and her hair thrown back. Talk about a religious experience. Sure beat my dad kissing Shana while wearing nothing but a fluffy bath towel.

Dude. How many times had she asked me to water her plants and bring in her mail when she was out of town? I totally surfed her cable and used her shower while I was there because she said it was cool and because I thought I was in the home of the girl who might someday be living with me.

Now I think I've been stupid twice in a row, and next time *he* can water her damn plants. The glass in my stomach is ripping it up in there, reminding me of everything I tried to forget last night. Or maybe it's the simple fact that I drank last night with nothing but a slice of day-old pizza in my stomach.

"I don't need to go out. I've got a massive hangover, and I gotta go teach a couple dozen kids how to make mosaics or whatever in a few hours. Just go away and let me die in peace." I grope around in my pile of laundry, looking for a shirt that's clean enough to wear.

Michelle hands me one that's hung over the back of the desk chair she's made herself comfortable in. "Take it from someone who knows, E. You can't hide out in your room forever."

I freeze with my shirt half on and half off. "Shit. You're right." Michelle has no idea, but she's just reminded me of something extremely important. Not only can I not keep hiding in my room, but I need to fucking move.

"I gotta get out of here. If I don't move, I might strangle my dad in his sleep."

She looks around. "Yeah, I get it."

Once my shirt is on, I give her a look. Has she heard something? "You do?"

"You just turned twenty. Take it from someone who lived at home way too long. Eventually you really need to not be the kid who still lives with their parents. I mean, your dad seems way cooler than my parents on a good day, but still. Getting your own space isn't a bad idea if you think you can afford the rent."

I relax against the doorframe between my bedroom and bathroom. Thank God. Not that I want to keep things from my friends, but I'm not ready to share this one yet.

"Yeah, well, luckily I can. It's not like I have a ton of expenses here, so I've saved most of my work-study money and whatnot. This guy from my poetry class might have a room I can rent for cheap, so I think I can work it out."

Also, since my dad's a professor at Pender Tech, I get my tuition for free. That part I keep to myself, because I know Michelle busted her ass for a scholarship and I don't need to be an even bigger dick right now.

Michelle jumps up. "All right. Make you a deal."

That phrase makes my eyes narrow. Michelle likes to try to solve problems. I suspect I'm her new project.

"Uh. What's the deal?"

"Get your shoes on and let's go find you a breakfast sandwich and something for your headache. And coffee. My treat. While we're out, we'll see if we can check out your friend's place. Sound good?"

It sounds like it involves sunlight, but as much as I want to go back to sleep, the life-altering shocks of the previous weekend have me dying to get my independence, and Alonzo did say I could come by his place this week to see about the available room he's got for rent.

"It's a nice offer, and I have to admit it might even make me feel human. Can we go to the coffee shop over by the vet college? I heard there was some sort of protest on the other side of campus today. As much as I love a good consciousness-raising, the noise might actually kill me."

"What are they protesting this time?"

"Dining hall conditions, I think. Fuck, where are my glasses?" I don't mind wearing them usually, but when I can't find the damn things and I can't see *to* find them *without* them, I get ragey.

"A worthy cause. Remember when you got food poisoning?"

My stomach makes a mighty heave-ho. "Please. Don't remind me."

"Yeah, well. Don't die, okay? I'm not strong enough to haul your carcass back here if you do." She's kidding, I hope?

Now that Michelle's not standing right in my face, I can't see her well enough to tell.

"Yeah. Well. If you promise me a fancy coffee drink with flavors and whipped cream on top, I promise to try not to keel over. And potato chips." Sounds gross, I know. Works for my hangover every time.

"And..." Michelle holds up a finger. "You'll come out with us tonight to re-celebrate your birthday."

Another groan escapes from my raw throat. I don't know if I was screaming a lot last night or chucking up all the junk I drank, and I'm sort of glad I don't remember.

"I think I might need a day to recover."

"You can't have pounding shots at some random party with strangers be the only thing you did to celebrate your birthday. Let your friends take you out. Have some actual fun and not mindless partying."

Once again, my mind goes to LeeAnne. Her cheeks flushed hot pink and her lips parted on breathy moans. The heat of her around my fingers. The taste of her on my tongue. Another groan comes from my mouth, and it has nothing to do with displeasure.

For a fleeting moment, I wonder how I could have been stupid enough to believe I had some kind of cosmic connection or whatever with Shana. One night with LeeAnne and I can't get her out of my head. I'm pissed she hasn't called, but I can't think too much or my head hurts. I guess getting sloshed worked out after all.

"Ethan?" Michelle waves her hands in my face.

I push away from the doorway and grab for a towel. "Yeah. Fine. We'll go out. But I don't promise to have any fun."

Then I turn around and walk right into the bathroom door.

#

Alonzo's place is an old house on the edge of Ever-green Grove. I could throw a rock from the back yard and hit the dividing line between Evergreen Grove and Pender, the larger city where our campus lies. There's a bus that goes from one to the other, which is useful since parking on campus can be a real bitch. Unless I'm feeling atrocious (like today), I could even walk.

It's clear Michelle disapproves, from the wrinkle of her nose and the careful, mincing steps she takes across a floor that hasn't been cleaned since maybe the last president took office? The one before?

"Ethan, this place is a sty," she hisses. "Why are we here? Surely there are better options."

"Kinda trying to find something in a hurry," I whisper back.

Jesse's passed out on a massive L-shaped sofa in the living room, which has clearly seen better days. He's watching Pro Wrestling, or at least he was when he was still conscious.

I'm greeted by a friendly and surprisingly alert Alonzo (considering how I left him last night) and a surly young blond lady who doesn't give her name or any other information; she doesn't talk at all, for that matter. Alonzo introduces her as Layla and leaves well enough alone. She's wearing warm-up pants and a sports bra, and from the look on her face and the shape of her arms, she could kick my ass. I decide it's best if I don't piss her off.

"So I hope you're cool with a little weed," Alonzo's saying as he shows me around. He points to Jesse, who's still dead on the couch. "Guy's a legit pothead, man. Good guy, but he pretty much lives in front of the television smoking up, you know? Here, let me show you where you'd be shacking up if you decided to take the place…"

Michelle trails behind me, looking like she's not sure whether she wants to vomit or call in an anonymous tip to the authorities. Me, I'm not sure whether I want to ask Alonzo if he's got another of the beers he's sipping, because suddenly I'm remembering that hair-of-the-dog thing my friends always talk about and wondering if it might not be such a bad idea. Or a bad idea with good results? Either way, my stomach feels better but my head doesn't, and something has got to be done.

"So the last guy who lived here, he kind of had some issues," Alonzo continues as he shows us up to the third floor. "Good news is, once you get everything cleaned up, you'll have your own bathroom. And a king-size bed, if you feel comfortable sleeping on the mattress. Griffin got a lot of action. You know what I'm saying?"

He holds up a fist for a bump but makes the mistake of aiming it toward Michelle, who looks at him like he's gone insane. "And how come Griffin left in the middle of the school year?"

Alonzo laughs and drops his hand, giving a "you got me" kind of shrug. "*Oh.* Yeah. He flunked out."

Super.

Opening the door, Alonzo points into the room and manages to sink all of my hope. The "clean everything up" he referred to isn't a simple matter of a few boxes or some sweeping. The place is bad. I mean, I've got some laundry piles in my room but my mom taught me how to make my bed and dust off all the surfaces once in a while.

This place?

"I can't believe it hasn't been condemned." Michelle voices my thoughts aloud.

"It needs a little elbow grease," I agree. That's a massive understatement but I can't manage to take it all in right now. The floor is almost black but I can tell it's hardwood. The walls wear a dingy layer of…I'd call it rotten avocado? Some area rugs have been left around but they're wadded up and God only knows what's been ground into the fibers.

This Griffin guy, whoever he was, must have had some mad skills in the sack if he managed to get girls to have sex with him in this room. Either that, or I have no clue about what it is women look for when it comes to guys.

Well, clearly that second thing is true.

"Seriously, Ethan, we could look around more."

I push my glasses up and meet Michelle's irritated stare. "Look, I walked in on Shana and my dad in her apartment. They were in what I'd call a compromising position. I refuse to live in that house any longer, and I don't want to spend time looking midyear. Student housing is all full. It'll be fine for now."

After a moment of stunned silence, Michelle says, "What? All right. That's messed-up. I get it. But this place is filthy, and I think you're looking at a frying pan-slash-fireplace situation, here."

Alonzo chooses that moment to get indignant. "Hey, man. Needs some soap and water, that's all."

"If by soap and water you mean bleach and a hazmat suit."

I let them bicker while I pull out my phone. One thing I *do* know is that waiting around for someone to notice you're there doesn't do any good. So I shoot a text to LeeAnne: *Hey. It's Ethan. I know the other night was kind of crazy, but I'd really like to see you again.*

You see me all the time. At the bar.

Huh. Can't tell if she's being cute or giving me the brush-off, and that lingering nice guy piece of me figures I should let it go. And I *will* let it go, if she's plain old not into me. Except the way she moaned my name and put her hands in my hair...those weren't the moans of a girl who wasn't into me.

So do I get to see you the way I saw you last time at the bar?

No answer.

Alonzo's defending the state of his den of iniquity. "It's not actually so terrible." He walks over to a bay window and throws the curtain open. "See, lotsa light."

"All that does is make it easier to tell how disgusting it is." Michelle turns and grabs my arm. "Surely there are other places. Let's see what else is available."

"I'm telling you, bro. You're not going to find a sweeter deal." Alonzo spreads his arms wide, standing in the middle of a braided rug that looks like it's from the seventies. Maybe it was even in the middle of an orgy back then. Either he's oblivious to the grime and piles of trash surrounding him, or he's hoping *we* will be. "Plus, Layla's in a band. We have house parties every month. All the beer and ass you can handle."

My phone vibrates in my hand.

Michelle comes around to stand in front of me. "Who are you texting?"

"Nobody."

"E, this really doesn't sound like the best place for you. Aside from the fact that it's disgusting, after what happened last night, do you really think it's healthy for you to get over your ex by moving to party central?"

Actually, at the moment, I'm not even thinking about Shana. In my few sober moments over the past couple of days, I've realized my anger at my dad is not entirely about that. More about the fact that I never entirely felt comfortable, like maybe it was an inconvenience to have me around. I love my dad, and I'm sure he loves me, but I've gotten the sense that my dad never really planned on having kids before I dropped into his world.

As far as Shana goes? Well, I get hard every time I think of LeeAnne since the other night. It was never like that with Shana. I'm beginning to think I just didn't have enough experience with other women to know the difference.

I slide my phone out to read LeeAnne's reply: *Ethan... You're sweet, but we're in such different places. You're*

*younger and you're still in college. I don't think it's good for
us to see each other again. That way.*

*I'm not that young and I'm not that sweet. And I know
damn well I made you feel good. Let me do it again. Please.*

Ethan...

Am I wrong? Wasn't it good?

Yes.

Fuck. Yes. I was about to throw in the towel when she
sent me back those three amazing letters.

Except she thinks I'm young and sweet. Yeah, definitely being a guy who still lives with his parents won't help
that image.

I make eye contact with Alonzo over Michelle's head.
"How soon can I move in?"

Alonzo shrugs again. "If you want it, the room is yours
anytime."

The faster I get away from my dad's place, the better. I
grab his hands and shake until my vision goes blurry. "I'm in."

\#

I started tutoring at Grove Elementary for senior-year
service hours. After my hours ended, the teachers asked me to
come back and I liked the kids, so I kept going. Honestly, it's a
good way to keep from turning into a hermit on those weeks
when I'd rather hole up in my room with nothing but my TV
and my paints.

Today, however, I could pass. For starters, there's the
a-hole in the beaten-up truck who cuts me off on my way into
the school parking lot. Then there's all the bright and happy
that threw up on the school walls on my way in. Most days I
love kids' artwork, but I am so not in the mood for all these
rainbows.

In spite of it being after three when I get to the school,
my head still feels all throbby and I've only managed to keep
down half a piece of toast. It isn't pretty. Hopefully it was at
least a good lesson.

'Cause when I check in at the office and walk into the art room to the sound of a couple dozen kids yelling "Hi, Mr. K!", I'm about ready to turn around and leave. Not that I would, because a lot of these kids are here for more than doing crafts and getting help with their homework. Man, though. That headache rears up again, good and angry.

"Heya, Max." I make a beeline for the quiet kid in the corner while Mrs. Temple, the teacher who runs this whole thing, passes out the snacks. Pretty sure some of the kids in this program only come here for the free cheese and crackers, but at least they're here.

Max scribbles in a notebook, his face screwed up in the kind of frustration I probably get on my own face when a piece isn't coming together right. Class hasn't started yet, but he's working on his own sketch; some kind of half-human, half-robot thing. Seems to be attacking a village.

"Hey, so is that the bad guy?"

Max shakes his head. "That's Robitron. These people called him for help from the evil zombie boss. He's flying in to save them."

He flips pages, pointing to a lifelike rendering of the evil zombie with an arm hanging from its mouth. Even my queasy stomach can't find fault with the quality of his work.

"Wow. That's pretty gross, Max. Great work."

The smile I get from this kid. Man. It about chases away my headache.

Until I wonder how many people have told him his drawings have real potential. I know firsthand how hard it can be to have confidence in your own ability. "Hey, Max. Seriously." I flip to another page, a cityscape with shooting lasers and more robots. "These are really good."

A thousand expressions play across his face before he finally says, "Thanks. Hey, Mr. K. How can you tell if a duck is a boy or a girl?"

I'm stumped by this change of subject, but I play along. "I don't know. How?"

He shrugs, eyelids hooded and shy. "Ask it, I guess."

I laugh because I think he wants me to, and because I think for some reason he wasn't comfortable with my praise so he needed to say something different. Still though, I worry about this kid sitting in the corner who isn't being encouraged. No child left behind and all.

On my way around the room, I say hello to all the other kids who reach out to slap me five or wave. In a spur-of-the-moment thing, I whip out my phone and text Max's duck joke to LeeAnne, because I love goofy jokes like that and she's the person I want to share it with.

Plus I've got this crazy notion that if I can make her laugh, she'll want to keep me around.

The duck joke doesn't go *quite* my way with her. LeeAnne's reply:

Ha. Customer at bar is a duck watcher. Heard you can tell by the feathers. ;)

I'm tempted to stand here for far too long and analyze her reply (Was that sarcasm? I got a sideways winky face. Maybe she did think it was funny?), but I'm getting a scowl from Mrs. Temple. Not supposed to have my phone out when I'm working with the kids.

So I slide on over to say what I wanted to say. "Hey, Mrs. T? Have you taken a look at the drawing Max does? It's really good work."

She's busy getting out popsicle sticks and cotton balls for whatever it is we're doing today. "Oh, yeah." A dismissive wave of the hand makes my head pound some more. "He's been doing that comic book stuff forever."

"Yeah, but I mean, this kid's got real talent. He's special. I really think—"

"Every kid in here is special, Mr. K." She gives me a pointed look.

"Of course. But—"

"Help me pass these out, would you?" She shoves a tray full of supplies into my hands, and I get the idea this is her way of ending the conversation.

I grit my teeth and turn to hand out the popsicle sticks and whatnot, with a newly formed piece of glass poking me from the inside. When I get to Max's seat, I lean down and tap on his notebook. "Hey, bud. You hang on to that stuff for me. I wanna take a look at it later."

The kid gifts me with another blinding smile.

I've done some dumbass things lately, like most of all the copious quantities of beer I consumed the night before. Got this serious-looking kid to smile though, so today feels like a win.

Hopefully one of these days, I can get LeeAnne to show me such a winning smile.

5. SWEET

LeeAnne
I'm on edge working at Joe's tonight. In a big way. Keeping my hands steady to pour a beer takes more effort than usual.

Since Charles came in to talk, I've been looking over my shoulder. I thought it wouldn't bother me to know he was back in town, so long as he kept his distance, but day after day it gets worse.

Tonight, I could have sworn I saw him when I was walking in the door to the bar again, but he said he wouldn't bother me. At one time, I'd have expected him to be working. He used to have a regular route, driving medical supplies. I'd been grateful when we were together that his job kept him away for long stretches of time. Eventually the job fell through, like all things with Charles.

Thank goodness it's slow for a Saturday. There's a regular crowd here of course, including the guys who hang out to shoot the breeze over boxing and drink pitchers until their wives drag them home. A handful of kids are here from the college over in Pender, which is fairly new. More started coming when Joe hired Cassie to play the guitar. She's been out with a flu or something, so that helps.

Honestly, Cassie's sweet and the crowd here loves her. I can't complain. Not to mention she helped me out of a jam once, so I sort of owe it to her to be nice. Still…

My eyes scan the room, landing on my coworker, Jake. He's over by a table full of friends, saying hi. At one time, I'd thought Jake was going to be the white knight who rescued me from Charles.

Jake's with Cassie now. And I guess it was a good thing I grew up and realized there's no such thing.

So what, right? What was I thinking? My father always said I was lucky Charles had been willing to marry me. Too many of those fairy tales my mother read to me as a child. They're still in there, even if I'd be smarter to rip the book into pieces and throw them away. Which is why I shouldn't think about seeing Ethan again. A nice, smart college kid with his whole future ahead of him doesn't belong with someone who's this…damaged. Someone who's already old at twenty-two.

Morris Epson, the local taxidermist, gestures for me to get him another Mic Light. I make the mistake of glancing up in the middle of the pour in time to see Jake's friend Dante scoot his chair back from the table.

And the sight of the nerdy-hot guy behind him makes me pour beer all over my arm.

I knew he'd probably be back. That doesn't mean I was ready to see him tonight. Or any night.

"Dammit."

"You all right there, young lady, or did the beer do something to offend you?"

Morris is looking at me from over his mustache, like he thinks I might pass out. Meanwhile, I've committed alcohol abuse.

"I'm so sorry." Putting the glass aside, I force myself to focus while I start over but all I can see in my head is *him*.

Ethan.

Tell me you want more.

He's texted me a few times. Ridiculous things. Crazy things. Things I probably ought to ignore but can't seem to.

Ethan: *What do you call a vegetable that goes ding-dong?*

Me: *Your head?*

Ethan: *Ha. A bell pepper. Get it??!!*

I can almost see him holding his sides with laughter over the ridiculous joke.

Ethan: *That was my sister's favorite joke when she was little. All the rage at the preschool.*

Me: *And you think it's got flirting potential?*

Ethan: *I tutor fifth and sixth graders in the after school art program over at Grove Elementary. The ladies there love my sense of humor.*

Me: *You're comparing me to a twelve-year-old?*

Ethan: *Just hoping you'll find me as cute as they do. ;)*

At first, I worried. He'd gotten my number by picking up my phone from the bar, and did that speak to a guy who didn't respect boundaries? But then this happened:

Me: *Ethan, I think it's better if we're just friends.*

Ethan: *Truth? Do Not Want. Just friends is hard to do after I've had my hands on your skin and I know what you taste like, LeeAnne. I want more. But if what YOU honestly want is for me to leave you alone, then say the word.*

I didn't answer that day, knowing that in saying nothing, I was sort of making a decision anyway. The truth was that I hadn't gotten the way he'd made me feel out of my head. And him offering to walk away? Made me want him to less, somehow, even though I knew he should.

As I watch Ethan, my pulse picks up. Joe is supposed to be at the bar, but tonight our cook is sick so Joe's in the back. Jake and I have been running around all evening, and I'm so distracted I hadn't noticed Ethan's presence. I'm not sure whether I'm disappointed or relieved that he hasn't yet come over.

Great. Now that I've spotted him, he's approaching. With Dante's girlfriend, Michelle. She's a sweet one, too. They're all sweet. Not like me.

Next to all of these college kids, I feel like I'm four tires away from being trailer trash.

"Hey, LeeAnne. How're you doing tonight?"

"Really good. You?"

I have to say that or people ask questions. In reality, smiling hurts my face. Ethan is smiling also, standing a step behind Michelle. He's wearing a black T-shirt with white letters, bearing the statement, "ARTISTS DO IT WITH BOLD STROKES."

No. I most certainly did *not* just try to picture what that means.

Behind Ethan's innocent boy-next-door-looking glasses, I see all the things he isn't saying out loud. Those text messages, which seemed so safe and distant when I was lying alone in the dark, now broadcast from those warm brown eyes:

You've been thinking about me, haven't you? I know you loved how I touched you, how I made you feel special and wanted. How I made you light up like nobody else has. Bet you can't walk into that back room without remembering what we did there.

And I can't, either. Every time I head into the kitchen to grab an order or even to refill a bottle of ketchup, I willfully avert my gaze to avoid the pull of that spot where Ethan made me feel things I didn't think I was even capable of.

Michelle's talking to me. Asking something. Ordering something. I don't even know because I can't get the picture of Ethan on his knees in front of me out of my head.

I'm filling a glass with water to try to cover the fact that my skin is on fire, when Ethan's jaw turns to stone.

I follow his gaze and spot Randy, Charles's old friend that Ethan got into that dustup with the other night.

They're staring at each other, nostrils flaring and all but whipping out their dicks so they can piss on each other. Randy's got his fists clenched like he's already in the mood to start a fight. Ethan, approaching Randy with his arms crossed over his chest, isn't looking much better.

The bar's gotten quiet, chatter and laughter dying away at the tables as people see them squaring off. Dammit, why couldn't Randy have been too drunk to remember?

Joe comes out of the kitchen to deliver a plate of nachos. "What seems to be the trouble out here?"

I brace my hands on the bar, willing Ethan—either of
them, but mostly Ethan—to back away. As much as I appreciate what he did to stand up for me, I can't have them starting a
fight during business hours. Joe will ban him, for one thing.
For another, I can't be involved with a guy who solves every
single one of his problems with his fists.

Charles was that kind of guy. I don't want to find out
Ethan's the same kind of person. I really don't.

#

Ethan

"You're gonna break your neck, buddy." Dante seems
to think my fixation on LeeAnne is funny as hell.

When that dipstick glared at me from the bar with his
jeans slung low and his lip jutting out full of tobacco, I took
one look at the horror on LeeAnne's face and backed away.
Not before I made it as clear as I could to that fucker that I had
my eye on him. I may be wiry, but I'm pretty sure if I knocked
him down once I can do it again. I'm not sure of much, but I
don't stand for guys shitting on me for funsies. Or the people I
care about.

At some point though, I figured she'd stop by the table.
Say hi, maybe. I can't decide whether she's only busy or point-
edly avoiding eye contact. Or both? During our late-night texting sessions, I got the sense that maybe I'd broken through and
she was starting to bend on my not being datable.

*You're young. You're sweet. You need a nice college
girl,* she'd said in one of her messages.

*I'm 20. You're 22. This isn't exactly a Harold and
Maude scenario. And I said I'm not that sweet. The glasses fool
everyone. Ask me about when I vandalized the school bathroom. *suspense music, here**

Because I was feeling ballsy, I also added, *If you want, I can do that thing again where I take the glasses off and get between your legs until you come.*

Uh...I don't know who Harold and Maude are.

I tried not to take it as a bad sign that she'd ignored my blatant come-on. Which was way better than my vandal story. My buddy Lucas and I'd used a bar of soap. As vandalizing went, it wasn't super hardcore.

Emo twenty-year-old falls in love with a woman who's like...80? It's a cult classic. We'll watch it together sometime.

You're awfully sure of yourself, aren't you?

At the time, I'd fired back a reply about how of course I was sure and she was definitely going to want to go out with me. Seemed like the way to play. Truth is, I'm not sure of myself ever, at all. I question everything I do, every day. *Every* day.

I question my artistic ability. I question my friendships. Even the friends I think I can trust (especially after what happened with my dad and Shana). If I say or do the wrong thing, will they turn their backs? Will they lose their faith in me like my high school buddy, Lucas, did?

Used to be I worried maybe my parents would decide I wasn't worth the trouble. It's why I've always tried to be so fucking agreeable. Like that's gotten me anywhere except stepped on.

People would probably laugh if I said I was afraid my parents would give me away, but such is the life of an adopted kid with free-floating anxiety. It's a bitch. Then again, so are lots of things.

The big difference lately? I've decided on doing the thing I actually want instead of the thing that seems safest. Safe never got me anything good, and I'm gonna worry no matter what. So fuck it.

Dante snaps his hands in front of my face. "Boy, you got it bad. Still in there?"

I realize I've been staring across to the bar where LeeAnne is pouring beers, and Angry McTrucker Hat is hunched in his flannel shirt with one surly eye on me and the other on whatever's happening with the TV above his head.

"That guy," I mutter. "He was bothering LeeAnne the last time I was in here. The night before my birthday."

My words are short and gruff. They hide my internal panic, I hope. What if that guy starts trouble again? What if he rattles LeeAnne?

I'm usually pretty good at keeping my misfiring nerves on the inside. My desire to go over there and shove that guy out of the bar myself covers everything lurking underneath: Is LeeAnne all right? Would she rather I leave? Would she rather I'd said something to him? Am I wasting my time here, thinking a few text messages mean she's into me at all?

Everyone at our table is now passing around greasy appetizers and pouring beers. I was hoping nobody'd notice me rapidly switching my focus from the pretty, ponytailed bartender on the other end of the room to the shady townie hunched over at the end of the bar. Or the way I'm gripping my fork.

Jake, who stopped by the table to say hello, glances over to the bar. "Yeah, I think that guy's buddies with her ex. Probably isn't a fan since she and Charles split, but as far as I know he's mostly harmless."

"Yeah, well he kind of tried to shove me into a wall," I mumble, right before cramming a cheese-laden nacho in my mouth. Really though, I'm not feeling that "harmless" explanation at all.

"Hey, man, let's not go stepping into trouble now. How about we throw some darts." Dante nudges me, so I wipe my fingers and jump up from the table. Sending something sharp and pointy at the wall sounds like a good distraction.

Partly because I'll take any excuse not to sit in the corner and stare across the room like a stalker. Partly because

Dante Ramos asked me to play darts, so hell freaking yeah I'll play some darts. Used to watch him on TV with my dad when he boxed professionally. While I may be mega pissed at my father right now, it hasn't taken the coolness out of the fact that one of my best friends is living with a guy I've cheered for from my living room couch.

The caffeine I keep drinking isn't helping my jitters. Or my distraction. My gaze keeps straying back over to the bar.

"Hey, careful there, buddy."

While watching LeeAnne have a tense conversation with that guy who gave her trouble the other night, the dart I threw missed the board by a country mile. In fact, it's imbedded in the drywall by an ancient Jukebox. A goatee-wearing dude in a backwards baseball cap gives me an evil glare. Looks like I missed his shoulder by a few inches. Can't blame him, though, for being pissed.

"Shit. Sorry man," I give a little wave.

Dante claps me on the shoulder and goes to grab the dart. He smiles at the grumpy customer and gives him a warm "How's it going?" before offering to buy beers for his table. It's easy to see why Dante is so popular.

As I stand there, I find myself beating back a hint of jealousy. Dante is tall—like, definitely taller than my five feet, ten inches (and a half, if my posture's excellent, which it hardly ever is), with muscles bulging out of his toasted-pecan skin. He walks around with this cocky swagger, as if he's totally at home in his body. I'm surprised G-strings and jock straps don't just hit him in the face as he passes people on the street.

I've never had that kind of self-assuredness and I wonder what it must be like. Right now, I'm a big faker walking around.

Dante's hand lands on my shoulder again. "So. You're into LeeAnne?"

"Uh…" Guess I was staring again.

"Don't know her all that well, but Jake does." He points over his shoulder with his thumb. "Could ask him to put in a good word. Talk you up?"

"Nah. I should really do it myself." Especially since we breezed right past the getting-to-know-you stage and headed straight on to naked.

Sort of naked.

I don't want to say so to Dante, but I get the sense that asking Jake to talk me up would be a major step backwards. Massive. Like, all the way back to having him stick a note in her locker that says, "Do you like Ethan? Check yes or no."

Then again, a note like that would certainly clear up a lot of ambiguities.

"Hey, I heard you offer that guy some beers. I should go get them."

Dante waves me off. "Nah, buddy. We're here to celebrate your birthday. It's on me."

That's a great offer, and since I'm gonna have to actually pay rent from now on, I'd love to accept. However, I really want another excuse to go talk to LeeAnne.

"Thanks, but it's cool. I'm gonna go get the guy his beers."

Dante looks at me and angles his head toward the bar. "Ah. Aha, I got you. Good luck, buddy. Don't do anything I wouldn't do."

"Uh. Yeah. Something tells me that leaves me pretty wide open to getting my face slapped."

Dante's booming laugh fills the bar. "Hey, now. I'm practically a saint since I've been with Michelle."

I glance back and forth between the two of them, wondering again how their relationship works. Then I gather up all the courage two and a half Diet Cokes can instill in me and march over to the bar. After my ridiculous overindulgence the last few nights, I'm still disturbingly sober.

Chances are excellent I'm going to get my ass handed to me or beer dumped on my head. In the interest of optimism, I push up my glasses (using the sides and not the nose piece so it's slightly less geeky) and I lead with my best grin.

When LeeAnne spots me, a crease appears in the middle of her forehead, and suddenly I'm wishing I spent more time hanging out with Dante and Jake, and less time painting and reading alone in my bedroom.

"So, a bunch of penguins walk into a bar," I say as soon as I pull up in front of her. Sometimes she actually pretends to find my text jokes funny, and sometimes all she does is send me a thumbs down emoji. I think she likes them more than she's letting on, so leading with one now feels like a good strategy.

She's moved away from Douchey McTrucker-Hat to clean up a spill at the other end of the bar. Even if he hadn't started shit with me, I'd hate the dude on principle. LeeAnne's smile appears so rarely, and he's in here stressing her out. I can tell from the tight curve of her shoulders and the lines around her mouth.

She gives me an eye roll now, but the barest curve of her lips tell me I'm on to something with the joke. "Let me guess. One of the penguins ducks?"

"Please. Penguins. Ducks. Totally wrong climate. No way." I slap my hand on the bar. "So these penguins walk into a bar, and the bartender says 'We don't serve your kind here.' So the penguins say…"

I give her a little jazz hands maneuver for suspense.

She pours a beer and hands it to a customer. "I can't begin to guess."

"Oh, no! Waddle we do!"

Some dude next to me snorts into the beer LeeAnne just handed him. "Heh. Because penguins waddle."

She smirks and shakes her head. "That's horrible and you should be ashamed."

"Aww, really? The kids I tutor love that one."

I see her steps stutter in the middle of grabbing some glasses from behind the bar. "I'm not sure what it says that you keep telling me jokes meant for kids."

In spite of her protest, the groove in her forehead eases up. Her eyes are practically crinkling at the corners, the way a person's eyes do when they're smiling. We're making progress, baby.

"Hey, how about this one? Oh. Could you send four of the house special over to that table with the broody guy and his friends?"

One hand goes to her hip. "Is that the joke or do you actually want to send four beers to that table?"

"Four beers to that table, please. They're technically from Dante, if that helps. Also, did you hear about the donkey that fell into some sugar? Wait for it..." I put my hands up for the big reveal. "Now *that's* a sweet ass."

LeeAnne's answer is more of an agonized groan. Her hand is gripping the beer tap with some force, and her head drops almost like she's about to clunk it on the polished mahogany in front of her. I kinda wonder if she'd maybe rather be wringing my neck.

When she stands up again though? Man, I can see she's fighting a smile. There's even some light in her eyes. That right there is what I hold on to.

"Come on," I say. "Sweet ass? That's hysterical. I laughed for fifteen minutes when Alonzo told me that joke. I *actually* cried a little."

The dude next to me seems to agree. He's chuckling so hard I think he might fall off his stool.

"See! *He* thinks it's funny."

Her smile brightens some as she plunks four mugs on the counter. "Maybe you should go out with *him*."

I lean across the bar so I can get close to her. Get a better look at that amazing smile. "Gosh, he's a good-looking guy and all, but I kind of have a thing for this really special girl. Can't stop thinking about kissing her again."

LeeAnne rolls her eyes, but I can tell I've gotten to her. She can't hide the vibrant rose blush that washes across her throat and the tops of her cheekbones, even if she'd like to. "You're insane."

"That's one interpretation."

"Uh-huh. Now hand over your ten bucks and get out of here."

The tiny half smile hasn't left her face but I don't want to push my luck. "Yes, ma'am."

I gather up the beers and turn away. Just as I do, fingers grab my arm.

"Hey. Wait. I'll take the beers over. And, uh, I'll text you later."

Yes! I'd do some sort of victory dance, but I don't want to knock over those beers.

Down the bar, I see that a-hole fidgeting with his phone and giving me the evil eye. *Yeah, fuck off, buddy.*

6. No to Stretchy Pants
LeeAnne

It's Monday morning and I'm at the gym with AJ. I've been staying at a place he owns since Charles and I split, and he's been helping me to learn about boxing and self-defense.

It's a lot of work, but I'm slowly building confidence. AJ and his boyfriend competed in the Golden Gloves last year, so he's a good teacher. Dante, who co-owns the gym, is a former professional fighter. Some seriously hardcore guys come here to train, so it's a wonder I manage to get myself through the door. There's an awful lot of testosterone swimming around this place, and every time I'm here I do my best not to run and hide in the dressing room.

Supposedly, AJ's showing me all the same stuff Dante showed *him*, but I feel as if he's got me on the kiddie ride. I'm too nervous and awkward for anything else.

"This is always sort of unsettling," I tell AJ. I'm talking to his reflection in a big floor-to-ceiling wall mirror. We're using it because he wants me to watch my form, but all it's doing is making me feel small. If I look beyond my reflection, I can see men twice my size sparring in a ring, hitting a heavy bag or lifting weights that would crush me to death. Those plates are, like, the size of a tire.

How are we even pretending I fit in here?

AJ stops to grab some water. "What part? Are you having trouble with the moves? If you want, we can take it slower."

God, no. Already we're practically standing still. "It's not that. It's..." I throw up my hands. "I mean, look at me. I'm no athlete. Besides, watching myself in the mirror makes me feel like a dope."

Show me a woman who's comfortable looking at herself up close in yoga pants and I'll show you someone who's had at least two shots of tequila. At which point, she's on the bar and ready to take off the yoga pants. So, you see. Just say no to stretchy pants unless you've got your butt covered or you're home alone.

AJ smiles like he understands, and I'm sure he does. Right now though, that smile makes me itch. Around the little town of Evergreen Grove, I get a lot of those smiles, especially since I left Charles.

Oh, how ARE you, sweetie? You look like you're hanging in there even though you're all alone. Bless your heart.

What that phrase really means is, "Boy, didn't you get the shitty end of the stick?"

And if they're all around now to ooze syrupy sweetness, how come not a single person knew I needed help? The embarrassment and shame made me keep it to myself. The guilt and fear made me stay. But sometimes I was convinced the whole world could tell.

Charles wasn't always the way he is now. A bit of a temper, but nothing like he was...after.

AJ's still watching me, and I can't rub away the prickles from the back of my neck. Since I've been on my own, the paranoia, the queasy fear of being watched and discussed, follows me everywhere.

"LeeAnne, the stronger you are physically, the stronger you'll feel mentally and emotionally. Trust me."

The deep breath I suck down sears my lungs. He's right. I know he is. I know AJ is only trying to help. "I wish I knew why this all feels so impossible."

More hive-inducing sympathy oozes from his blue eyes. "You're scared. And things have been a certain way for so long that any change hurts. Even if the change is good. It took years for things to get to be the way they were, so you can expect results won't be fast either."

AJ's eyes aren't just blue; they are a clear, deep blue, like the ocean. Something about them is so earnest that my chest deflates. "I'm sorry, AJ. You've done nothing but be a good friend and help me out of a bad situation and here I am, arguing with you,"

"Hey." He puts his gloved hands into the air. "I am the master at that stuff. I'm telling you…ask Dante sometime, how much trouble I used to give him when he tried to train me. And speaking of which? It took me a lot of time in here to make any progress happen. If I can do it, so can you."

He motions up and down his body, showing a muscled landscape that I have to admit is awfully nice. His lean chest and arms are well defined and covered in tribal tattoos. Honestly, he almost looks like a model. A few scars and a dimpled chin add to the ruggedness of his physique. Both handsome and kind with a fabulous sense of humor, we could all use an AJ in our lives. I instruct myself to use him as an example of what I can accomplish.

Ethan's latest text pops into my head:

Ethan: Hey. What did the egg say to the boiling water?

LeeAnne: I'm afraid to ask.

Ethan: Might take a while to get hard. I just got laid by this chick!

*LeeAnne: *crickets chirping**

What a pants-flaming lie. It had been my first time ever laughing at anything while lying awake in the wee hours of the morning, but it felt like giving something too big away to say so.

Ethan: Oh. Come. ON. I'll get you to laugh yet, missy.

Me: Missy?

Ethan: Would you prefer ma'am? Queen? Princess? Queencess? Tell me what you like and that's what I'll call you.

Remembering Ethan and his goofball jokes, the way he asked me what I liked, pushes my lips into a smile. It reminds me of, well, *that night*. It creates a strange, fluttery sensation in the center of my body. Heat centers between my thighs. All sorts of confusing things have happened with Ethan.

A guy like him almost makes me believe I'm worth more. That what I want matters. I don't know if that's something I can honestly trust.

I look at AJ, staring me down with frustration and concern. "I'll keep trying," I tell him. "You're right. Maybe eventually it won't feel so awkward."

AJ taps his glove on my shoulder. "You know, I get it. Maybe not the same way, but I do. The weirdness will fade as your confidence builds. Some of it maybe never will entirely go away, but I think a little paranoia can be healthy. Even in this quiet town, it's good to stay on our toes."

He says it with a smile though, and I smile back. "You make some good points."

"Eh. Sometimes my brain works. Either way, we've got to start somewhere. First step if we're feeling out of control is to find the things we know we can manage. Going fetal and watching infomercials fixes nothing. Believe me, I've tried."

I raise my eyebrows. Partly excited, because I totally do this. "Oh, really?"

"Hell yeah. I totally love that pasta maker, too. Hayden's gonna kill me though if I get any more gadgets."

Some of the tension bleeds from my body as I laugh. "Oh. Wow. Thank you. I needed to hear that. I almost bought home work-out videos one night, and I have no DVD player or any room to work out."

I couldn't bring myself to stay in the house I'd shared with Charles. The place AJ's given me to stay is nice. It's clean. But it's only got room for a bed, a dresser, and a small table. There's no way I'm doing the *Fifteen Minute Ab-Sanity Workout* on my little postage-stamp sized floor.

"Hey, if you're ever really dying for a gut-buster, I'll tell you about the rainbow-colored toilet bowl night light I ordered for our bathroom. For now, though?" He taps his gloves together. "Back to work."

"Wait, is that like an actual light on the—"

"Back to work!"

He puts me through the usual cardio exercises, shuffling left and right to work on my foot speed, and jumping rope. That part's honestly my favorite because it brings me back to the simplicity of my childhood, when I'd go out to jump rope with my friends and then run home to sit in the kitchen while my mom cooked dinner. That was a long time ago.

"Water break." AJ tosses over a bottle.

"Ohmygod, thank you." It's crazy. I hadn't realized I was so thirsty from a little jumping around, but I guzzle the water greedily.

So much so that I almost choke when AJ asks me, "So I stopped by the bar Saturday night. Looked like you were getting kind of cozy with Ethan…uh, whatzisname… Kinney?"

The coughing fit buys me some time before I have to answer, on the bright side. "Uh…" *Oh, good, LeeAnne. There's the mature response you were going for.* "You know more about him than I do. I didn't even know his last name."

And how embarrassing is that? I've let him say, text, and *do* all sorts of unmentionable things to me. I kissed him for the craziest of reasons. Not once did it occur to me to ask his last name.

I could've gotten it. His last name. He pays with a credit card sometimes when he comes into the bar, or I simply could've asked. That's what I tell myself while looking utterly fascinated in the plastic label on my water bottle. *Oh, look. Bottled at the source. What does that even mean?*

God, I can't believe I was so distracted by how a guy made me feel that I wasn't even thinking about who he was. Am I a teenager all over again?

"Hey, so when do you think the weather will start warming up?" Maybe redirecting AJ will work. Because I so don't want to explain the whole, *well I was sad and lonely and a little scared so I let a customer kiss me and things got way out of hand so I dropped my new rule not to get involved with any new guys faster than a fresh piece of gossip hitting the town airwaves* thing.

But I still think he's cute. Those glasses. That chin. I never knew I had a weakness for such a baby face.

AJ ignores my weather question. "You sure? Because when I came in the other night, you guys seemed pretty deep in conversation."

Damn. I stop to wipe my mouth on a towel, still unsure how to answer. "Uh, no. I just stopped him to tell him…something." Something! Excellent. I'm winning at this game.

"All right." AJ chuckles. "Well, whatever. He and Michelle are good friends. Seems like a nice guy. Smart, kind of quiet, but decent, you know? You could use a decent guy in your life."

My chest burns. That's sweet of AJ to say, but I don't know if I know what to do with decent or nice. Frankly, I'm not sure decent could handle *me*. That stuff he said about Ethan? I'm getting the sense that it's all true. And all reasons why I should probably stop encouraging Ethan and answering his texts.

Ethan's a good guy. He's smart. He's in college. I didn't even go. He deserves someone smarter, right? Someone with plans and a future.

Charles used to have plans and a future, and being with me turned him into someone else. I don't want to ruin another good guy.

#

Ethan

"Class, don't forget your product rebranding triptychs are due on Friday. Also, if you show up at my gallery opening, you'll get your quarterly grades back early." That's Alisson Sloan, our special visiting Advanced Graphics professor, who's practically my age. Apparently she's some kind of insane prodigy and getting her to teach at our little school this year was a massive win.

Half the guys in the class think she's smoking hot, but I can't manage the interest. For one thing, she's friendly with my dad, and I keep rotating between wondering if I got into this class because of him and not my talent, and wondering if she and my dad have also had sex.

At this point, I'm wondering who *hasn't* slept with my dad?

I save the design I've been working on, of a woman blowing music notes into the night sky, to the university server. Then I grab my backpack and hightail it out of there before anyone can try to make small talk.

Professor Sloan slaps a folder in my hand on the way out the door. Last week's homework. "Excellent stuff, Ethan. Please see me during office hours at the end of the week. I have some things I'd like to discuss."

With a vague smile and a nod of acknowledgement, I push my way out of the room. There's a knot of students waiting to fawn over the ultra-cool young professor, so I'm relieved to be free of the pack. Heat spreads over the back of my neck when I open the folder to take a look at what I'd turned in.

Oh. Yeah. That.

Honestly, it's nothing great, and Professor Sloan is probably blowing sunshine at me because of my dad. I was in a hurry to get the project done... Well, I'm always in a hurry to get a project done. In my head, there tends to be the stuff that's so urgent I practically have an aneurism over it and the stuff that isn't urgent yet so I ignore it until the aforementioned aneurism.

So at three in the morning on the day this project about socially motivated design was due, I did a graphic rendering of a graffiti wall and threw some awful iambic pentameter on top.

Bam! Poetry class and graphics assignments taken care of all in one swoop.

Not my best work. Hardly even work at all, if you don't count the fact that I was dragging ass once my three cups of coffee stopped working. Poetry is a class I took to fulfill my English requirement, but except for when I have to pick apart some dead guy's symbolism, I actually kind of like it. I've been scribbling emo shit in the margins of my notebooks like a good geek boy for years anyway. Why not use it for an easy A?

For all the crap I used to hear about how girls love a guy who's in touch with their feelings, you'd think it'd get me laid more.

"Ethan."

Shit. That voice behind me is definitely Shana's. No need to even glance over my shoulder—and no, I really don't wish to speak to her. At all.

With a deep breath, I hike my bulging backpack up on my shoulders and speed ahead, weaving in and out of all the students hustling to get to and from class.

"Ethan!"

Aaargh. *Go away, Shana.* A few times this week, she's spotted me on campus, but I've managed successful evasive maneuvers. I'm not really ready to talk to her, on account of I can't look at her face without remembering the last time I saw it. Why can't the girl pick up a phone?

This time she's right behind me, so I have no choice but to acknowledge her. Well, I suppose there's always a choice, but it would be pretty ridiculous to keep on ignoring when she's stepping on my heel. "Shana, I've got to go," I growl over my shoulder.

For a more pleasant distraction, I pull out my phone to text LeeAnne: *Hey. Wanna go to an art gallery opening with me? My professor is having this thing. Extra credit. I think there'll be snacks.*

LeeAnne: *I don't know if I'm an art gallery kind of girl.*

Ethan: *Don't knock it 'til you've tried. What kind of girl do you think you are?*

LeeAnne: *I don't know, yoga pants and potato chips?*

Honestly, I kinda love that about her. I see some girls on this campus who dress up to go out to a bar in the winter and then they're so damn cold they have to huddle just to walk from the bus stop. Or they show up in the dining hall for breakfast wearing full-on makeup. LeeAnne's not out to be perfect, which makes her perfect. To me, anyway.

Ethan: *That's totally hot. So when's this yoga-pants date of ours? I don't own a pair so I'll need to be ready. Unless you're willing to let me borrow a pair of yours?*

Texting these things to LeeAnne makes me smile even as my chest tightens and my palms sweat. I'm not used to walking up to a girl and being all, "Me: Ethan. You: Want me." It feels awkward and foreign. Part of me is convinced she's gonna realize I'm faking this badass confidence and laugh in my face. And not just because I keep cribbing jokes from my roommates and the kids I tutor.

I shove my phone in my pocket, walking faster.

Fingers brush my arm. "Ethan, wait. Can't we just talk for a minute?"

"You know I'd like to, but I remembered I'm late for an aneurism. Also, I don't want to."

She manages to pull around in front of me even though I've sped up and she's got shorter legs. Motivation is a powerful thing. "God, Ethan. I'm sorry. I really am. Is there any chance we can still be friends?"

I run a frustrated hand through my hair, but it gets caught in my uncombed curls. The bathroom at my new place is still a biohazard site, and I refuse to get naked in that room until I perform a full-scale decontamination. I've cleaned up at the gym some, but it's not ideal.

Meanwhile, my hair probably looks like some woodland creature made a nest in there. Then some other asshole woodland creature came along and trashed that first little creature's nest but good.

Fuck it, right? Nobody around I need to impress.

I stop by an empty bench and drop my backpack for a minute. My body is tired and strung tight. I always did like Shana as a good friend, but right now, I'm still kinda pissed. The chance is real that I'll say something I shouldn't.

"What else do you want to hear, Shana? You want me to ask how long it's been going on? Cuz I don't want to know. Should I ask if my dad is the reason you never wanted to so much as kiss me? I'm pretty sure I already *do* know. Nothing about what I walked into that morning was good, Shana, especially not when I walked in there like a fucktard thinking for the hundredth time that maybe if I kept showing you what a nice guy I was, some piece of you would start to see me differently. Jesus, talk about insanity. You must really think I'm the world's biggest sucker."

Her lip trembles. "Of course not. I swear I didn't. I just—"

I don't want to hear her answer. I can't. "Did you even ever care about me at all, or was I like"—I wave my hand around, looking for the right word—"your student beard, or something? You can't date a professor, especially not one in your department, so when I asked you out, you figured what the hell? Close enough?"

More lip trembling. No answer.

"Yeah. Leave me alone." I grab my backpack with a rough pull and walk away. I'm being a dick, and whatever I think of Shana right now, I don't like the venom I'm spewing all around myself. Fuck though, I feel cheated. If she'd been honest with me, I might have understood. I don't know.

Guess I never will know.

Shana's hand wraps around my wrist. "Honestly, I did-n't want to hurt you. We didn't want—"

"Please don't finish that sentence." Because it did hurt. It still does. Even if seeing Shana and my dad that way ripped the rosy glasses off my face, even if it was the thing that pushed me to make a move on LeeAnne, hearing her say no-body meant it sounds completely hollow right now.

I just can't. Not even a little.

"Uhm...Ethan?"

I turn again with a flat stare.

"You're not going to tell anyone, are you?"

For a moment, I consider messing with her. Like I said, I'm pretty damn mad.

No energy for head games today, it turns out. "How-ever fucked over I might be feeling, and I gotta say the score on the fucked-over meter is high, I don't want my dad to lose his job. Not that I'm intimate with the ins and outs of the Pender Code of Conduct, but something tells me not even hav-ing tenure saves you from the ramifications of screwing your students. Especially not ones you're also paying to work for you."

Cuz yeah, Shana's in my dad's Angles and Perspec-tives class, in addition to occasionally modeling for his Life Drawing class. I have no idea how that factors with the code of conduct, but it seems sticky to me. Her pale skin gets even more ghostly when I mention the possible precariousness of their situation, but she straightens up pretty quick. "Ethan... Thank you."

She's squeezing my hand again. The idea of her touch-ing me is now slightly nauseating. Or maybe that's because I was drinking cheap beer again last night.

It wasn't planned, but when my new roommate came banging on my door at midnight yelling, "Hey, E, I need a beer pong partner!" I decided it was better than lying on my questionable mattress, contemplating all of my worries and the meaning of my life.

The meaning wasn't coming out well in my favor. I do know I've gotta put my foot down with Alonzo next time.

With as much pleasantness as I can muster, I pull my arm away from Shana and give her a forced smile. "Don't take this the wrong way, but you can thank me by leaving me alone. It's not that I don't get why you hid it or anything, but I really wish I hadn't gotten dragged into the middle of things. I'm beginning to realize I probably didn't love you the way I thought I did, but leading me on was a dick move. Anyway, you know if I don't tell someone else still could."

If I never see that lip of hers tremble again, it'll be too soon. "I really am sorr—"

"Yeah. Take care, Shana."

I walk away before she can finish. I have to.

My stomach growls, which surprises me, since I haven't had much of an appetite in days. I pull out my phone again to see if Michelle's on campus and wants to grab lunch.

"Hey, what's up? Everything okay?" She sounds awake at least. That's good. I always feel like a douche when I catch her in bed with her boyfriend.

"Ish. Ran into Shana. Originally, I was planning to go home and grab the rest of my stuff, but I think my dad has office hours late on Mondays. I could use some friend company. You game for lunch?"

"Sure, but I'm still at home. Should take me about half an hour to change and get to campus, or we could grab some of the good coffee at Delia's if you want to hoof it downtown. Cassie's been working with Delia's son on a new lunch menu. They said I could get free soup and sandwich in exchange for an honest opinion. Bet they'd have enough for two."

"Free lunch? Hell yeah. I'll see you over there." If there's one self-evident truth, it's that no college student turns down a free meal.

After I hang up on Michelle, another text message comes from LeeAnne. A response to my latest jokey attempt to get her to agree to a date.

I would love to see you in yoga pants.

That almost seems like a yes.

What are the chances things are actually looking up?

7. PRETTY COLLEGE BOY IS PRETTY

LeeAnne

I'm getting coffee and a muffin before my afternoon shift at Joe's Bar. AJ's beside me, chattering about what he thinks we should do with my "training" going forward, and how I should really be eating more protein, or something to that effect.

Not that I can focus when Ethan's coming up the sidewalk.

The bell above the door jingles and I almost jump out of my chair, even though I knew he was probably heading this way. Plus, the door makes that noise every time someone comes in and I shouldn't be surprised.

"Doing all right there, ace?"

I turn to look at AJ. "Ace?" Why does everyone insist on giving me nicknames?

Queen? Princess? Queencess? Tell me what you like and that's what I'll call you.

I actually smile a little thinking of Ethan's text. It's funny but I think he's pretty much the only person who's ever asked for my opinion. On anything.

AJ taps his forehead. "Gotta get yourself into a winning mentality, you know? You're a fighter. Start thinking like one."

"A fighter, huh?"

I scowl and dump a ton of milk into my coffee. I admit it, I'm kind of a wuss where coffee is concerned. It's the get-up-and-go I like, not so much the flavor. Charles used to make fun of me. "That coffee hardly looks like you could take it serious anymore," he'd say. He mostly stuck to beer though, unless he had a route to drive, so I don't know why I ever cared what he had to say about coffee.

Heat rushes to my face anyway, remembering the way I let his opinion affect me so easily. It's just that when he didn't like the way things were, he wasn't happy. And when Charles wasn't happy, *nobody* around him was happy. Living with someone whose moods turned on a dime gave me a reason to cater to *his* needs instead of my own. I'd sort of gotten used to it already, after living with my dad.

At least, that's what I tell myself to try to feel better.

Since I'm still looking in the direction of Ethan and his conversation with his pretty college friend, I guess AJ mistakes the reason for my furious blushing.

At least I assume so when he elbows me in the ribs and clucks his tongue. "I totally get it. Pretty college boy is pretty."

"What? No."

"Uh-huh. I saw that look."

"You didn't see any look." I'm such a liar. There was all sorts of looking. As much as I want to tell myself not to, it's hard to look away from the one single guy who's managed to give me an orgasm since I knew sex was a thing.

Honestly, I thought people were lying about all that stuff. The feelings and the toe curling and the tingles. No lie, my toes curled. It might've been because I was on a chilly countertop, but they curled all the same.

Ethan looks up, so I look down, skin flaming as I search for a coffee stirrer. I need a place to sit, to hide, anything. Anything other than this conversation with AJ. Or the fact that I just got busted staring.

In spite of my desire to make tracks for the door, I know I'm going to be on my feet for the next eight hours, and I've got fifteen minutes before I need to be upstairs at Joe's Bar, so I plant my butt in a chair. "AJ, I'm recently divorced. Charles and I got married right out of high school. What do I actually know about dating? Besides, Ethan's like a world away when it comes to life experiences."

He smiles. "There *is* that old saying about not knocking something before you've given it a fair shot."

It's impossible not to glance across the room at that cute smile again. His jaw is deliciously dusted with dark stubble today. Why is that so distracting?

"You might be right. It's just hard to feel comfortable when I've been so epically wrong before. How do I know I want Ethan for the right reasons?"

Marrying Charles was supposed to get me away from the painful living situation I'd been in with my dad and provide a safe shelter for me and my future child. In the end, neither thing happened.

When Charles and I first agreed to separate, I tried snagging my coworker Jake, because he was a nice guy who seemed like he could take care of me. Also a fail, and now working with him is slightly uncomfortable. I don't want Ethan to be another broken safety net.

"It takes time." AJ nods, thoughtfully scratching the back of his neck. "Could be you need to get your feet underneath you before you get serious with someone else. Nobody can answer that question except you."

"That's what the therapist I talked to said. And I agreed." I did. Really. It all made so much sense, but every time I talk to Ethan, I feel completely torn.

He nods towards Ethan. "Anyway, Ethan seems cool, for what it's worth. I don't think you'd be walking into another Charles-situation."

Ethan does seem great. Really great. It's hard for me to trust my senses after the track record I've had, but he's adorable—like a puppy if that puppy told goofy jokes and had great abs and a super talented tongue.

Honestly, I like him more than I feel like it's okay to admit. Suddenly I'm jamming piece after piece of blueberry muffin into my mouth in order to stop myself from turning this into one big overshare. Things like, *he's the first guy to give me an orgasm with his mouth. My vision went white, it was so amazing. He asked me what I liked. Why hasn't it occurred to me to even think about that before?*

AJ has been nothing but helpful to me since I left Charles. I can't subject the poor man to sex details on top of everything else.

Tell me if what I'm doing feels good.

Oh God, and it had. The memory floods my lady parts with heat.

So not the place, LeeAnne. I smack my hand on the table, drawing the stares of everyone in the cafe. Including Ethan, who had turned to place his order at the counter. When his eyes widen and his lips part at the sight of my probably crazed expression, I admit I feel another rush of heat. Heat, and something else that makes my stomach go funny.

It's the way he's looking at me...like I'm fascinating. That's what it is. For this one moment, I almost believe I could be.

Only that's impossible.

"Earth to LeeAnne." AJ snaps his fingers in front of my face.

"I'm right here."

He laughs. "Sure."

"No. I—" My mouth works to make words but nothing's coming out. I glance at AJ and back over to Ethan.

Ethan smiles slightly, his eyes dark and wide behind those thick-rimmed glasses of his, leaving me unsure of what to say.

Ethan *isn't* the sort of guy I'd usually go for. The guys who'd captured my interest in the past were the types of guys I was raised around. Guys who worked with their rough, calloused hands. Guys who are at home in shredded jeans and unafraid to get dirty.

Like Charles who helped his dad at his roofing company before he entered the army. Jake, who I started seeing after Charles and I separated, he's a mechanic on top of working with me at the bar. Though I can admit now that part of the attraction was his nearness and the fact that he was nice enough, which made him seem like an easy match.

So yes, Ethan is different. He's standing by the bakery counter with a knit cap covering his curly hair, wiping his glasses on the hem of one of those graphic T-shirts he likes. The kind with a reference I know is supposed to be funny or smart, but I don't get at all. Today he's wearing one that has a giant "E" tipped kind of up and backwards like a giant claw.

Is it another artist joke? A movie reference? Would he ask me out again if I go over and talk to him about what it means? Not that I want him to. Do I?

I turn back to AJ. "He's nothing like Charles, I can say that much. Maybe change is good."

AJ shrugs. "All I'd suggest is to proceed with caution, sweetie. You're still finding your independence."

I get the feeling he's about to say more, but there's a commotion outside the shop window. AJ's boyfriend, in an expensive-looking coat, waving and jumping to get his attention. Next to Hayden is a stunning redhead I've never seen before, but she's waving also. And when I say stunning, I mean Marty Foreman from the Grove High football team just crashed his bike into a light post while pedaling past her.

Poor kid. He needs to save the hits for the field.

"Uh…who's that?"

AJ grits his teeth. "That would be my boyfriend, and the mega-smoking-hot ballerina he was engaged to when we met."

Holy Crown Royal, Batman. "That's his ex? Wow, she's…"

He sniffs and takes a gulp of his coffee. "Yeah, I know. Don't rub it in."

"Sorry. But what's she doing here?"

AJ's jerky shrug seems so unlike him. He's the most laid-back guy I know. "She's got stuff going on. Decided a small-town getaway might clear her head. I don't know. I'm trying to be Zen." He says this as his legs bounce so fast under the table, I'm afraid he might upend all of our drinks.

"If I didn't know better, I'd think you're jealous." I may not be savvy about my own relationships, but in my years of tending bar, I've witnessed every relationship scenario you could possibly imagine. Even in this itty-bitty town. Seriously, I know who's into kinky stuff, who's in a love triangle, and who likes his wife to pretend he's a stranger when he comes into Joe's.

It's info I'd rather not have, but there it is. I manage to know stuff even when I don't ask.

"Are you nervous because Hayden's still, you know, into women?"

If you ask anyone in town, Hayden's gay. If you ask Hayden, he'd likely say the same. I guess to keep from confusing people. This little place hardly knows what to do with an actual gay couple, let alone a guy who could have chosen what's behind door number one, but didn't. I've seen Hayden's interested glances when a pretty girl walks into the bar. I've *also* seen the way he looks at AJ. No contest. Really.

Everyone in the world would kill for the kind of love Hayden has in his eyes when he looks at AJ. Even I would, and I spend most of my nights convincing myself that love doesn't exist.

AJ sighs. "My boyfriend's ex is a gorgeous ballet dancer. I think I'm allowed to be a little concerned."

"Weren't you telling me to work on my confidence?" Looking out the window at the way Hayden's smiling face is patiently broadcasting his want for AJ to come join him, I see that I'm right. "You know why I left Charles, right? Do you think I'd go back to him?"

"Honey, I would beg you not to."

I squeeze his hand. "I wouldn't. It took so long to get the courage to walk out for good, and I can't go back. We had problems. We would have had problems even if he'd never once hit me. Don't you think the same is true for Hayden and his ex? Surely he didn't leave her only because he met you."

AJ huffs a breath. "You may have a point. I guess I worry he'll decide he'd rather have the alternative."

I lean in and give AJ a hug. "Who could possibly want anybody else? You know, you have done so much for me since I left Charles. I can't thank you enough. You ever decide you like girls, you give me a call."

He blinks. Surely he must know I was kidding, but it's cute how he gets a little flustered. "Uh, right. I mean, you know I'm happy to help."

"I do know. Now. Right now, I have to be at work in ten minutes and you gotta go. Your boyfriend is outside looking at you like you're the only thing in the world that he cares about. I'd kill to have a piece of that action. I think you need to go spend some time together so you can stop worrying so much about whether or not you two are solid. Let me eat my muffin in peace."

"Uh-huh. Aaaand there's a handsome college guy over there looking at you like you're lunch." He tweaks my chin. It's a very little-sister type gesture, but it's sweet so I don't mind.

Or I wouldn't, except Ethan is walking this way, and now I'm feeling embarrassed.

I glance at Ethan, then back at AJ. "Uhmm. Maybe. Go. I'll be at work for the next eight hours. Spend time with your family so you can be the happy, un-stressed AJ we all recognize."

He kisses the top of my head. "Call me if you need anything."

"Sure." We both know I probably won't.

As AJ rushes away, I try not to cringe. When I look up, Ethan's warm eyes sparkle with humor.

He smiles and sits down with a large cup of coffee and two sandwiches. "So. I was hoping you could help me with something."

\#

Ethan

Sitting in front of LeeAnne with a nervous stomach and two sandwiches, I must look like the biggest dork on the face of the planet. I figured though, after the way she'd been nervous about a date before, maybe I needed to take a different approach. Something less formal. Perhaps bring the date to her?

Wooing, or pursing, or whatever…it's definitely not my area of expertise. I've gotten intimate with two girls ever.

Two and a half? Two. Anyway…

Didn't seem like such a lame number before. Waiting around for the right person, and all. Now I wish I had more experience backing me up. More real relationship stuff.

Considering the closest thing I've had to an actual girlfriend was only using me while she, I dunno, secretly got with my dad, I don't think she counted. Does my high school hookup with Maria Poindexter count as a date? Maybe, but it wasn't dat*ing.*

I sort of had a date to my junior prom. Midway through she ditched me to "go to the bathroom" and when I found her, she was under the bleachers making out with Lisa Warren from the cheer squad on a pile of wrestling mats.

So total legit girlfriends? Zero. And what is it with girls using me as a prop?

If I thought LeeAnne honestly wasn't into me, I'd go lick my wounds and move on. As much as I want someone to feel connected to, and I can admit that I do, I don't want a person who doesn't want me back. I've been there and done that plenty. The issue here is I can tell LeeAnne does want me. I see her skin flush and her eyes widen every time I come close. Who can walk away from such a potent reaction?

Wish I knew what was holding her back.

So I'll give it another shot before I throw in the towel. Invite her to share my lunch. Worst case, I've got my new favorite pastime of scrubbing the toxic room I've rented and my merry band of roomies to keep me company. Which reminds me, I've got to pick up some tub and tile cleaner before I lose my mind.

"So what did you need help with?" She's looking at me and I realize I've kind of been staring for way too long. In my defense, her eyes make me want to paint things.

Haven't had that urge for a little while. The quiet hum of inspiration in the back of my head sounds so sweet I don't want to look away.

"Oh. Yeah. Glad you asked." I push one of the sandwiches her way. "I need help with *this*. Cassie and Hayden are trying a new lunch menu and I was asked to taste-test, but I can't eat two sandwiches. You look like you might be the kind of girl who enjoys a turkey and Swiss."

She wrinkles her nose. "What's the other one?"

"Called it wrong? Damn. How about egg salad with dill? Looks positively gourmet."

With a look at her watch, she purses her lips. "I don't know. I'm more a peanut butter and banana gal. Anyway, I have to be at work in a few minutes."

I nudge the egg salad. "Would you at least try a couple of bites so I can have a second opinion?" I pick up half and chew. "Personally, I think it's sassy and oniony, with notes of paprika and a delightful but pretentious streak of sweet gherkin and vinegar. You?"

She laughs and takes a bite. (She laughed! Yes! Gooooooaal!) "I think it tastes like egg salad."

"Yeah, me too."

A pretty, unadorned hand flies to her mouth. "Oh, re-aaally? What was all that stuff about sassy onions and pretentious vinegar?"

I shrug. "Part of my ongoing quest to turn your frown upside-down. So is this." While we've been talking, I've been doodling on her napkin. Nothing fancy, but a tiny little bunny with a turtle, playing checkers.

Turtle's winning.

Normally I wouldn't brag on my drawing, but I do love the way her eyes get big. Also, I don't miss that she folds up the napkin to slip it into her bag.

When she sits back and lets herself swallow, I'm flooded with excitement. Maybe this is working. This is the kind of rush I usually get from clearing a level of *Vamps and Vandals*, as if I'm one step closer to a final victory. Even better, there's another real-live human being involved. A beautiful one.

"I really ought to get to work." She wipes her mouth and grabs a half-finished cup of coffee. "It was nice of you to share your sandwich with me."

"No," I correct. "It was nice of you to help me eat." Not that she ate much, but still.

"If you say so." The way she bites her lip brings back the memories of touching her, kissing her, and the way she looked at once unequivocally sexy and surprisingly unsure. I decide to tell her so.

"Hey. I wanted to say again that I had an amazing time with you that night...you know." Remembering draws heat and tension low in my gut every time. The way she sits up straighter and crosses her legs, I wonder if it does for her, too.

"It, uh, it really was," I continue. "Kinda had the feeling we both needed someone that night, and I know I've talked a lot of smack, but honestly, I hope I made you feel as good as I felt, getting to please you." I take a chance on leaning close and brushing my fingertips against hers. That's all. A few tiny molecules of skin, but a zing of awareness rushes through me all the same.

She swallows. "It was definitely... Good. Yes."

"Good, huh?" I wish she'd tell me more. What I want to hear is that I'm in her head like she's in mine, but maybe I'm hoping for more than I can get.

Her eyes widen. "It was, but Ethan, I'm honestly trying to straighten myself out after making a lot of bad decisions. Dating isn't something I'm looking for, and you deserve better than a girl who's got more issues than *Time* magazine. I'm not saying what happened that night was a mistake, but I'm not so sure it should happen again."

Right. "Listen, I've decided honesty is really important to me. Especially lately. So I want to be clear about something. I've got my own issues. You could fill a library with 'em. Plus the archives. Probably you'd still have a few left over to donate to your local dentist's office so folks have shit to read before they get their teeth cleaned. Entertaining stuff like how I hardly talked as a kid but now I don't shut up, since silence never helped a damn thing, or how you're only like the third girl I've ever kissed, but I wouldn't mind if you were the last."

Letting all the crazy hang out, aren't I? Well, the girl's already doing her best to blow me off, so it's not as if I'm out anything if I tell her something she doesn't like.

She shakes her head and acts like she's going to brush my hand away. She doesn't though. Our fingers catch and they wind up partway curled around each other. "Ethan, you're so nice, but you're still in school and—"

Oh, no. *Nice.* I've heard that one before.

"Sure. Yeah." I jump up from my seat. "My mom raised a polite boy. To this day, I don't get fed at her house if I don't say 'please' first when I ask for stuff. But don't mistake my being nice or being a stupid couple of years younger for being not good enough. Not without giving me a shot."

"Oh, God." Her eyes widen. "That's not what I think. That you're not... You're great. You're *too* good."

"Too good? What the fuck—"

Out of nowhere, she sucks in a sharp breath, scanning the sidewalk outside the window. "You know what? Let's drop it. I'll give it some thought, okay? Right now I need to get to work. Would you mind walking me upstairs to Joe's?"

By the time I turn around, whatever had her spooked was gone. Unless that old dude who feeds squirrels on the bus bench is the one who got her wigged out.

I don't argue. Instead, I seize the bittersweet opportunity and accept the hand she reaches out. Together, we walk outside, up the back stairs to Joe's Bar.

8. WORK IN PROGRESS

LeeAnne

I trudge up the stairs to work with all the enthusiasm of a scolded child, shuffling off to see the principal. My skin prickles with the awareness of Ethan at my back, my face sizzling with memories of what happened between the two of us. He presses a comforting hand to my side, and my nerves are too thin and too tight to want to push him off.

Part of me wishes I hadn't sent AJ off when I did. Well, that's not true. AJ deserved his time with Hayden. After everything he's done to help me since leaving Charles, I don't regret letting him off the hook from keeping an eye on me. Besides, nobody wants to feel like they need a babysitter.

All of that was canceled out the moment I glanced out the window of Delia's and saw Charles's truck drive past. I couldn't help the panic that seized my brain. Did he see me? Where was he going? Was he finally leaving town?

That last option would be a good one if I believed he'd finally moved on, but after our talk the day he came by Joe's, I'm worried.

"Seriously, is everything okay?" Ethan's walking me past the door to the kitchen where we...

Do you want me to stop?

I don't... I like you.

I can tell we're both thinking about it as we pass. Ethan's eyes go warm and sweet like amaretto again, and me? I haven't managed to forget. I haven't exactly wanted to.

Ethan was right. The night we hooked up, I felt more alone than I ever had. The way he touched me and spoke to me woke me up from a numbness that had actually become painful. Since that night, it's so easy to pull out the heated memories to keep me warm when I feel shaken and worried about the future. Even though I know all the reasons why Ethan could do better than a small-town bartender who got bad grades in high school.

That night, he made me feel so good I want to stay in that memory all the time. Ethan may not be an addiction, but sometimes he feels like one.

Inside the still-empty dining area, Ethan says hi to Joe and perches himself on a stool while I stow my things. I guess I looked so spooked, he doesn't want to leave. Now I feel like a jerk. Except I actually don't *want* him to leave.

"Honestly," I whisper. "You don't have to stay here and hold my hand. It's just that having my ex back in town reminds me of how small this place is. Now and then, I see the bill of his favorite ball cap or his truck driving down Main Street. Not sure if it's really him or if they're my own paranoid delusions. It's crazy."

Ethan's glasses lift up when he scrunches his eyebrows together. It's kind of cute. "Could be I just really *want* to hold your hand."

Well, that's so sweet, I don't know what to say. I hardly even mean to open my mouth when I blurt out, "Why?"

He blinks and removes his glasses, frowning as he wipes off the lenses on the hem of his T-shirt. I can't tell if his displeasure is aimed at my question or some stubborn smudge he's working on, but I'm betting there isn't a smudge at all. I'm getting the idea that this is something he does when he needs a moment to think or doesn't want people to see the expression on his face. For all of his joking, I've caught hints of brooding. And drinking. Like with Charles. I won't say that doesn't worry me a little.

But when his body rocks on the aging, split leather of the bar stool, my heart breaks open a little more. He's going to leave, which is exactly what I've been saying he ought to do this whole time, but it doesn't feel the least bit good. Feels more like I've been downing pitcher after pitcher of that bad batch of microbrew Joe got a half-keg of last week, only twice as nauseating.

"Is it really such a bad thing, me wanting you?" His question is quiet. I can hear his hurt, but it also sounds like he genuinely doesn't understand the problem.

I nearly drop a glass in the middle of restacking the ones on the bar. "Ethan, you wanting me is pretty much the best thing that's ever happened. I've made so many mistakes though, and I'm trying to make sure nobody else gets hurt by my bad decisions. I'd never want to hurt you."

With one hand, he grabs his leather jacket. With the other, he reaches across the bar to slide his hand over mine. "I know the phrase is 'college kid' but I'm actually a grown-ass adult, you know? So how about you stop thinking you're doing me favors by pushing me away?"

He's right. Standing taller than I am with his chest puffed, his eyes and jaw hard, it's clear that there's a man—a strong man—behind the playful jokes. Why haven't I wanted to see that? "I guess I'm—"

"LeeAnne, how you holding up, sweetheart?" Big Joe comes out of the kitchen and puts a giant hand on my shoulder. He's a massive, balding bear of a man. Sweet, albeit a little nosey and overbearing. I guess since he likes being in everyone's business, tending bar suits him.

"Hey, Joe. Doing fine."

"You sure, sweetheart? Looking a little spooked."

Just having an uncomfortable relationship conversation with the guy who gave me a mind-blowing orgasm in your kitchen. Why?

My face catches fire. "It's fine. I thought I saw Charles's truck outside. Just a little on edge."

Joe gives my arm a squeeze and then throws a friendly wave to two ladies who wander in to sit at one of the little dining tables. "Hey, now, sis. You know I love you. Now I was thinking to myself the other day, it's gotta be extra hard with

Charles back in town. You ain't taken hardly a minute of vacation since you started working here and I bet you could use a good long break. Why don't you let your young gentleman give you a ride home? Take some time off, until things have calmed down."

The pity on his face makes my stomach hurt. God, I didn't even take hardly any time when Charles bruised my face. Thank goodness for concealer. "That's sweet, but there's no need. Really. You know I love working here."

Honestly, I don't know if nachos and five-dollar pitcher night is anyone's idea of a dream job, but it's a good place. Joe's a good boss. I know I'm lucky.

"Honey, but you've been under a whole heap of stress. Something's gotta give."

Ethan gives my hand a gentle squeeze. In my surprise, I squeeze back.

Hell, I don't know what to do. How would I even stay occupied if I took time off? I'm not good at having nothing to do. But if I try to stay, Joe will give me grief. He might even put his foot down, which would be embarrassing in front of the ladies chattering amongst themselves across the room.

And the big question is, "Joe, am I being fired?"

"Course not, sweetheart. Like to see you focus on taking care of yourself for a little while, is all. I'll even pay you for the time. You give yourself a couple of weeks and if you want to come back, we'll all be here waiting."

"Why wouldn't I want to come back?"

Joe lifts one heavy shoulder. "Met the wife at an outdoor country music festival in South Carolina. She was on vacation from Atlanta. Brought her back here to Evergreen Grove and that was the end of the story. Plans change."

Ethan gives my arm a little shake. I reach over with my free hand and grab onto him. I'm too stunned, and frankly I need an anchor right now.

"Listen, it's cold out," Ethan says. "Let me drive you home."

I don't know what else to say, so I don't say anything. I squeeze his arm and let him lead me to his car. We get out into the cold, and Ethan immediately sets about warming up the interior of his little yellow CRX.

"Cute car." This is me trying to act normal as I swivel my head, not so secretly glancing around while I buckle my seat belt. The street is empty of people except for us right now, as far as I can tell.

"Thanks." He pats the dash. "She's my baby. Since until recently I was still living at home, I splurged and got a sporty car. Then I had to move out, so I guess it wasn't my smartest decision." With a shrug, he puts the car in gear and cuts the wheel so he can pull out. "Anyway, where to? Home?"

Home. It's a nice word, but I don't know what it means. Home is a piece of the couch by my mother's feet while she slept. I haven't been home since I was nine.

"No...I..." Home, such as it is, will be lonely and chilly. "I've been staying in what used to be the Grove Inn that AJ fixed up for people who needed help during life transitions. It's okay, but I don't feel like going there right now."

"We could go get something to eat," he offers. "You didn't have much of that sandwich I tried to share. Some friend you are."

It's not his usual goofball silliness and it doesn't make me laugh, but I appreciate that he's trying to cheer me up. His deep chuckle sounds good in my ears.

"Thanks to a steady diet of coffee and insomnia, I can't say I've been hungry much lately." Usually I'm not good at telling people honestly how I feel. Being open is a weakness, and one I can't afford. Maybe because I'm feeling like a wrung-out dish towel, I don't know how to hold in how tired I am.

Ethan feels solid and he makes me laugh. For once I hope I've judged a man in my life correctly.

"That sucks." Ethan pulls out of the space and flips a neat U turn in the middle of Main Street. You're not supposed to do that here but nobody shows up to stop him. "I've had a little trouble with that myself. Anxiety and whatnot. Not the same reasons I'm sure, but I guess I could relate."

"Oh yeah? You seem like a guy who's got it all together. What's keeping you up?" For some reason, this makes me feel better. Charles always slept hard. Sometimes he had nightmares that made him toss and turn, but thanks to alcohol and painkillers, he usually passed out cold and stayed that way until his bladder forced him to lumber off to the bathroom. After which, he'd pass out again until his shift at work, if I was lucky. Until God knew when, otherwise. Like me, not having anything to keep him occupied was Charles's biggest weakness.

Ethan chuckles. "If I seem like I've got it all together, then I need to consider switching my career to advertising or some shit. Let me tell you, LeeAnne, I've got exactly nothing together except the clear and definite plan to buy a ton of cleaning products to finish decontaminating my new living space." He leans his head toward me, grinning. "The previous tenant was apparently the most disgusting creature on the face of the planet. Not counting my dad."

What was wrong with his dad? Did he drink, like Charles? Did he hit Ethan? Was he like my father, so anxious to get rid of the responsibility he'd been saddled with that he pushed a child who wasn't ready into an awful marriage?

I'm dying to know, beyond simply curiosity. God, I need to know I'm not the only person who got the short straw in the Happy Childhood Lottery. AJ's always saying pain isn't exclusive to any one person. That's got to be true, but that isn't how it feels when I'm awake at night, watching some perky model show off her amazing workout routine on television.

Maybe if I understood Ethan's, it would help. "What's going on with your dad?"

Ethan's lips thin as he presses the gas. "He screwed my ex-girlfriend. Is. Present-tense. Or I guess, she was never really my girlfriend. She lied to me. They both did."

Oh. Okay. "That sucks, I'm sorry."

There's a tumble of rocks in my stomach as we navigate over Evergreen Grove's back roads. Whatever I expected him to say, it wasn't that his father slept with his ex whatever. And now I'm wondering...

"Uh. Ethan? Are you and she still... I mean... Do you still like this girl? Is that why you're so mad?" The answer to this question feels intensely important. It worries me how the strain and anger on his face are making me queasy.

"No way. I thought I did, if that makes any sense. It's more like Shana and I were friends for so long, I assumed we'd work our way around to being together again, and I liked the familiarity of her in my life. My parents adopted me sort of as an unexpected thing, and I never really felt totally comfortable, I guess. I think the fact that Shana was someone who had always been there made me think she was someone I could connect to. Maybe I'm not making sense."

"Wow, that's... No, I think it does make sense." I'm not sure if I'm supposed to say something here. Offering my condolences doesn't seem right, even though I do hurt for what I think he's lost.

It's sort of funny how in spite of the short time we've known each other, I find myself feeling a little protective. A little bit of *how dare you* aimed in my head at both a nameless, faceless ex-girlfriend and an equally blank birth mother. I understand, as someone who got pregnant too young, that sometimes you simply aren't ready to be a mom. Even so, the idea of someone giving Ethan away hurts my heart.

He shrugs. "Anyway. Whatever it is I had with Shana, that night you and I were together at Joe's made me realize my feelings for Shana were all an illusion."

Oh. Double wow.

He taps his fingers on the steering wheel. "It's the fact that I was lied to. You know, they made me look like an idiot. Let's not forget my dad abused his power as a teaching professional. Anyway, you wanna be a dumbass and abuse your power, that's your funeral. Don't lie to your kid to get it done."

Hurt shines in his eyes. Maybe he didn't have to endure what I did, but it's clear this was hard for him. "I'm sorry."

"I'm not as mad as I was when it first happened. Obviously, it's a work in progress."

"Is it okay if I ask what you mean by you being unexpected?"

"My mom and my birth mother were friends. My birth mother died shortly after I was born. Complications with a severe illness, they said. So my parents adopted me. Not sure my dad even wanted kids. That's the short version, anyway."

I put a hand on his knee. "I know what that's like. Not being wanted."

Our moment of sharing is interrupted when I look back at the road and realize I've got no idea where we are. Evergreen Grove is a small town and pretty hard to get lost in, but this looks way strange. "Ethan, where on Earth are you taking me?"

#

Ethan

I hadn't decided for sure where I was driving us; it's more like I aimed the car down Evergreen Grove's winding, tree-lined back roads without meaning to.

There are things I haven't told my friends, places I go that I keep to myself because they're nerdy or super weird or too personal. My buddies are okay, but I can't risk them throwing shit at the stuff that matters to me.

LeeAnne is different, which sort of makes it seem easier. Like the night we got together, I feel like we both need something right now. Something to shake us up from the way we're both kind of twisting in the wind.

I can't see inside LeeAnne's head, but I sure as fuck could use a break. From that jagged bit of glass in my gut that's always twisting. Tighter and tighter. When I'm with her, it doesn't feel so sharp or so tight. Not that night I made her say my name in Joe's kitchen and not when I can tell she's trying not to laugh at my ridiculous jokes.

When I was with Shana, I was always a little bit worried. Always afraid to do or say something stupid that would make her decide she didn't want to hang out with me anymore. With LeeAnne, I do whatever the fuck I want since I'm on edge no matter what. Somehow she keeps letting me come around. Guess we'll see if that changes. For now, I'm gonna roll around in this thing we have like...something luxurious you'd roll around in.

Not really an expert on rolling in stuff.

We come to the turnoff for a dirt road marked haphazardly with a tiny wooden marker. You'd miss it if you weren't looking, thanks to the close bunching of trees with long needles that reach into the road. I take the turn, hoping LeeAnne doesn't get creeped out that I'm driving her to a spot in town that's pretty much been forgotten.

"I found this place one time when I went over to Jake and Cassie's place for movie night. Made a wrong turn. Wound up the good kind of lost."

"Good lost. I'm not familiar with that concept."

I shift and let up on the gas, easing onto the rolling, curved road that's gotten pitted and cracked from neglect and disuse. We won't be leaving Evergreen Grove, but we'll be making a wide circle around the outside. Further in are most of the homes and stores. There are a couple of houses down this road too, but I think they're all empty.

"Where does this go?"

The tension in LeeAnne's voice makes me cringe. Last thing I want is to make her nervous. "If we went far enough, we'd wind up out by The Ridge." That's what people call the nicer part of Evergreen Grove. Where the small handful of large, affluent houses are. I believe the mayor lives there, and a few others. One home's been turned into a small art gallery. I've tried to get a showing there, but no luck. Apparently even in a speck of a town like Evergreen Grove, my work isn't evolved, or high-brow enough, or what the fuck ever enough.

Doesn't pair well with champagne, that's all I know. Elitist dicks. Fuck 'em.

"The Ridge…" LeeAnne taps her fingers. "You come at it from up on Spruce. I thought it was a dead end."

I shake my head. "Technically is. There's one of those big yellow signs at the end of this road. The kind that they put up to warn cars they're about to drive off a cliff or whatever? I don't really know why, unless maybe there are falling rocks along the cliff face or it's dangerous for some other reason. Could also be that they just didn't want to have to maintain the road. It's pitted and uneven in some spots out here from disuse. I'm pretty sure nobody at all ever comes out this way."

Almost to illustrate my point, the left side of the car dips as I hit a divot in the road. Usually I know which way to go to avoid them, but I'm paying more attention to LeeAnne and the way she's clutching at her armrest.

"Look, maybe we should head back. I don't want you to feel nervous." The tension radiating from the seat next to me is pulling that glass into my gut. I edge the car off to the side, tires crunching on gravel.

We're at a bend in the road. It's an easy place to make a U-turn.

"No. Wait." She grabs at the steering wheel, her hand landing on mine. "I— Yeah, I'm really nervous right now. Joe basically gave me no choice about taking vacation, and I've never taken time off unless I've been sick or hurt. I'm still a little worried he might try to let me go, even though he said he wouldn't. And then there's how I'll meet the gap in my budget with no tips. But I think the last thing I should do is go home and be by myself."

It's hardly necessary for her to tell me she's stressed. I can see her anxiety from the corner of my eye in the way she fidgets. I can hear it in the breathless way her words stumble out of her mouth.

"So what do you want to do? I was going to take you some place I like to go when I need to chill out. If you're *more* keyed up about me taking you there, then that defeats the purpose. You sure you don't want me to just drive you home? Or, did you have a friend's place you'd rather go or something?"

She straightens in her seat, pulling her jacket around her. "I want to see what it is you were going to show me."

"Is that why you look like you're bracing yourself for impact?"

She's got her arms around her body like she's shielding herself from something, and I hate thinking she needs to shield herself from me.

I can try telling myself over and over that Shana didn't want to be with me because secretly she was already boning my dad, but it doesn't help that what sticks in my head is the part where she didn't want me. Not being wanted is kind of a thing with me.

The rejection burns. Such an unwanted feeling, but there all the same.

LeeAnne, I know she's got stuff going on. This stuff with her ex, and her ex's friend who started trouble at the bar. Her job. This isn't about me, not really at all. Whatever else is up, she seems to want to be with me. Except I can't shake the whispers telling me that maybe she's right. Maybe we're too different and I can't be the guy she needs.

Shit. I cough and clear my throat. "LeeAnne...I... You've been saying a lot of stuff about how you and I aren't a good fit. I've tried to play it off, but I don't honestly think things will be pretty if I start to really care and then you toss me out on my ass."

Fuck. Until now, I've done an okay job of pretending confidence with her. Right now, that sharp edge in my gut is sinking deeper, opening up a whole mess of uncertainty.

"I want to see what you'd like to show me," she repeats. When I look at her with all of my confusion hanging out, she continues. "I'm not good at trusting, Ethan. That goes most of all for myself. You have no idea how many decisions I'd unmake if I could. Falling for you scares the pants off of me. I feel like I can't afford to be wrong again. God, that sounds horrible. I'm sorry."

With a hard breath, I turn my attention back to the road and pull forward, leaving the shoulder in a cloud of dust and gravel. Pieces of rock hit the side of the car and I don't miss the way LeeAnne flinches when they plink on the steel. Shit.

"Don't apologize," I say. "I'm having a few trust issues with myself lately. Not trying to frog-march you into hanging out with me, that's all."

I figure there's a difference between not being nice and being a total toolshed. Best to stay on the right side of that line if I can.

She seems to find that amusing. With a quiet chuckle, she says, "Maybe we both need this."

"I'm saying, that's what I thought the night you let me go down on you." I pull into what was probably supposed to have been a parking area. A large dirt rectangle sits cut into the pull-off, but the pavement wasn't finished.

LeeAnne's lips part. "Are you saying you thought I needed to get laid?"

My surprise makes me stop the car with a jerk. "God. No. You looked sad. Sort of scared. I was feeling kind of the same way, to be honest. Like nothing in life was good right then, you know? For me, something opened up that night. For a little while, neither of us had to be alone or...or *feel* alone, I guess. People need contact with each other. It's kinda how we're wired."

That night she and I shared at Joe's mattered to me more than I'm comfortable saying and for far greater reasons than simply getting her off. I needed to be wanted. I needed to know I'd done something right.

Making art is a struggle for that reason. It's the thing I love, but there's no knowing you've done it right. There *is* no right when you're creating art. For some I bet that's empowering. For me, someone who relies on feedback, it's fucking scary. Cue the glass shards.

LeeAnne reaches over to grasp my leg. Mother of cats, you wouldn't believe how fast the warmth of her hand soaks into my pants.

"Ohmygod. Ethan. There's a playground out here?"

"Yep. Can you believe nobody knows about this place?" I point through the trees where you can barely make out the flaking painted bars of a swing set. "Well, someone must. I find the occasional beer bottle or condom wrapper when I come up here, but I never see anyone, so it must be a pretty well-kept secret."

Up ahead of us, surrounded by overgrown trees, is a rust-worn merry-go-round, a small swing set, and one of those metal play sets with a slide.

I wave my arms as we walk. "Some time ago one of the rivets at the bottom of the slide came off, so it isn't useable anymore without risking tetanus or whatever. Still, there's this little childhood throwback hidden here, and it's the absolute best. I'm guessing someone tried to put up these high-dollar homes along with a play area and all, but I don't know what happened. I only see one that ever got finished."

LeeAnne shrugged. "Evergreen Grove has never expanded much. We have a few rich folks, but I think it would be hard to find people willing to pay for a massive plot of land unless they could use it to hunt or farm."

I reach over and give the merry-go-round a spin. It squeaks and groans some, but still works fine. "Whatever the reason, stuff like this fascinates me. Places people simply walked away from. Things that nature's reclaimed and things that managed to stay standing."

My body's hot while I'm standing there in the chilly February weather. Letting people in on my secret interests isn't something I generally do. "Guess that sounds weird."

"Not weird. It makes you wonder, right? What happened? Did people leave by choice? Out of fear? Was there a disaster? Like..." She snaps her fingers. "I saw pictures once of some island in a magazine at the library. Thousands of apartment homes with dishes left out and everything. Like everybody vanished in the middle of breakfast."

"Yeah." LeeAnne's acceptance makes me smile.

Shana used to say, "Ethan, you're so strange."

This coming from the girl who was getting it on with her forty-year-old professor.

LeeAnne hums to herself as she hooks her finger on one of the bars of the merry-go-round, stopping it enough so that she can sit down on the flaking surface. "Sometimes I wish I could vanish." Before I have a chance to answer, she adds, "It's nice and quiet here. I can see why you'd come here when you need to think."

I draw a deep breath. Do I ask her why she said she wishes she could vanish? I want to. Desperately. But there's an absent, dreamy expression on her face and I wonder how often she looks that way. I don't want to chase it off so soon.

"You can use it," I tell her instead. "Anytime. If you need a quiet place to think or whatever, it's yours."

The brightening of her smile tells me I said the right words. Goddamn, do I ever feel like I'm a billion feet tall right now.

So I decide to try a few more. Grabbing the rusting metal bar of the merry-go-round, I lean over her.

"So. I'm gonna push you."

9. BREATHLESS

LeeAnne

Sitting there on that rusty piece of playground equipment while Ethan smiles down at me, I don't feel as old as I usually do. Or, not so much older than him.

"You want to push me?" Everything around him glows under the golden light coming through the trees, and his cheeks blush such a dark red, I could swear he borrowed my favorite compact of "Very Berry" to color his face.

"Oh I am *so* going to push you." Ethan nudges the metal disk underneath me a little but he doesn't put much speed behind it. I get the feeling that in spite of his insistence, I could say no, even tell him to take me home, and he'd stop in an instant.

Every step of the way, even when he's made it clear he wants me, Ethan's made it just as clear that I had a choice. If I told him to stop texting me his silly jokes about vegetables and farm animals in the middle of the night, he'd stop. I know he would. I never ask him to because even if I can't manage to say so, those messages keep me company when I'm lonely at night. Even when I try to tell myself a guy like him could do better.

But he'd leave me alone if I asked. He'd stop texting. Stop trying to spin me. He would.

Having a choice in one's own life shouldn't be a luxury, should it? And yet, up until now, nobody's ever asked me what I wanted. Nobody but him.

Even AJ, awesome friend that he is, can get rather pushy. Telling me I need to get myself in shape. I need to eat more. Take better care of myself. It's done out of love, but it's still telling and not asking.

In spite of my nerves, I find myself leaning toward Ethan's grinning face and drawing my knees to my chest so that my feet no longer touch the ground. "If you really want to push me, sure."

His smile widens as he pulls on the metal bar in his hand. "Awesome. You ready?"

There's a lurch and screech of metal that makes me yelp and brace my hands. "Okay, let's go easy. You don't want me to vomit on you."

Ethan laughs. With a running jump, he makes the whatchamacallit turn, then lands on the platform beside me with a metallic thud. "Yeah, my new roommate was so drunk he pissed on my shoes this morning, so you puking on me might actually be an upgrade."

I glance down at his battered boots.

"Different shoes. Not these." He pulls his feet in and sits up cross-legged.

Now I worry that I've made him self-conscious, so I try to come up with a goofy joke like the kind he's always telling to ease the mood. "So, a pirate walks into a— Whoa." The wheel we're both sitting on wobbles and jerks, sending me sideways.

"Hey. Sorry." He scoots to the center of the circle where there's room for us both and pulls me against him. Carefully. It's a secure, front-to-back kind of hold, but we're both seated and not facing each other dead-on, so we could easily slide apart, or we could scoot a few inches to put our faces right in kissing range.

"It's...no problems—problem, I mean." I'm noticing now how his eyes have a little ring of green around the outside of the brown and how his lips are sort of dark and full.

And how his hands fit so nicely over mine. "And?"

"It seems like every time I see you, I notice new stuff," I murmur. That wasn't at all what I meant to say, but it slipped out. My hand goes to my lips, covering that silly mouth from telling any more secrets.

For a flash of an instant, I worry he might make fun of the information I just gave him—Charles would've mocked me for saying something so flowery.

All Ethan does is smile and say, "I hope it's good stuff."

"It is."

I'm about to shield my eyes from the dazzling brightness of that smile when he says, "Tell me the rest of your pirate joke."

I laugh and bury my face in my hands. "Oh God. It's awful."

"Come on."

"Fine. The pirate walks into a restaurant. He has a steering wheel in his pants. The waiter asks what's up with that, and the pirate says 'Arr, it's driving me nuts.'"

"Oh man." His laughter vibrates against my back. "That's fucking great. You've been holding out on me."

I shake my head. "I heard that one from my ex, Charles. Back when we were still friends."

Behind me, Ethan gets still. "I guess it's tough when people grow apart."

"It was more than growing apart." I realize his arms are around me when I find myself pulling them tighter for warmth. "We had a couple of dates in our senior year of high school. I got pregnant around graduation. My father pushed us to get married. Truthfully, I *wanted* to get married because it meant getting out of my father's house. Charles joined the military to provide for us, and came home from his first deployment a changed person. Paranoid. Mean. Violent. In the end, it was all for nothing because I miscarried right after he graduated from boot camp."

I go cold inside when I realize he's gone rigid behind me. "God, I'm so sorry. I wasn't trying to bring the mood down."

"We came here for you. Say whatever you need to say." There's no denying I like the way his hands knead my shoulders.

For a second I let myself lean back against his shoulder. "I say…you're pretty incredible."

"Hey," he murmurs. "I have a good friend who's been through some stuff. She said it can be a habit to blame yourself when bad stuff happens because it gives you the illusion that you had some control to change the outcome. Sometimes you just don't. I don't know if that helps, but…"

It does help. It does.

I turn to face him. His nostrils flare and his hand tightens against my shoulder. He's got a fistful of my coat and he's leaning in like he wants to kiss me, but it's clear I'd have to meet him halfway.

Do I want to?

Actually…yes.

My heart speeds up at the thought. Without even thinking about it, I lick my lips and swallow. Our noses brush, and then our lips, only slightly. Just enough to make my breath catch and my head feel light.

Then I chicken out, pulling back enough to put air between our bodies. "So how come your roommate peed on your shoes?"

Ethan laughs, letting me go and leaning back against one of the posts on our little metal island. I can only hope from his reaction that I haven't hurt him by pulling away.

I'm not even sure why I've done it. What am I still afraid of? Repeating history, I guess.

"Well, I've got like four roommates. A couple I never see—one's some kind of health nut, and the other's an architecture major, which apparently involves sleeping on his drafting table. The other two…always partying. The party guys share a room but one of them was in the bathroom, so the other came running up to use mine and mistook my closet for the room with the toilet…" Instead of finishing the story, he waves his hand in a gesture that clearly implies I should fill in the rest. Which, of course, I can.

The wind whips past, and I shiver. Pulling my arms around myself isn't quite the same.

To cover my discomfort, I laugh at Ethan's story. "I guess that sounds like a legitimate mistake."

"Dunno. I just moved in but I get the feeling this sort of thing happens a lot. We'll see how things shape up. To his credit, Alonzo promised to get me a new pair of sneakers. Dude seems to have plenty of money, so I'm not sure why he lives with so many people."

Ethan shivers too and pulls his coat tighter. I resist the urge to draw closer to his warmth. My phone therapist thinks I have a bad habit of leaning on men. I ran to Charles when my father didn't want me. I tried to use Jake to get away from Charles when things got bad. Nothing is clearer to me than the fact that I need to stand up and rely on myself.

Is it so wrong that I want to lean on Ethan right now? It all feels different. *He* feels different. I just don't know if *I* am.

My frown must have been interpreted as a response to what Ethan said about his roommate, because next he says, "Well, I figure I should see how things go before I decide to turn around and move out."

"Oh. Right. Absolutely."

"Besides, this time of year, housing options are limited. I'm not moving back in with my dad, and going to live with my mom would mean changing schools and leaving the area, which I'm not sure I want to do. So, right now, I wanna try and get along with these guys." He shrugs. "'Sides. A little piss never hurt anyone, right?"

"I…really don't know. I do know that I've now officially thought about urine more than I ever wanted. So thank you."

When he smiles big, he has a dimple. "Well then, I think," he dusts his hands, "my work here is done."

Something shiny catches my eye in the gravel beneath us, some little gold charm that someone must have dropped here however long ago. I lean over the side of the merry-go-round to grab it, awkwardly sticking my butt in Ethan's face.

"Aha." It's a nautical star. The jump ring is broken but I have more at home.

"Pretty." Though the way Ethan's looking, I don't quite know if he means the jewelry I just found.

I cough and close my hand over the small piece of metal. "Oh. Yeah. I started picking up buttons and beads and things to make jewelry out of. Gives me something to do."

"I think that's great. I'm all about recycling found objects. Used to search for stuff like that with my mom on the beach. I had a definite shell and sand dollar period in my artwork. So, whatcha thinking? Time to go?" He rises up on his knees. The way he's poised, he could either move away or get closer just as easily.

"Oh, I don't know. I'm not dizzy yet." Not that I honestly want to get dizzy, but we've gotten a little too serious. After Ethan brought me here to have fun, I want to lighten the mood.

With his hands deep in the pockets of his leather jacket, Ethan leans in toward me again. "I thought you didn't want me to make you dizzy."

I didn't think so. Yet here we are, hot breath puffing in the cold air between us. My lips tingle as he leans close. It's impossible to forget the way his hands explored me so carefully before. The way his tongue tasted me like he wanted to keep on tasting me forever.

"You remember that first time you kissed me?"

His cheeks turn a deep merlot. "Damn right I do. I remember thinking it was the best kiss I'd ever had."

Well now. I'm pretty sure if I wasn't sitting on something cold and metal, I'd have just melted right into the playground gravel.

"It was the first time I'd kissed someone because I wanted to, and not because I thought I should." My chest feels strange when I confess this to him. Like it's full of butterflies or bees. Lighter but nervous. And oh God, my heart is just bouncing every which way.

As his hair brushes my forehead, his dimple deepens and his eyes get darker. "I'm glad you wanted to kiss me, LeeAnne. I've been dying to do it again."

Maybe…maybe I don't have to lean *on* him. Maybe I could just lean in again. Meet those wind-chapped lips halfway. That'd be okay, right?

I wrap my arms around my knees and smile. "I think I've decided I wouldn't mind getting a little dizzy."

His lips brush mine so fast, I'm left breathless when he jumps from the merry-go-round to give it a spin.

"Hang on tight," he says.

So I do.

#

Ethan

"We really don't have to do this now."

I'm facing a shelf full of cleaning supplies at the SaverSmart. No clue what ninety-nine percent of this stuff does. While I fulfill my job of holding the basket, LeeAnne plucks bottles and cans and boxes from here and there to toss inside.

We'd stayed at the park until we were both too frozen to do more than clutch at each other for warmth. Fun though that was. After we ran back to my car and blasted the heat, and LeeAnne let me warm her hands in mine for a minute before things got a little weird.

Mostly because I was staring at her lips and thinking about kissing her some more, but worried my car's front seats were too small to make fooling around comfortable.

Like I said. Weird.

When I offered to drop her at her place, she got antsy, so now we're here. Picking up antibacterial wipes and trash bags, like all the romance guides tell you to do. If I were going to call this a date, I'd say it was the strangest one ever, between the frozen playground escapade and now wandering the grocery store aisles looking for stuff to make my hardwood floors less sticky.

"Vinegar will work fine for the floors." My startled head jerk finds LeeAnne right beside me, leaning in to whisper in my ear. "And this isn't really a date. You said you had a ton of cleaning to do, so I offered to help. No stress, right?"

Wow, I've got to pay more attention to what I say inside and outside of my head. I cover by grabbing some paper towels from the shelf and flipping them into the basket. "I'm not sure I know the meaning of no stress. So you're saying this is a friend thing?"

I consider how I feel about that concept. Shana's "just friends" kept me confused forever and I've already told LeeAnne I'd like to be more. All that being said, I think I like her too much to simply drop her if she said friendship was all she wanted.

"Maybe. We're friends, too, aren't we?" She presses her lips together and squints hard at the spray bottle in her hand. Mildew remover. Excellent thinking.

Friends, too. The way the words settle comfortably in my chest, like they belong there. She's suggesting we could be both, and that's a far better deal.

"Well." I take the bottle from her hand. "You know what? I say we are. Not only are we friends, I say we're good friends. Great friends. Best friends."

A small laugh escapes her. Trash bags come off the shelf and so does a package of disposable rubber gloves. Jesus, maybe I did a little too well in conveying the level of biohazard the dude in my room left behind.

"And how do you figure we're best friends, Ethan? I thought Michelle was your best friend."

She piles in the trash bags, the gloves, some fabric spray, and a lemon-scented wood cleaner. Not that I can't handle the weight, but I use the growing burden as an excuse to put the basket down and slide closer.

"Michelle's a great friend. Except I don't think even *she* would volunteer to come over and help me decontaminate my new place." When I pause for breath, I get a deep and gratifying whiff of LeeAnne. Apples and winter and a little lingering beer smell from the bar fills my nostrils. It's a smell that's down to earth but fantasy at the same time, kind of like all of her.

"Even though," I continue, "I'm pretty sure you only volunteered because for some reason you really don't want to go back to where you live. That's cool though, because best friends let each other hang out whenever they want. They're even willing to listen. Should you decide you want to talk more about why it is you don't want to go home."

I brush my knuckles against the back of her hand. Her fingers are turning white on a can of disinfectant spray, and I want her to know it's okay to let go. Whatever it is she's holding on to for dear life, I'm willing to listen.

I really am, too. Not only so I can get laid. That's not even…I mean, I'd be lying if I said I had no interest in being with LeeAnne again, because of course I do. I want to kiss those pouty lips when I'm stone-cold sober and to feel the smoothness of her silky-looking hair between my fingers. I want to take off her clothes so I can feel all of those curves that lead from her hips to her backside and down a pair of killer legs that don't deserve to be hidden by layers of clothes.

But.

Buuut.

I can also be a friend. If I could be there for Shana while she *figured herself out* for months on end and gave me nothing but glimmers of possibility, I can be there for LeeAnne.

Feels like I've almost convinced myself of that when LeeAnne leans closer. The sweetness of her breath fans across my cheek, making me turn to meet her eyes. They're so close. So's her mouth.

Those lips. They're parted like she might speak. Or maybe…

"Ethan—"

"My goodness, you see that?"

"I think she's dating again… too soon."

"Always throwing good after bad."

"Some people just keep making wrong decisions over and over."

"Wonder if he knows she cheated on her husband with that bartender…"

LeeAnne freezes. Her face is a mask of horror, and it doesn't take long to figure out why when I glance down the aisle. The women talking nearby, they're looking at us.

Talking about us. Whispering. About LeeAnne. Picking her apart into little pieces of gossip, as if she's not standing *right here*. They've lowered their voices so I can't make out what they're saying anymore, but it's enough to see the stain of embarrassment on LeeAnne's face.

I turn to shut them down. "Hey."

"Ethan. Don't." LeeAnne reaches down to give my hand a hard squeeze, stopping me when I might have walked away.

Her fingers wrapped around mine interrupt the furious rant building on my tongue. The momentum I had gathered to stalk over there and give them a talking to, like my mom would've done, fizzled at the frantic shake of her head.

"They have no right."

"You don't even know what they're talking about. You shouldn't be defending me."

10. HOT AND COLD

LeeAnne

I'm not crying because of the way those ladies were gossiping about me. It was Ethan. The way he got in their faces on my behalf. Silly, right?

Ethan is clenching his jaw as he drives. "Sorry. I guess I didn't need to get in their faces and everything. I have trouble sometimes, not saying what's on my mind."

"You handled it fine. I... I can't believe you did that." I'm not sure what to say. Living in a tiny town like Evergreen Grove, you get used to the way everyone knows your business. Or the way they think they do. I've heard folks whisper all my life. About my mother's death, about my father's drinking, and sometimes even about Charles.

I should be used to it. I am. Sometimes though, I'm just tired.

There's so much judgment. People don't have to live my life, but they sure as hell decide that they know better. That they'd have handled things differently in my shoes.

Well, I'd love to see them *all* in my shoes. I'd love to see them walk a mile without blisters and bruises and bloody cuts.

"Hey. No way was I gonna just let them talk smack about you, LeeAnne. You all right? Where'd you go?"

The car is stopped. Ethan is wiggling his fingers in front of my face the way you do when someone has zoned out. Which I guess I have, actually.

"I'm okay. Honest. I'm just...trying not to let what those women said get to me."

"Sometimes our skin isn't as thick as we'd like." Ethan's shoulder raises as he pulls his keys out of the ignition. "Believe me, I know. I'm someone who someday hopes to make a living off work that is completely subject to people's opinions, but even in class when someone gets nasty about a piece I've put time into, I bleed. It hurts."

His confession is painful and raw. I see and appreciate so much the vulnerability he's trusting me with. At the same time, I remember the Ethan from our first night together in Joe's Bar. He seemed like he knew himself so clearly.

"So how do you keep going if the criticism hurts?"

He smiles sadly. "Sometimes I think I'd quit if I knew what else I could do with myself. I don't, so I carry on. My biological mother was supposedly this amazing painter. My dad's an art professor. He paints. Also does ceramics and sculpture and stuff. My mom runs a little tourist art shop up at the cape. Feels sometimes like creating is what I was born to do. But sometimes that also feels like pressure."

My heart balls up nice and tight. "Well, my mom died young and my father is a semi-functional alcoholic, so I really hope we're not all destined to do what we were born into."

His brow scrunches. "Sorry. I didn't mean—"

"No. It's okay." I grab one of the grocery bags at my feet and force a smile. "You know what? My mom used to say a great way to chase away a bad mood was to clean things. Grab the bag with the lemon-scented stuff in it and let's get going."

Ethan's lips smush up, kind of pursed and wrinkled at the same time. It reminds me of when we kissed. Of course it does.

"Cleaning's supposed to put you in a good mood? I don't get it," he says.

"It clears out the junk, literally. Gives you a sense of accomplishment. When things feel out of control, it's something you have control over."

That dimple I've grown fond of so fast appears. "Ah. Lemon-scented accomplishment. Got it. Let's go."

When we get inside, I realize he wasn't kidding about the level of caked on yuck. "Wow. I'm afraid to even ask what died on that rug."

"Right? As soon as I get a new one, that's going in the trash."

I roll my eyes and hand over a sponge after making a quick run to the bathroom to fill a bucket we grabbed from the store with water and vinegar. "Okay, you get on the floor and get started with this stuff. I guarantee the hardwood isn't supposed to be that color."

With a grin, he whips off his jacket and then drops down with a loud thud. "Man, not too many women would get me on my knees this easily." He winks, but he's blushing hard even as he proceeds to dunk the sponge in his hand.

"You flirt better when you're sober." I nudge him with my foot but I have to turn my back before he sees how his comment affects me. He's been on his knees for me before, after all. Glasses coming off, curly hair going every which way. No shirt.

When his arm brushes mine, I shiver and jump. How had I not heard him come close? "And yet I got you to let me put my mouth between your legs," he whispers in my ear. "I must've done something charming that night."

How does a person get both hot and cold at the same time? Because that totally just happened.

"Yeah, I think it was the part where you started groping yourself and laughing at your own jokes." All right, that was goofy and I shouldn't try to make up jokes. Mine aren't as good as his.

"What?" He looks up toward the ceiling. "I definitely did not do that, but I'll have to write it down. Nothing whips the ladies into a frenzy like being a douchebag. Did I tell my lawnmower joke? That one never fails to melt the panties."

The laughter bubbles out of me before I can even try to hold it in. God, I really do like this guy. He's funny. He's...different.

Good.

I turn my back again so he can't see the blush that I'm sure is rising to my face. "You might need to work on the douchebaggery some more. On a scale of one to dickhead, you're hanging out around at best a decent human being."

He looks truly confused, all wrinkled forehead and squinting eyes, like I've given him a riddle to solve. "Seriously? I was pretty sure I'd nailed the ultimate d-bag award after getting you off and then running away from Joe's Bar."

He reaches forward, but stops short of touching my face and only pushes an escaped strand of my ponytail behind my ear. "I mean, I guess it would've gotten you in trouble with your boss if I'd stuck around shirtless in the kitchen. Felt wrong though. Leaving, that is. The rest felt very good indeed. I'd seriously like to do it again. And again."

This guy.

Thump. Kathump. *Thump-thump-thumpthumpthump-thump.*

"I meant what I said before, you know? I honestly like you."

He says it with a smile and I can see his eyes crinkle from behind those Clark Kent glasses of his. His words feel so genuine, and I'm gut punched by his closeness.

I stand there with my lips parted, searching for the right response. Anything I can think of feels so trite.

He leans closer so I part my lips more. Drawing a breath, I decide to tell him the truth. "I honestly—"

Someone knocks on the door to Ethan's room. "Yo, roomie, get your ass out here, we're playing beer pong!"

Ethan grimaces and gives me an apologetic look. To the door, he shouts, "No fucking way. On a weekday afternoon?"

"Pre-gaming, dude, come on!"

"Go. Away!"

"'Kay! We're heading to the big house party over on Castle Street later if you wanna join." Party Dude's footsteps retreat, finally, and I'm left feeling like the odd man out. The closest I've ever gotten to a party was serving drinks over at Joe's.

"Sorry," Ethan says. "They seem to think it's pretty much always beer o'clock."

I wrap my arms around myself, suddenly chilled. "I hear that's how it is in college."

He comes toward me, his face serious. "That's not how *I* am. I've gone a little overboard lately. Fuck knows you met me on a bad night. Honestly though, that's not me."

"You're a student. This is supposed to be when you have fun." Admittedly, this side to his life does make me worry. Charles could be a heavy drinker, and I can't be with another. I can't. Even though I like Ethan. And I couldn't ask him to put his college experience on hold.

"Sure, I had some fun. Also plenty of headaches. What about you? What do you do for fun?"

The way he's studying me makes me take a step back. "I don't..." At first I try to think of an answer. When nothing but tension stretches between us, I finally give up. "I make jewelry and watch infomercials. Other than that, I guess I'm not much fun."

"You were fun today. At the playground."

"That was just being silly."

"Silly can be fun."

I suppose he's got a point, but... "I don't feel like I have time for silly."

"So maybe you need to make time." He's standing way too close. "It could be good for you to let off some steam. We can't survive if we don't laugh."

I think about how Ethan always manages to make jokes, even when he's upset about stuff like his dad and his girlfriend. He definitely seems to have a better outlook than I've had.

"I'm not sure how you seem so positive. I feel like I've been stuck in this habit of assuming things will turn out badly my entire life." At some point, I stop wiping down dirty wall marks, the container of antibacterial wipes still in my hand. With a shake of my head, I put them down.

He pokes a finger at the corner of my mouth. "Don't let the knock-knock jokes fool you. I really do have plenty of issues. Do my best to stay on top of 'em is all. Laughing helps. A lot.

It's like I keep seeing different sides of him. Right now his face is stern and maybe even a little sad, but I still find myself envying him. "I wish I could be more like that."

"Hey, no. No way. You shouldn't wish that."

"Why not?"

He puts his hand behind my neck. I don't think I've ever loved the feel of someone else's stubble against my cheek this much before.

"Because," he says. "You're perfect the way you are."

#

Ethan

Couldn't focus in class worth a damn all week, and I nearly poked a pencil in my thigh during a studio drawing class as an excuse to leave early. No question, I'm distracted.

Since things went to hell with my dad, the thing I loved to do most has felt like torture except for some tiny inspirational bursts after hanging out with LeeAnne. That piece of glass in my stomach keeps pushing deep when I try to put my paintbrush on a canvas.

When things get this way, I need to move. To do something to get out of my head. Yesterday I tried hitting Roy's Gym to spar with Dante, but on the way in, some guy got in my face while I was parking. Tried telling me I needed to stay away from his property. If you ask me, his truck wasn't anything worth worrying about but I left anyway because some days you don't wanna fucking deal.

Today's Friday, so I've blown off my Critical Theory lecture to drive up and see my mom. I need a change of scenery and she's been asking me to visit, which has me a little curious. My mom's from England, and she's always been a pretty cool customer about get-togethers. "We'll see each other when we see each other," she usually says.

I dunno if that's an English thing or a *her* thing, but it means we don't hang out a ton. Doesn't help I guess that when she left my dad and moved to the beach, I wanted to stay where things were familiar. We've simply never been close.

I park on a paved strip surrounded by sand and trek up the creaky wooden stairs to her place, wondering why she's been nudging me to visit. I did just have a birthday, so maybe that's why. Usually she just sends a card though. Is it too much to hope that this year she got me something especially awesome like tickets to U2 or a pony?

My sister's reading a book at the kitchen table when I show up at their beach house in Cape Carteret on Friday afternoon. Yeah, a beach house might sound great, but it's winter. Even though there are some permanent residents, everything feels kind of deadsville to me in the off season.

I'm cranky from the long drive, and my mom's not in sight, so I take the opportunity to pester my little sister.

"Hey, buttface." For the kids I tutor, this sort of thing causes a fit of giggles. For any child ages six to sixteen, butts are hysterical. Not so for Rain, who's always been wise beyond her years and super serious. No joke, my sister could probably start college tomorrow and get better grades than I do.

"Mooom, Ethan called me a buttface!"

I don't even know why I give her such a hard time, when the honest truth is I love that kid to the moon and back.

In a heartbeat, I'd kick the shit out of anybody who even breathed on my baby sister the wrong way. But I guess it's a little hard not to be jealous. When she was born, I was so much older, but I still couldn't help but worry that my place had been usurped. After all, she was mom's *real* kid.

"Ethan, don't call your sister ugly names. You wouldn't want to be called a buttface, would you?"

At the moment, I'm tempted to argue with my mom that a) buttface isn't even close to the most offensive thing I've ever been called; and b) I don't think I'd take it too seriously if that was the best crack a person could come up with. Something tells me she wouldn't like the argument though, so instead I sling my arm around my sister's shoulders and ruffle her long, uncombed hair.

"She knows I'm kidding. Don't you, Rain?"

"It still wasn't nice." Man, my sister's got the art of pouting *down*.

"Okay. I didn't mean to hurt your feelings, and I'm sorrier than I've ever been sorry. What can I do to make it up to you?" I already know I'm going to regret asking.

When she puts her finger to her temple to illustrate how hard she's thinking, I *know* I'm going to regret it. "You could come to my soccer game tomorrow! I'm the goalie."

Uh. Groan. Standing around in forty-degree weather to watch a bunch of eleven-year-old girls cluster around the ball because they don't know their positions? Pass. "Not even Channing Tatum could keep me away."

My sister wrinkles her nose. "Who?"

Oh. Come. On.

I turn to my mom, who's turned off the burner under a steaming tea kettle. "I guess I'm not up-to-date on my pre-teen heartthrobs."

She tsks and shakes her head. "And we pay good money for that fancy school you attend."

"Mom, I go to school for free because Dad's on the faculty."

She smiles and pulls a mug from the shelf over the sink. "Then I suppose we're getting our money's worth."

A gasp slips from her mouth as a mug tumbles from her hand to the counter, luckily unbroken. She steadies herself and reaches for another, but I place my hand over hers.

"Let me get the mugs."

"Thank you, sweetheart. Can you pour the water, too, please?"

"Yeah. Sit. I got this."

I grab the tea and the milk, and make three cups with cream and sugar. I may be a card-carrying cappuccino fiend like any proper American, but being raised by an English woman means I really do enjoy a "nice cup of tea." With milk. Lots of milk.

When I sit with the mugs, she pushes an envelope across the table. "For your birthday."

I push it back. "Mom, no. You know I don't need you to give me money."

My grandparents left me some cash when they kicked it. My biological ones. They died before I was born, but I guess it's cool because I didn't know my mom, either. I know when I graduate from college, I'll get this money I'm not even sure I want. Point is, Mom's got her and Rain to take care of, and I'm away at school with free tuition and a trust fund waiting for me.

Damn. LeeAnne was right. I've got my issues. Boy, do I. But I'm in a pretty cushy position at the moment. Kinda wishing she was here so I could tell her. She's hella easy to talk to, especially on a merry-go-round.

Oh. And if you're wondering about Rainbow's father, we all are. All I know is he's some guy who showed up during tourist season and disappeared after he got Mom pregnant. I guess she's not good with picking reliable guys. Which sucks. When I think about it, I guess I could add myself to that list.

I mostly visit on the holidays.

Shit. Here I've been feeling like I'm the one who got the short end of the family stick on account of my biological mother being dead. But I hardly visit the one who raised me. I'm a terrible kid.

Mom pushes the envelope back. "Don't give me a hard time. Soon enough you'll be out in the world, being a responsible adult, and you'll long for the days when you had a little something in your pocket to blow for no reason at all."

I'm already longing. Frankly, I'm afraid to check my bank balance.

"I'm good, really." When she gives me a stern look, I relent and slip the envelope into my jacket. "Okay. I'll take it, but only because I'm afraid you can do magic with your eyebrows. And thanks."

She grips her mug with both hands and takes a sip, looking satisfied.

I lean across the table and squeeze my mom's arm. "So what'm I doing here, Mom? You asked me to drive up so you could give me some money? I always love to see you, but you could've put that in the mail."

She smiles slightly and reaches over to tug on a piece of my sister's hair. "Do us a favor and let me speak with Ethan alone, dear. You can read upstairs in your room."

My sister's jutting lip makes another appearance. "But it's boring up in my room and the Wi-Fi is down."

"Then I suppose we'd better throw away all of the toys and dolls you have upstairs if it's so boring up there. You must have nothing worth playing with any longer."

Rainbow scowls and scampers off.

"Damn, Mom. Nice one."

"One to remember when you have children of your own someday."

There's a scary thought. "I can't even begin to think about that sort of thing," I grumble as I drop my chin onto my balled-up fist. "Besides, maybe that's not a good idea. What if I turn out to be a serial cheater like dad?"

My mom's open-mouthed expression tells me my theory was correct. She was Dad's grad student back in the day. They started dating and got married after Mom's neighbor passed away suddenly and left behind an infant who needed to be cared for. So Mom and I could use his insurance, or whatever, I think. Poor bastard got stuck on the hook for a kid that wasn't even his.

Now that I really think about it, kinda explains a lot.

"So I'm right? Dad's slept with his students before? Is that why you left him?"

My mom seems to have trouble with what to do with her hands. She fidgets nervously, sighing and frowning with apparent frustration.

"Mom, I caught him and Shana together. The whole naughty-professor gig is out of the book bag. You're not exactly protecting me from anything."

There's a look of sadness on her face when she leans back in her chair. "Oh, honey. I'm sorry. Your father was always good at being your mate. Your friend. That's what you need to remember. That doesn't change even if he's made some poor decisions. And if you're like him, I guarantee it's the good parts."

I put my hand on hers. "Mom, it's fine. I moved out. Give me time and I won't be pissed. It was just kind of a kick in the nuts, you know?"

She sighs. "I can imagine. But he did a good job taking care of you. Better than I could've imagined. This business with your girlfriend aside, he's been a responsible father. He loves you. You might have been a surprise, but you weren't a burden, sweetheart."

Something's weird here. "Mom, I don't get it. This isn't his parole hearing. Why are you defending him?"

She reaches across the table to ruffle my hair, a little clumsy but affectionate. We haven't been close since I was about Rainbow's age, maybe. I kind of feel myself needing my mom right now, and for a few minutes I'm lighter than I've been. It's nice.

"You and your father have always had a good relationship," Mom says. "I hate to think of all those years in ruins over a single moment."

"It's not about the moment, it's about—"

"Ethan, life is short, sweet boy. And when you get to be my age, you'll realize everything is about the moments. We try to fit the pieces of our lives together to make a complete picture, but some of those pieces, those moments, we can't get back once we've thrown them in the rubbish bin. Take it from someone who knows. I'd do a lot in my life differently if I could. Your father's done wrong, but don't toss him in the rubbish bin just yet. Don't lose the moments you have left."

My chest hurts and I don't know why. Something in my mom's voice has my throat tightening up. Her words sound loaded, and I can't process the meaning.

"Mom, where is all this coming from?"

Her hand lands on top of mine. "Oh, honey. Well, you see, the thing is… I'm afraid I'm dying."

11. MY PANTS ARE RIPPED

LeeAnne

A child is crying and it's all my fault.

"It's okay. Sometimes we drop a bead here and there. I have a whole bunch of them right in this container. Why don't we pick another?"

"But I wanted that one!"

I'm babysitting for one of the other ladies staying here at AJ's "family center," the old hotel he's turned into a place for those of us to stay who've gotten our lives kind of turned around. Truthfully, I don't love caring for small children. It brings up a lot of feelings about being unable to have a kid of my own, and Joy's little girl gets super emotional.

But we all have to help each other out around here, and Lord knows I have needed the backup now and then. Plus, the kid's sort of cute when she isn't stomping her feet.

Like now.

"Oh, I know you wanted that bead. But once they've rolled into the air vents, I have to call Mister AJ to come and get them out. Maybe you could choose a different bead to just hold its spot, until that happens."

Her lips purse and her forehead wrinkles like she's making the biggest decision of her life. I guess for a four- or five- (or however many) year-old kid she is, the big sparkly bead debate is a major one. Sometimes I spend a lot of time going over which items to string on a piece of wire too, but that's because most days I find the even bigger decisions far too daunting. Beads I can do. Beads are easy.

Especially when you're comparing them to handsome guys with glasses who make your knees feel weak.

"Ow! Mommy!" More crying.

I look over from the container I'd been sifting through to see a red line across the little one's knee. Okay, she was fine a minute ago, and even *I'm* not good at breaking a kid that fast.

"All right, what happened?" Picking her up from the table where we've been doing our craft and carrying her to the bed takes more work than it should. My arms are shaking. I've got a crying child on my hands and her mother is going to come home to find her injured. This wasn't part of the plan.

"The table bit me!"

"The table...what?" When I reach underneath with my fingers to see what she means, I realize the stupidity of my plan. Or rather, I realize it when the table bites *me* ,too. "Ow!"

"See?" Well, the little girl may have an annoying case of the I-told-you-sos, but at least she's no longer crying.

"You're right, there's a sharp edge under there. I don't usually sit on the other chair so I hadn't noticed. Let's get a bandage on your knee and we'll find out if we can cover over the spot until it's fixed."

"My pants are ripped."

"Good news. Your mother left me with clean clothes in case you had an accident." Yes! Pants. One problem I have a solution for.

"She didn't mean that kind of accident."

I look up at the ceiling. "God save me."

"We had a man come to the door once who said God saves everybody. But Mommy's boyfriend told him to take his Bible and shove it up his—"

Knocking on the door saves me from having a spiritual debate with a tiny person. Or one about words that kids shouldn't use.

"LeeAnne, it's Joy. I'm back."

Oh, thank God. Or...whoever.

When I open the door, I give Joy the biggest, brightest smile I can manage. "Hey, you're back! We're so glad to see you. Aren't we, kiddo? Aren't you glad to see Mommy?"

Joy drops her bag next to the chair her daughter recently vacated. "You hated it, didn't you?"

Wow, I must have a worse poker face than I thought. "No! Of course not. We had a fantastic time. Didn't we, sweetheart?"

Only ten, maybe fifteen times was I tempted to text Ethan to see if he knew of any ways to help me keep the child entertained. He tutors kids after all, right? Something told me if I called him, he'd come over to tell her jokes or we could've taken her to that playground together, but stubbornness kept me from dialing. As much as I wanted to lean on Ethan, I needed to prove that I could handle a stressful situation on my own.

"Mommy, my pants are ripped and I'm bleeding."

I turn to Joy with a helpless sigh. "Okay, so it wasn't a walk in the park, but we were fine. Honest."

Joy puts her arms out. "We'll get that checked out, honey. No worries." To me, she says, "Thank you for watching her. I've got to get a job closer to here, but Evergreen Grove isn't exactly the employment mecca of the USA. I'd leave, but until I get my dad's house sold, it isn't an option."

"You and me both. Joe's been good to me at the bar, but I'm worried that I've about worn out my welcome over there."

"I don't get it. You've worked there for years, haven't you?"

"He made me take time off. Maybe he honestly thought it was helping. I'm not sure"

I shrug and then throw a hand up in time to catch an airborne hairbrush that Joy's little angel has launched across the room. "Uh-oh. Let's not throw things, please."

This kid, I swear she gets into everything. That's probably completely normal child behavior, but it's another thing that makes me glad her mother is about to take her home.

I don't think little people used to bother me so much. Since I lost the baby, my tolerance for the normal whining and carrying on of little kids is so low, it's like something crawling under my skin. Right now, I almost feel the way I used to when I was with Charles. I'm going out of my mind with wanting to walk away, but I feel so guilty about it that I keep my jaw clamped shut.

"You're so good with her," Joy marvels when I turn to put the hairbrush away.

God, am I? No. No, I'm not.

"Well listen, I'm glad I could help. Sorry again about the cut. I had no idea that was a biting table." *Please take her with you now.*

"Yeah, accidents happen. Luckily, she's had a tetanus shot. Thanks again."

What I want to tell Joy is please, please don't ever bring her adorable little girl over again, because it's not that she's a bad kid, it's just that I am not as good with kids as she thinks and I'm afraid I'll lose my mind.

But instead I say, "Absolutely. Anytime." Because I know Joy would help me if I asked, and that's what people should do for each other.

Joy picks up a bracelet from my dresser. One of my favorites, made from found charms and wooden craft store beads. I had to move all my jewelry up there to keep it from tiny, curious fingers. "Hey, this is cute. Where'd you get it?"

"Keep it if you want. I made that one. I find stuff and fill it in with bits from the craft store. Keeps me busy, but I have a ton lying around."

"Fun. You know, I took up knitting. Mostly scarves and hats and stuff. AJ helped me open a shop online. They're selling surprisingly well. I could add some of these if you're interested?"

"Oh. Wow. Definitely." I had no idea you could sell jewelry made from recycled parts, but it can't hurt to try, right?

Once again, I check my phone after they leave. No messages from Ethan. It's been a couple of days since I went over to help him clean, and I haven't heard from him since. Not sure what's going on, and I have a decision to make. If I really think Ethan and I are no good for each other, I should assume he's changed his mind about me and let it go.

Except I don't want to give up. And I've waited long enough. It's time for a different approach. So I open up a new text message: *Knock, knock...*

#

Ethan

Fuck. Fuck fuck fuck.

I've been lying here on my bed since I made it back from my mom's last night. Exhausted as shit. Can't sleep.

The awkward fumbling and the tremors in her hands? I'd assumed it was nerves. It wasn't. She's losing them, she said. Her hands. My mom, who used to bake everything from scratch and who used to custom-sew Rain's Halloween costumes, she's losing the use of her hands.

It sucks.

It sucks for her. For my sister, who's still so young. Selfishly, it sucks for me. My sister's dad isn't around. My parents are divorced. Mom says I don't need to worry, but who the hell else will be there to help her if it isn't me?

Even though I haven't lost her yet, it's eating at me. I lost my mother before I could even know her. In high school, I lost my best friend. He didn't die, but he might as well have.

I pick up my phone and squint at the display. My dad called earlier and I let it go to voice mail. There was also a text from LeeAnne. The beginning of a knock-knock joke. By the time I got it, she'd probably gone to bed, but I call it a good sign that she sent anything. Especially since my current spaz-attack has caused me to drop the ball.

When the sun peeks in through my newly washed windows, I roll out of bed and hit the deck for some push-ups. When the big piece of glass digs in deep, I've got to have the discipline to work out or I spiral like a fucking champ.

"One…two…" I only manage to knock out twenty before I let the fact that it's been a shitty weekend convince me to take a break. Shitty weekends are when I should work the hardest, but sometimes you don't have it in you.

Instead, I cue up *Purple Rain* on my laptop and pull out my paints. When I took one of my first painting classes, the instructor was this amazing lady who wore scarves on her head because she'd recently undergone cancer treatment. She played Prince every day during studio, and told us there was God in his music. That it'd help us connect to our muse. At the time, I'd thought maybe she'd hit the medical marijuana too hard and I didn't like having someone else's "oldies" crammed down my throat. These days it's my go-to when I take my brushes out.

Even though I'm still not feeling inspired, I've decided it's time to sit down and make some damn art anyway. It's funny when something that's such a part of you feels so out of reach, and lately my painting has been. Even if my fingers are missing their usual ease, it's good to be creating again.

While I let my hand wander, making a sea of thick acrylic swirls on white canvas, the voices start to come back. The ones that tell me to make this line thick or that line light and wispy. The ones that say *no, less technique and more feeling*, and root around in my brain until I can find the feeling and what color it is.

Right now? The feeling is helpless. The color is midnight blue.

I think about the text from LeeAnne. At first I didn't get her message because I'd been driving back after a long day of my sister's soccer game, dinner, and pretending like not a fucking thing was wrong. By the time I did, I was too wrapped up in overthinking my life to send her a reply.

So when I'm ready to change colors, I stick my brush in the plastic Pender Tech mug I've used since freshman orientation. Hopefully my two-word reply plays the way she wants it to:

Who's there?

A beep reminds me that there's an unopened voice message. From my dad. Shit. As much as I'd like to keep avoiding, I suppose I should hear what he has to say.

"Ethan, it's your dad. Listen, first you move out without saying a word and then Professor Sloan calls to say she asked you to come by her office and you blew her off. Now, I understand you're under some stress, but if this has something to do with your being angry at me, I hope you'll reconsider. Allison Sloan is a talented artist, and it's a significant deal if she's taken an interest in your work. Don't squander an opportunity for emotional reasons."

Well that's some bullshit. For one thing, artists are emotional. Isn't he the one who's always told me emotion is what makes the work resonate? For another thing, he doesn't know what's going on with LeeAnne or with mom but I guess a guy who needs to sleep with progressively younger students as he gets older would have a big enough ego to think things are all about him.

Geez.

It's weird to see my dad so differently. The hero thing, I guess. Now a piece of his armor has fallen off, and I can see what's underneath.

My mom is right. He's still my dad. I'm just realizing how incredibly human he is, too.

No, I'm not going to stay mad forever. Not even sure I'm still mad now. In the aftermath of your mom saying she's maybe only gonna be around for another three to five years, seeing your dad kissing a girl you thought you loved seems like a hill of stupidness.

In spite of that, I can feel a dark rush inside of me. The way my heart beats too fast when I'm freaking out, and my thoughts buzz in so many directions I can't grab hold of one.

My mom.

My sister.

LeeAnne.

My classes.

My dad.

My missed meeting with my professor.

I need a job.

I need…shit. Shit, I don't even know.

I need to get up. I need to move.

When my head gets jammed like this, I know the first thing I need is to take inventory. Eat. Get some water. Make sure I've taken my vitamins. Those little things make a big difference. If I sit and let my thoughts swirl around, they'll make a black hole and crush me in their vortex. Or whatever. I'm not a science major for fuck's sake.

What I know is it's paralyzing if I let it be. I don't want to be paralyzed.

My hand's come to rest on the little table where I keep my portable paint set. It's been minutes since I made a mark on the canvas. "Come on, Ethan. Get your pansy ass moving. Go find yourself some food that isn't booze."

Things you learn living with four roommates. The beer in the fridge is fresh. The milk probably isn't. All the same, booze only loosens that piece of glass temporarily.

Once I've trudged to the kitchen and found water and a protein bar, I pull on shoes and head down to the basement. When I was doing my laundry the other day, I saw a heavy bag by the machines. My hand wraps are still packed, but I don't even care. Punching something would feel awfully good right now.

When I get down there, things don't go quite as planned.

I intend to start with some warm-up jabs and then maybe just a few power punches. My right hand is still just a little sore from that fight at Joe's, so I intend to go easy but I don't. I do start with jabs. Light ones. Hard ones. Harder ones.

Left hooks. Right hooks. Next thing I know the rush of adrenaline feels so good I'm practically punching right through the bag.

"Gaaaaah!" So maybe I let myself get a little worked up. At least I haven't been out doing drinking games with Alonzo.

"Man, I am going to kill whoever is comin' in here to wake my ass up at this hour."

When I see what looks like a rumpled pile of laundry rising up from the corner and a hand pushing out, I realize I'm not alone. There's an actual person in there.

"Shit. I didn't come here to wake you. Didn't know anyone slept down here." I address the athletic shirt draped over what I assume is a head rising up from the pile.

"Alonzo was supposed to tell you." The guy pulls the shirt off his head to reveal a weary-looking face. "My man's got some communication issues when he's high."

"He's... Yeah. I'm not sure that only applies when he's high." I really like Alonzo, but I can tell he's crazy smart and I can't help but think he'd be kicking ass and running the world if he weren't drinking or baked 24/7.

The guy whose sleep I interrupted runs a hand over his close-cropped hair. "Listen, I'm only trying to crash for a minute. If you've got a thing to do in here, I can find someplace else to—"

"Hey, no. It's cool." I throw up my hands and then put them down even faster. I'm not sure, but it looks like my hand might be swelling up again. "I mean, it was shitty of me to come down here and wake you. I couldn't sleep so I came to get some hits in on the bag. I can wait until later."

Now, before you think I'm falling back on my nice-guy ways, Nice Guy Ethan would have probably asked if it was okay to use the equipment at all. Hell. Nice Guy Ethan probably would've frigging offered to do the dude's laundry and make him breakfast as an apology for stepping into his morning unannounced, because Nice Ethan couldn't handle it if anybody didn't like him.

And if you think this moment isn't causing my stomach to churn, you're as high as Alonzo. I don't think worrying about being kicked out of the pack disappears overnight. But fuck it. I picked myself up once, I'll do it again.

Still. Refusing to let people treat me like high-traffic Berber doesn't mean I can't be considerate.

"It's cool, man. I'm up now." He groans and pushes a pile of stuff to the side. "Do whatever you need to do."

"Uh…thanks. I'm Ethan, by the way." I hold out my hand but I have to work not to wince when he reaches over and gives it a solid pump.

"Tyler."

I nod and step back, trying to be casual as I eyeball his sleeping arrangement. As far as I can tell, he's got a sleeping bag thrown over an old folding cot, and half of that is taken up by what I can only hope is his laundry.

"So listen. I don't wanna pry…"

"Then don't."

"Look, I have a lot of extra space upstairs in the attic. Probably way more comfortable than shoving yourself into that corner. I mean, you're a big guy and that can't be good."

He reminds me a little of Dante. Not quite as large and muscular, but he has that same sort of build.

Tyler's eyes widen first, then sharpen with mistrust. "Why would you wanna have some stranger sleeping in your room?"

I look around the room with its painted cinderblocks and piles of discarded junk. "Eh. It's a big room, and this looks like a shitty place to sleep. And that cot you're sleeping on? My dad used to have one. Not comfortable. If Alonzo let you crash here, you're probably not a psycho. He's a stoner, but he's a decent guy. I'm assuming you are, too."

The guy relaxes back against the basement's stone wall. "Well thanks, but I'm solid. I hope I won't be in town long. Kinda like having my space."

"Sure. I hear you." I bob my head and turn toward the bag, deciding to be stubborn and get a few hits in since I'm here and everything.

I manage a few more hooks before I hear instructions coming from behind me. "You need to widen your stance. Put your hips into those punches. Throwing a weak-assed punch like that is gonna break your hand. Probably why your hand is sore."

I don't know how he can tell, but it's not like I can argue that he's wrong. For a few hits, I do as suggested without question, adjusting my feet and putting more of my body in when I throw the punch.

"There you go. That's more like it."

This time I stop, turning to him with my eyebrows raised. "So you're a boxer?"

"Got into competitive MMA for a little bit. My brother was a boxer."

Was? Wonder what the story is there?

"He's dead."

Oh. Fuck. Did I think out loud again? I really do know how to step in it sometimes. "Sorry. I figured maybe an injury or something."

"You could say that. He had skills, my brother. Started young. This sick fuck fight promoter gets his hands on 'im. Says he used to be a coach and he can help Terrence get ahead, but after that everything goes straight to hell in a wicker basket. Messed him up real good."

"Shit, that's... I don't even know what to say."

He rests his head back against the cinderblock wall. "Nothing to say. Sometimes things are just bad."

"Yeah. So, uh, you know Alonzo from school?"

He shakes his head, eyes still closed. "Foster brothers. Came up in South Carolina. He lucked out and got placed with some rich folks who paid for his schooling. Offered me a spot to crash if I ever needed. Didn't think I would until I found out this boxer my brother talked about is around here. We have an enemy in common, so I've been looking to talk to him."

"Hey." I snap my fingers, but damn does my hand throb. "You don't mean Dante Ramos, do you? I know him." How many boxers in Evergreen Grove could he be looking for?

Tyler sits up. "Oh, you bet your ass. No way. You know him?"

My phone chimes quietly in my hand. God, I hope that's LeeAnne responding to my text. I want to know what she says, but I can't look yet. Thanks to having my head up my ass lately, I haven't been much of a friend. I know Dante's been looking for someone who has information about his ex-coach, and it sounds like this guy might.

I focus on Tyler. "He's dating my best friend. I know Dante's looking for people to testify against this d-bag ex-coach of his. It sounds like you guys might have something in common."

Tyler's face darkens. "Yeah, it's a possibility."

When I sneak a peek at my phone, the message from LeeAnne gives me new life:

Can't think of a good way to end the joke so I'll just say I'm at Roy's Gym with AJ and Dante now and then church. Maybe we could talk later?

"Hey, Tyler. Just heard Dante's at the gym over on Main Street. We could head over and have a chat. Just real quick. No pressure."

Not that I'd ever use a guy's pain as a hookup plan, but the timing feels supremely lucky. I can see LeeAnne. He can talk to Dante. All kinds of win.

After a minute, Tyler unfolds his long body from the pile of laundry and throws on a shirt. "Okay, man. That sounds good. I've been looking to talk to your boy."

I send a text to LeeAnne. *I have another idea...*

12. NO SEX FOR YOU

LeeAnne

I have to admit, when I first let AJ talk me into learning to box, I thought he was nutso. I mean…I spent years afraid that Charles would come after me with his fists. Why would I want someone to come at me with them intentionally?

It still doesn't make sense.

And yet…it does. Every day I resist going to the gym, but once I get in there and start, I realize how good it is for me. How the speedbag in the corner has a nice rhythm once I find my groove with it, and how the weight of the heavy bag is satisfying under my fists.

Back when AJ first dragged me in here, I gasped and wheezed like crazy just from the warm-ups. I was self-conscious being in this sweat-scented setting with old mirrors and pitted metal and men who all grunted when they wanted to borrow the equipment you were using.

It's familiar now, and I'm sort of getting comfortable. Nobody here looks at me twice. Outside of being coached, nobody here tells me what I should or shouldn't be doing. You get used to the smell. Grunting aside, everyone's respectful.

Especially Dante, who has run the place ever since poor Roy had his stroke. He's a huge guy, and he used to hang around the bar with this wild party-boy persona that I found sort of daunting. Actually, it turns out he's pretty sweet.

When he isn't trying to make me speed-jump rope.

"Okay, let's give it another try. A little more oomph this time and you won't keep tripping."

I pull my hair back and wrap it in a ponytail holder to stall for time. "When I jump super fast, my boobs whack each other and all the fat on my butt jiggles. It's honestly painful."

Wow. I don't think he could look more uncomfortable. Maybe if I tried talking to him about tampons. "See, the thing is, jumping rope helps you improve your coordination and body awareness. There isn't—"

"Anything wrong with your butt, which is awesome, by the way." Ethan sidles up next to me with a smile. "I mean that in whatever manner doesn't sound completely pervy, by the way."

Dante turns to him with a shake of his head. "Man, even I've got better control over my brain-to-mouth filter than you do."

Ethan shrugs. "Maybe I do use a filter. Maybe that's only the tip of the iceberg, and I've got about a thousand things that are way more messed up that I'm not even saying." He taps his temple with his index finger. "Think about it."

Dante scowls and wraps the jump rope around his hand, momentarily distracted by Ethan's appearance. I can't deny that I'm a little relieved. I really do hate it when my boobs bounce around.

"Damn. Okay. So as much fun as it is to play a few rounds of 'who's weirder,' I'm in the middle of a training session."

"Oh. No. It's fine…" My feet are in motion already, carrying me backward, making space so the guys can talk. Dante's being generous, really. I'm not paying him for this. It's a favor for AJ since he had to duck out early, and like so many things, I'm feeling the press of how much I rely on others weighing on me.

"No." Dante's long arm manages to hook around my shoulder. "This is your time. Ethan, can we do this later?"

"I guess so…" He's looking around the room, shuffling his feet with apparent discomfort. "Real quick though, I wanted to introduce you to one of my housemates, Tyler. He says he's been looking to talk to you. His brother trained with Arlo Specter."

I don't know that name or why it's important, but suddenly Dante's a different person. His normally friendly face sharpens to something angry and cold.

He looks over Ethan's head to the broody guy hanging back by the drinking fountain. "Who's your brother?"

"Terrance Thacker's my brother. Was my brother." The guy who answers is wearing only basketball shorts and a hoodie despite the cold weather outside. I've never seen him in the bar before, but if I had, I'd have offered him a free appetizer to try to cheer him up. His face is so handsome, but he looks so unhappy.

Dante's face gets even gloomier. "Ethan. Help LeeAnne run some cardio drills, would you?" He jerks his chin at the guy in the hoodie. "Let's you and me talk in the office."

They head off toward the back and I'm forced to turn my attention to Ethan, who's standing reeeeeaaally close. He's not doing anything outwardly suggestive—unless you call holding the jump rope Dante handed him and smiling suggestive—he's just standing. There. In front of me. Being Ethan.

Seeing him lights a tiny spark in my belly that I never knew could be lit. Something I didn't feel with Charles. Not even with Jake.

I'm honestly happy to see him.

Jake was my way out. Jake was safety, I thought. An escape from Charles.

This guy. With his glasses and his blinding smile, all I can think of is the way I'm freer than I've ever been when I'm with him, and I don't want to lose that feeling.

"I guess this is a little awkward," he says when Dante's out of earshot.

"Yeah, sorry, I…" *Don't know what to say. Missed you more than I should have. I'm glad you're here.*

"Hey, I think I get it. You've been under some stress, right? Your ex and your job. I've had some stress, too. I have an idea though that I think might help."

"Oh?"

"Right. So. Uh, new career opportunities. A job in the moisturizer industry. Best advice I can give you? Apply daily."

Moisturizer. Apply daily. "Oh my *God*." I throw my towel at him. "You know, for a minute there I honestly thought you had helpful advice."

The funny part is, I'm not actually even annoyed. It's nice to be able to pretend I am. I didn't speak my mind when I was with Charles. I didn't do it with Jake either, because I worried I'd scare him off. The freedom to be honest is unbelievably refreshing.

Ethan unfurls the jump rope in his hand. "See, I thought I'd get you with that one."

I snort a laugh. "Gee, thanks."

He points a finger. "*But!* But the thing is, it's like I was saying before. Sometimes things suck and all you can do is laugh, you know?"

"Ethan." Oh, good Lord. His words. And his mouth. God, his mouth.

He clicks the jump rope on the gym floor, bringing my gaze back up from where it had settled. Well, in my defense, those lips are rather full.

"Yeah? So, I think there's a chance Dante's going to be a while. Maybe you and I should get out of here. Find a way to have some fun when everything feels like it's in the suck." He's standing so close to me. Whether he's trying to be suggestive or just discreet, the tickle of his breath on my neck makes me shiver.

"You don't have homework or anything to do?"

"Nothing more important than you," he whispers in my ear. "Come with me. Stop worrying so much. We'll go over to Pender Tech and hang out on campus where there are no old lady gossips and nobody gives a tiny flea's dick about what either of us did or when we did it, yeah?"

My thin yoga pants are no match for the warmth of his palms on my hips. I shiver, wishing I could go and take a shower. Make my hair look nicer. But I guess he's already seen me looking a mess.

"Yes. Okay. I'd like to spend time with you. I'm not sure what there is for me to do on a college campus, but I'll bite."

"So I'll have to prove how much fun you can have. And maybe I'll even do it without biting." He's got that glint in his eye, like he just told a dirty joke.

And why is that? "Ethan, are you thinking we're just going to go and get naked?" If I'm being honest, my body purrs whenever Ethan touches me. But I'd like to know that's not all I am to him.

He looks around. "For real? Of course not. Come on. Come with me. I had the shittiest last couple of days, and spending today with you is the best thing I can think of. Let me show you we can be good together. We can even do it without having sex."

I see the way he's eyeing my legs, and I'm not sure I believe him. "Really?"

He turns and does a not-so-discreet adjustment of his sweatpants. "Defiinitely. Hey, you're gonna have to hold yourself back. If you can manage to keep your hands off me, I can be good."

There's something about how devious he seems behind those glasses of his. He looks like a mad scientist, and oddly that gives me some strange and unusual fantasies involving restraints and lab tables.

Good grief, what is wrong with me?

"You honestly think I can't keep my hands off you?" Really. I'm asking. Can I?

"I think— Wait, you were gonna go to church."

I rub a hand over my forehead. "It's okay. I'm still not really sure how I feel about going, and missing one Sunday won't kill me."

He smiles again. "If you're sure. Okay. I'm going to show you a good time." He holds up a finger. "And no sex for you."

#

Ethan

I can't believe she left the gym with me. Left the gym, got in my car, and agreed to hang out with me, to let me prove I could show her we can actually enjoy hanging out like a real couple would. Without getting naked.

Actually, what I can't believe is I promised we wouldn't get naked.

I am *dying* right now. Having her next to me in the car fills my little vehicle with her smell. My body knows the taste and the feel of her and it's totally bummed about the idea of not getting skin on skin.

Part of me though, most of me actually, is pretty fucking excited. She agreed to spend the day with me, none of that "we shouldn't be together" crap. This is gonna be great. I'm gonna show her all the ways I can make her smile.

I can work with this. I might torture the shit out of myself, but I can sure as hell work with it.

First though… "Okay, I don't know about you, but I am dying for an extra-strong cup of coffee. So that'll be the first stop on our tour."

LeeAnne turns her head so fast her ponytail whaps me across the face. "You already passed Delia's."

I try to muffle my laugh. "You know that's not the only place to get some around here, right?"

Delia's Bakery and Cafe is where all the good folks of Evergreen Grove get their java, their oversized muffins, and their soup-and-bread combos at lunchtime. Much to my disappointment, that big chain with the green logo hasn't yet heard of Evergreen Grove, and I don't know where they'd put a store around here if they did.

We've heard rumors of one with a drive-through a couple counties over. Huge deal, that one. I've considered driving the half hour out of my way just so I can be a lazy asshole who gets his brew without getting out of the car.

"Delia's is great. We're not going there."

"But it's the best coffee in town."

"Yes. But the campus coffee shop has milkshakes."

"And you want to get a milkshake for breakfast?"

"Ever tried it?" I ask, but I can tell from her horrified gasp that she hasn't. Most days I wouldn't either. I try to avoid a ton of sugar, to prevent the massive spikes and dips in blood sugar that can possibly put me into a shitty mood and make my anxiety worse. But I've been feeling shitty for days now, frankly, and a milkshake sounds damn good. I promise myself I'll get a breakfast sandwich, pretend I'm healthy with some protein. That's as far as I'm willing to go in the direction of adult responsibility today.

I've got a whole fucking lot of it waiting for me. My mom. My sister. My dad. Gotta go talk to my professor sometime. Right now, I'm all about LeeAnne and a coffee-flavored breakfast milkshake.

Plus a sandwich with bacon. Hard to be sad when you're eating bacon. (Shana's a vegetarian. I tried. I did. The thing is, ham is delicious and I'm a weak man.)

"So. Milkshakes for breakfast. That's something you think we might have in common?"

I take a chance on reaching over and threading my fingers into hers. "I think if you've gone twenty-two years on this earth without trying one, then you've been missing out."

She slaps her free hand on her hip. "I think junk food first thing in the morning is not what I need."

I squeeze her hand in mine. "Well, while we're freely sharing opinions here, *I* think that's no way you'd speak about another person, so why're you doing it about yourself? And I'm talking about us treating ourselves one time, not making it a daily habit. So relax."

She eases back into her seat. "I guess you make a decent point."

"Sometimes I do." I trade my glasses for a pair of sunglasses. It may be winter but the morning sun can really throw a glare.

"Uh. You can still see, right?"

"No, LeeAnne. I am, as my mom would say, 'proper fucking blind.' Unbelievably nearsighted. So much that I literally cannot read text without my glasses unless you hold it up to my nose. But I hate when the sun gets in my face so…you know. Hope you're feeling lucky."

When I glance over, she looks mighty freaked, so I decide to let her off the hook. "I'm kidding. They're prescription sunglasses. Damn."

A laugh sputters out of her. "Sorry. I figured you were joking, but I didn't want to be wrong. Don't people who are that blind usually have super-thick lenses on their glasses?"

"Welcome to the reason I didn't get laid in high school." *Oh man. Shut the fuck up, dude.*

Except she's smiling at me with her cheek resting on her fist, and she doesn't look horrified anymore. "The way you looked at me just now from over the tops of those sunglasses, that wasn't the look of a guy who didn't know how to get laid."

"Oh yeah? I see." I want to laugh, because she's got no idea. I hold it in hard though, because if she thinks I'm laughing at her then I'm fucked.

"And what is it you see, exactly?"

I glance over again. "You. Trust me, honey. This is all kinds of a new development. I think you bring it out in me."

I throw my arm over the back of the passenger seat. The tips of my fingers brush at the back of her neck and I could swear I feel her shiver.

When we arrive at the campus of Pender Tech, I park in a gravel lot way the heck out by the cow pastures. "Sorry." I go around to get her door. "I know this is kind of far out, but most of the spots near campus have time or permit limits. Plus the towing company is run by bloodthirsty jackals."

"I don't mind walking."

"Great. Oh. Sec." I grab my glasses and toss the sunglasses back on the seat. "Almost forgot. I hate walking into places with prescription sunglasses on. Can't see without them so I have to hang out looking like a hungover rock star. Sorry they're not as cool looking."

"Uh...Ethan?"

"I haven't been drinking this time though. Swear." She hasn't come out and said so, but I've gotten the distinct impression she doesn't like that stuff. Fine for me. I wasn't bouncing back so great from all that partying.

"No. I was going to say I really like your glasses. That's all."

I can't fight the sudden urge to turn and press forward. Using one hand to close her door, we're body-to-body, with LeeAnne between me and the rear window of the car. Her stomach meets mine, her chest surging in and out.

She fits against me exactly perfectly. "I'm gonna kiss you now."

I said no sex. Kissing wasn't mentioned.

When her lips press against mine, followed by a tease of tongue, I can take a guess that she doesn't mind. Then she presses her pelvis into me, and sucks in a quick breath. Clearly the firm declaration of my interest is pressing against her hip.

"Ethan..." God, I love the way she breathes my name.

"Hmm." My hands skim up her sides, pushing her sweatshirt up a little so I can relish the satin smoothness of her skin. My back prickles for a moment at the feel of chilly air on the base of my spine. Hands knead my skin, sliding to my ass, pressing us even tighter, and I almost entirely forget where we are.

Until some vet students in blue scrubs stumble past on their way to the coffee shop and whistle at us.

LeeAnne jumps to the side. Her cheeks burn a bright fuchsia. "Hey now. You said no sex."

"Mm-hmm." I hook my pinkie finger with hers. "That wasn't sex. That was kissing. Plus some other stuff. Milkshakes have a lot of calories. It's good to work up an appetite. Some deep knee bends. Some stretching. A little tongue action."

"God." She buries her face in her hands, but she's laughing.

"Aha! Yes." Man, I'm so psyched, I actually jump in the air. "Made you laugh! I actually. Fricking. Made. You. Laugh."

"Did not." I can see it though, the curve of her lips and spark in her eyes through the cracks in her fingers. She's smiling. Fucking great.

When she reaches out to grab my hand all on her own, I'm pretty sure I go ahead and give her a piece of my heart right then and there.

We take our milkshakes and walk over to the veterinary school.

"Now, I know what you're thinking," I tell LeeAnne as we head toward the rear entrance behind the emergency animal hospital. "It's a classy guy who brings a girl to a building full of sick animals for a date. Like I said before. Try your best to hold on to your hormones."

She laughs as we enter the building. "This is all incredibly weird. And by the way, I'm freezing from drinking a milkshake outside in the cold."

I pull my hands out of my pocket and put an arm around her shoulder to pull her close. "All part of the plan, honey."

We stop at a nondescript door with a "STAFF ONLY" sign on the stainless steel. I knock a couple of times and step back to wait for my friend to answer.

After a couple of minutes, my buddy sticks her head into the hall with shifty eyes, as if I brought an outsider to the secret club. "What's going on, Ethan?"

"Hey, Simone. This is LeeAnne. I hoped we could help walk the dogs today."

She sighs. "This isn't the park, you know. You just can't go bringing all your friends over to play. I could get in trouble."

"We're taking homeless dogs for a walk, not asking to see the super-secret bacteria cultures. And I brought one friend. Not all my friends and their little sisters."

Simone grumbles and pushes the door wide so we can come in. The rows of kennels are full of dogs in various states of medical healing, with some looking peppy and excited to see us. Others, not so much.

"Stay away from that cage," Simone grumps to LeeAnne as she leans in to look at a sleeping French bulldog.

"Sorry." LeeAnne jumps up. "He looks really sweet."

"He bit a technician in the butt last week."

"Seriously?" I'm sure it was painful and shitty for whoever got a set of dog teeth in their ass, but I find the mental picture hilarious. I poke a finger in LeeAnne's side and shoot a look her way. I'm gratified to see she's biting her lips together, cheeks red like she's holding back laughter.

"You think that's funny?" Simone's look of nastiness is aimed at LeeAnne again.

"Hey, Simone. Lay off. You know damn well it's funny. That's the sort of thing they write into romantic comedies."

My cranky buddy rolls her eyes and gives me the finger. Simone's cool, honestly, she just…doesn't do people. Or winter. Or mornings. We met when I helped at a fundraiser for the Labs for Vets program she works for where she trains service dogs for injured service people part-time. I think she's much more animated dealing with dogs than she is with people on a chilly Sunday morning.

"See, I'm gonna let that go on account of I've seen you in your Power Rangers underwear. And also because you're letting us see the puppies."

Simone gives me the double finger this time. "You can walk Humphry, the puppy that flunked out of the Labs for Vets program." She hands over a slip lead and lets the excited black and brown lab mix out of his cage.

With a cigarette in her hand, she points to the door at the other end of the room from where we entered, which I know from experience leads out to a grassy field behind the vet school. "I'll be by the door having a smoke and some coffee, and if you do anything to get me in trouble—"

"I know, I know. You'll have me neutered. You're a good friend." I slap her on the back and hand the leash to LeeAnne, who looks at first startled and then amused when the brindle lab takes off at a clumsy, enthusiastic gallop.

We get back out into the chilly air, and I have to hustle to catch up with LeeAnne, who's basically just running along behind the dog.

"Hey. Hang on. You've never owned a pet before, have you?"

She turns to me with a massive blush on her face. Not sure if it's the cold or my question, but either way I love the look on her. It reminds me of the furious way her cheeks reddened when I put my hands between her legs in the back room of Joe's Bar.

Aaaand now I'm sporting what feels like inappropriate wood in front of a puppy.

"I guess it's obvious?"

"Eh. Kinda." I tip my head to the side as Humphry runs circles around her and she spins with him, trying to catch up before he turns the lead into a straitjacket. "You're supposed to walk the dog. Not the other way around."

"I know!" One hand flies up to cover her face. "Or at least, I know in theory. He just...keeps going."

"Here." I grab the lead and shorten it in my hand, putting an end to Humphry's shenanigans. With my other hand, I pull LeeAnne against my side again so she can walk next to me and the dog. And because I like the way she feels underneath my arm.

"So, uhm, what are we doing?"

I point to Humphry. "Duh. We're walking a dog."

"Thank you for clearing that up." She laughs. "Why? When you said you were going to show me a good time, I didn't envision sick animals and angry...what, ex-girlfriends?"

This time I'm the one who laughs. "No way. Simone and I have known each other for a while. She does a lot of great dog rescue stuff and even works with training therapy support dogs for veterans and first responders. Me, I just like dogs. I've never been her type, though. Trust me."

Yeah, so I tried. Once. Ask me how many times she's threatened to have me neutered?

"Uh-huh." LeeAnne wrinkles her forehead. "What's her type?"

"Oh. You know. Broody. Damaged. 36-D. Her last girlfriend played bass in a punk band. Or a...funk band? Some kind of band."

"Oh. So you've never been in a band?"

"Most importantly, I've never had boobs, although I'm a big fan." I tug Humphry away when he starts sniffing at LeeAnne's shoe. "Don't get any ideas, buddy." I clear my throat. "And I was not in a band, I was in *the* band, which is completely different. Still think I'm hot?"

"Hmm." LeeAnne watches the dog for a while. He sniffs at some grass, takes a piss, and then takes off after some invisible thing as if it's a matter of life and death.

She doesn't say anything more, and I wonder if maybe I've just screwed myself. She was saying I was too sweet there for a while, but maybe what she means is too nerdy. Marching band carries a pretty high nerd factor.

It can't be all about that stuff though. I'm not blind. I've seen the way she looks at me. She likes me even if she doesn't want to.

I turn to face her, reaching to turn her chin toward me even though Humphry is trying to pull me out toward the staff parking lot. "You think maybe I'm not your type either?"

She smiles, but it's a sad smile. I hate to see her look that way. "Well, I'm not a lesbian. But I'm also not in college, I'm not well educated. We don't have anywhere near the same life experiences."

"You keep saying that stuff, but I don't care about all that because I like being with you. I *know* you like being with me." I do a little jump. "I'm gonna prove it. That's what this whole day is about."

"I thought the whole point of this was to prove we could enjoy each other's company without sex."

"Sure." I pick up Humphry and pile him into her arms. "See? Impossible not to have fun while you're holding a puppy, right?"

Sure enough, she starts giggling when Humphry goes to town licking her face. "Okay. You're right. This is fun. And it's not sexy."

See, that's where she's wrong. Or maybe it's because I'm a guy. Looking at her now, hearing the music of her laugh and seeing the sparkle of her green eyes in the morning sunlight, I'm totally thinking about certain things.

"I disagree," I murmur in her ear. "Because the way you throw your head back like that when you laugh, all I can think of is how much I want to make you do it again. Including when we're naked and in a bed."

She gasps and puts Humphry back down in the grass. Her eyes are wide when they look into mine, but she doesn't pull away.

13. GEESE ARE MEAN

LeeAnne

I let Ethan drag me around campus all day. Even though I kept telling myself I needed to let him get to his homework. I should go home and do laundry. He was right; I was having fun.

We played pool, air hockey, and bowled in the basement of the student union. Sometime during our game, Ethan got a strike and did a silly victory dance complete with pumping fists and pelvic thrusts. I laughed so hard that I shot orange soda out of my nose, and I couldn't help but think that I didn't know any guy who would've been silly in public that way just to get me to laugh that hard.

He also treated me to lunch at the dining hall. I tried to pay my way but he swore he had tons of money on his meal plan, thanks to the fact that he'd been living with his dad. It was an experience, being in this giant cafeteria-like place that was about quadruple the size of where I'd gotten square pizzas and succotash in high school. Better food, too.

Coulda lived without hearing Ethan's tales of food poisoning from dining halls past.

My favorite? The duck pond. Totally worth being out in chilly weather wearing yoga pants.

It turns out that in winter, most of the ducks have been smart enough to flee, but a few hardy geese remain, waddling around the pond perimeter like a tight-knit pack. I half expected to hear some music from *West Side Story* as they approached us.

Apparently, geese who live at a college duck pond get pretty used to people. And aggressive. By that I mean once we ran out of bread, we had to make a run for it, and I honestly thought I might have to leave my pants behind when one of the geese clamped down with its beak.

OMG, did you know they have little tooth-like things on their bills? Beaks? Whatever. Ethan found out when one of them bit him on the finger and then on the butt.

Geese are mean.

We ran like crazy, but we wound up laughing all the way back to his car. So hard that the cold burned my lungs and my nose and eyes ran. I don't know if I've ever laughed so hard.

By the time we reached Ethan's car, all I wanted was to see his amaretto eyes sparkle again. Call me selfish, but I wanted him to make *me* laugh again. The way he'd done before.

"Hey, what do you call an octopus with nine legs?"

He looks up with surprise as he's buckling his seatbelt. "A nonapus? I don't know. What?"

"Well probably you should call it by its name or else it's rude, right?" It's terrible. I know. I made it up off the top of my head.

He chuckles. "That's good."

"Yeah? You think so?"

He leans across the gearshift and cups his fingers around my chin. "It is. I like it. Don't sell yourself short, honey. You're better than you give yourself credit for."

He keeps leaving me speechless.

Now though, we're at something called an anime party. Ethan swears I'll like it, but so far I'm in wait-and-see mode.

I see a group of folks dressed strangely. A cheerleader or something surreptitiously gives me the side eye while twisting one pigtail around her finger and chatting with some super tall guy dressed in what I think is an even skimpier cheerleader outfit? I can't really tell.

"I think I missed an important memo," I murmur to Ethan as I take in all the people.

"Please, don't sweat it." He motions to himself. "I'm not dressed up. You're not dressed up. Howie over there in the overalls is an animal husbandry major who only comes when we watch *Supernatural*, and you wouldn't catch him dead dressing up like Sailor Moon. Gotta hand it to Kellen, though. Dude's got killer calves in that outfit."

My own laugh surprises me. Again. Or maybe it's Ethan who keeps surprising me.

"I understand so little of what you just said, I'm not sure how to respond. I agree that Kellen does have nice legs. Who is Sailor Moon?"

Now Ethan is laughing. "You'll see. Anh's got a few episodes on deck tonight." He jerks his chin toward a grouping of chairs and beanbags. People are already filtering over from a table piled with giant bags of chips and generic soda. "I see the chairs are going fast. Why don't you go ahead and grab us a seat? Let me get us some munchies and I'll be right over."

It's with a heavy helping of reluctance that I leave Ethan's side. I don't know anybody here except him.

As I sit perched in what I can only assume is a chair stolen from a classroom, the lights dim around me. Ethan and some friend are over by the kitchen where light still filters in. She touches his arm and leans in to whisper to him like she has a claim to his secrets. Or he to hers.

And why should I care?

We aren't any kind of official couple. Wasn't it only a short while ago I was insisting we weren't a good fit?

But my hands are curled around the metal supports underneath my seat. My heart is galloping and I don't believe it has anything to do with the opening scene of whatever video just started where a masked man is riding a horse.

I think maybe this beautiful college student with her dark, braided hair and her adorably funny T-shirt with some complex math equation that is clearly supposed to be some sort of witty joke knows Ethan in an intimate sort of way, or she wants to, and either way, I'm seeing it unfold right here in front of me.

I'm the one who should be touching him that way. Not her.

"Okay, it's time to go."

A big guy with a ninja on his shirt turns to give me a loud "shhh!" before tossing a handful of popcorn in my direction.

I jump out of my chair and skitter across the room as fast as I can, hoping to avoid the wrath of all the people whose movie I'm interrupting. A group of cartoon warriors or whatever are duking it out in a sword battle on the screen and I'm hoping they think maybe I'm just super squeamish about cartoon battles as I make a beeline for Ethan and the Ms. Cutie Touchestoomuch. Who I'm sure is actually rather sweet and doesn't deserve my anger.

"Hey." I try and fail miserably to hide that I'm breathless by the time I get over to him. It's not like I just went running or anything, but the effort of pretending—all those godawful years of pretending—it's stealing my breath.

"Hey." He turns to me with a warm smile. "Keisha, this is my friend LeeAnne. Hey, are you okay?"

He doesn't wait for me to say hello to Keisha, or vice-versa, which is probably good. She looks annoyed that I've interrupted, but I'm a little annoyed myself.

"Hey. Uh. Sort of have this really bad headache. I'm sorry, but do you think we can go?"

His look of concern fills me instantly with guilt. Thing is, I'm not entirely lying. All that sitting and watching and feeling like I had no control, honestly my head is throbbing now.

Which I hate.

"Hey. Sure. Let me say goodbye real quick and we'll get going."

When we're out in the fresh air and walking to his car, the guilt sinks in further. Ethan is super good, hooking his arm in mine and checking in repeatedly to be sure I'm okay.

"You certain you don't want me to go and get the car? I hate having to do a lot of walking when I feel like shit."

If Charles were here, he would have told me to suck it up and stop being a pain. That's what he had to do when he felt like crap in the army, and so should I. I understood, but I still grew to resent his attitude.

"I'm feeling better now that we're out of there." Oops. "Now that we're in the fresh air."

No. You know what? No more lies. I don't have to lie with Ethan and I'm not going to fall into old habits now.

I stop next to a brick and bronze fountain. It's lovely and shiny, except there's no water flowing. I wish there was. Winter is so damn dreary.

"Actually… That's not it entirely."

He looks worried again, and there's more guilt. I can't tell if it's something in my DNA or simply a really bad habit.

"I just really didn't like it. The party. The way that girl was flirting with you."

I step back then, bracing myself. Ready for him to be angry at me.

#

Ethan

"Here." I hand LeeAnne a container of chicken lo mein. "I'd try to cook something for you, but that kitchen downstairs is a disaster. Plus I can only cook with a blender and a microwave."

We're back at my place, which, thanks to LeeAnne's help buying cleaning supplies, is actually reasonably clean.

We both calmed down but decided to come back here and chill instead of returning to the party. Less stressful for LeeAnne, even though she swore she was fine.

Gotta be honest, it did some stuff to hear her say she was jealous. Good stuff.

I mean, shit. Totally misdirected, all that jealousy. That girl was a friend. *Just* a friend. That's one of those problems I've always had. Females glom onto me because I'm a safe bet. I'm *nice*. I don't love it.

Not that I was really able to explain all of that to LeeAnne, because of how worked up she got. The red cheeks and stuttering movements. The way she walked out of the anime party with short steps and ragged breath, like someone had threatened her personally. Seemed like she expected me to be pissed, but frankly, nobody's ever been possessive of me before.

Feels awfully damn good to know you're wanted. I kinda had to kiss the shit out of her when we got to the car, pulling that adorable ponytail free of its confines and backing us both up against the passenger door until the chill got to be too much to take.

Back at my place we're busting into leftover Chinese food, which I've got tons of because I order it when I'm starving and then can't eat it all. I really gotta learn to cook.

LeeAnne sits cross-legged on the end of my bed and proceeds to slurp noodles more attractively than anyone I've ever seen. And the noises. Dear God, the noises. I'm gonna lose my shit.

"Mmm. Oh, wow. It's so good. I haven't had this stuff in forever. All the salt and the soy sauce and the little baby corn and the pea pods and oh my Goooood..." Maybe she says more after that, but I'm not sure. It's probably incoherent mumbling but I could swear I heard some sex noises and something about bamboo shoots.

I put down my beef with broccoli and pretend to get up. "You sound really into that stuff over there. Maybe I need to give the two of you some privacy."

"Oh, stop." She hits me in the chest with a fortune cookie as I'm sitting back against my head board. "I hardly ever get to eat Chinese food. It's my favorite."

Get to? "Is it like a diet thing? My sister's got food allergies so she doesn't get to have it either."

"No." Her face is red again. Like it was when she said she didn't like Keisha hanging on me at the anime club, except...not exactly. This is a deeper embarrassment, if I were guessing.

"So. Uh. Money? I guess it can get expensive to eat out. I'm trying to reign it in. This place has decent prices though, and they always give me free egg rolls and, uh..."

I shake my head. It's stupid but I don't know what to say now. I get it that LeeAnne hasn't grown up with much. If you were to ask me, I'd have said that I didn't either.

I mean, Dad's house isn't huge and his salary as a college professor puts us in what I'd call a middle-class bracket. Maybe a smidgen above? When I was in fifth grade, they recommended me for a private school for gifted students, but we didn't have the tuition. Believe me when I say I absolutely resented my dad. Back then I would've told you we didn't have enough.

Now? I think I get how lucky we are. I go to school for free, thanks to my dad. My bills have all been covered up until recently. My books and art supplies come at a discount, and my mom long ago taught me the art of thrift shopping. Shit has sucked at times, but it could have been a whole lot worse.

LeeAnne is staring down at her food. No longer slurping noodles and making noises. Shit, I'm talking too much again.

"Listen, I'm sorry. It's none of my business. My mom always says discussing money is rude, but sometimes I'm not great at shutting up—"

"My mom liked Chinese food." LeeAnne's declaration comes on a rapid rush of air, so thick I can practically see the cloud.

"Oh." What do I say? "Cool." *Brilliant, Kinney. Fucking awesome.*

Keep an eye out in the spring for my line of greeting cards.

She sets her carton onto the table. "She had a heart condition. My mom. She wasn't supposed to have food that was too high in fat or sodium or anything that really had flavor at all because it wasn't good for her. So for whatever reason, after she died, my dad kept the rule in place. No fast food. No eating out."

"That sounds kind of over the top."

She shakes her head. "He didn't handle her death well at all. He also started drinking."

Outside, the sun is going down. Shadows play across her face and I don't like what they show. There's a lot she isn't saying to me, and I'm not so sure we're at a place yet where I can ask her even more probing questions.

Hell. Right now, her bottom lip quivers and I sense the prospect of sobbing in my immediate future, if I can't come up with some way to bring back the sunshine. So to speak.

"Hey." I jump up and set my food on the tiny table by my bed, which in the short time I've lived here is already crammed with papers, pencils, a lamp that the bulb's about to burn out in, and a fantasy novel the barista at Pete's Place said would "absolutely turn your brain inside-out."

The first four pages have maps on them, which automatically turns my brain inside out.

I realize I've landed the food on top of my buddy's book, so I wince and turn around, scooping the book into my ever-bursting-at-the-seams backpack and go back to the far end of the room where my dresser and work table sit.

"Here. Let me show you something. This is why I wanted you to come over."

My worktable is a stacked couple of pieces of plywood on top of cinderblocks. Not fancy, but it works for now. A portfolio of sketches and some of my larger canvases lean against the side.

Honestly, I'm sort of nervous showing her my work. I know art's a subjective thing, and except for the assholes who seem to think a critique's no good unless they're shredding you verbally, I try not to mind much what people think. You know. Water and ducks' backs and stuff.

I mean, I once went to a gallery show where a dude's entire body of work consisted of rolling naked in paint and then doing the same on a large canvass. You can talk symbolism until the cows come home but all I could see was that dude's big ass print right in front of my nose. Personally? No thanks.

Your mileage may have varied. Or maybe you're into ass prints. I don't judge.

Either way, having LeeAnne here is special and her opinion means something to me. I painted this one for her. As a gift. She doesn't like it, then it might hurt. It *will* hurt.

Already, I'm hoping for the best but expecting the worst. Especially since, as I pull the small piece of canvas board off my worktable and hand it over, her mouth is open but she isn't saying a damn word.

14. SALT AND MICROBREW

LeeAnne

I'm pretty sure this painting Ethan's handing me is the most gorgeous piece of art I've ever seen. It isn't as large as some of the others in his haphazard stack. More like a picture window with the sun already inside of it.

Or rather, the sunrise.

A sparkling body of water laps around a dock, with the morning light glinting and playing over it as it paints the sky all sorts of golden colors. It's the kind of morning so few of us ever see because we're never up early enough, and when we are, we're in too much of a hurry to stop and appreciate the beauty.

"Ethan, this is amazing." But my chest is tight, and getting tighter as I look at the beauty of this painting. Since my mom died, the world has looked sort of flat and gray. I don't know what to do with something so sparkling and bright.

I don't know what to do with *him*.

Pushing the painting back into his hands, I almost choke on my protest. "It's too much. I can't."

"It's not anything at all." He pushes it back again. "I mean literally, except for the cost of paint and canvas, which— forget it. My dad gets a faculty discount at the student store on campus."

He's shrugging in this fast, twitchy way that makes me want to call bullshit. If he were one of my customers at the bar, I'd suspect him of having ingested something other than alcohol in the bathroom, because he's acting way too unnatural in his attempt to be calm.

"No." Finally, I take the canvass back before our tug of war causes it to get ripped or broken. That would break my heart. "No, it absolutely isn't nothing, and I won't forget it. It's gorgeous. It's only…nobody's ever given me anything like this. Nobody's ever given me anything they made. I love it. Really."

My mother used to draw pictures with me. And cook for me of course. I didn't appreciate those things when I was young because kids never do, and I have none of those little drawings left anymore.

"My mom has this place on the beach. The water is amazing first thing in the morning, and it's one of my favorite things to see when I go there. It helps me to remember that I can always find peace somewhere in the chaos, even if the chaos is inside my own head."

His words burn my eyes. He's whispering so softly and so close. I want to melt right into him and never let go.

He clears his throat, looking uncomfortable and a little red-faced. "I thought…" He points awkwardly. "You said the place you lived was small and dark. I thought maybe if you had a picture of the sunrise, it would help brighten things up. Maybe help you remember that no matter how shitty things feel, the sun will always rise. I think sometimes we all need that reminder."

No, I'm not crying. You're crying.

Fine, I'm crying.

Still, just when I think I'm about to lose my composure entirely, I realize there's more to the picture. "Are there words in here? Down in the water?"

He seems to blush harder. "Yeah. Wasn't sure you'd notice. It's a new thing I'm trying. Started with a homework project where I put some poetry kind of graffiti-like out of laziness, and then I decided to take it a step further. I, uh, sort of like writing poems. Sometimes I bury them in the painting. Sometimes I put them right out there. All depends on what I'm feeling and trying to accomplish."

"And what were you trying to accomplish here?"

"To make you feel good. You deserve that."

The painting feels hot in my hands. "I've never considered that before."

"You do. You deserve Chinese food every day if it makes you happy. You deserve a piece of sunshine in your bedroom. Hell, you deserve a giant fucking window with it hitting you in the face every morning, if that's what you want. You deserve the absolute best."

I catch myself rolling my eyes. I don't even know why. I guess I feel strange being so...gushed over? All the thick, naked praise being layered on me, it's too much. I grew up being told not to get too big for my britches and not to think I'm too special. Part of me wants to ask what's wrong with this guy that he thinks something different?

That he actually thinks I'm better?

"Tell me what the poem says," I say to redirect the conversation.

Instead of taking the painting from my hand so he can read it, he slides behind me and puts an arm around my waist.

He clears his throat again, but it's a low, raspy sound that sends a shivery puff of warm breath right across the back of my neck. The chill starts at the top of my spine and fans out at the bottom, going down each leg and curling my feet.

From a breath. A simple throat clear.

God, I need some help.

"Your skin tasted of salt and microbrew.
I dream of standing in the sun with you.
I think of that night I tasted you.
I dream of tasting more and more of you.
I dream of making love to you.
Of tasting every inch of you."

Honest to God, I'm speechless. I've spent the last two years working in a bar. Give me a gropey drunk, an angry asshole, two townies shouting at the game, and I've got a comeback or a way to diffuse the situation almost every time. At least I used to.

Now?

Now I've got Ethan's arms around my waist and his chest—which I know from recent memory is lean and carved and covered in a disturbingly sexy new tattoo—well, that chest is pressing against my back and moving in short, choppy beats of breath. Warm air from his open mouth continues to assault that sensitive spot at the base of my neck, and God help me if his lips aren't brushing gently over the fine hairs that are standing up from my skin.

"That was kind of a short poem." *Excellent response, LeeAnne. When in doubt, insult the guy who just gave you a heartfelt and erotic gift.*

"I ran out of room. And time."

"Time?"

"I got…turned on."

"Oh." I have no comebacks.

"Yeah. Oh."

His hand is drifting toward the waistband of my yoga pants and I'm both startled and thrilled to discover his fingers are aiming straight toward a strange but pleasant throbbing sensation.

Until Ethan, I didn't think I could enjoy sex unless I was having it by myself. Something so simple as getting aroused beforehand? It might sound basic and easy, but it never was. Which is probably why I lost my mind with Ethan that first night at Joe's.

Something that once seemed like a basic chore now feels kind of like magic.

Not kind of. It *is*. I thought I had a broken piece. Faulty wiring or a broken button. Maybe I just needed this quirky, glasses-wearing, college guy to touch me in all the right places. I'm trying to remember why I thought Ethan and I were all wrong for each other.

Now I think Ethan and I are like pieces from two different puzzles that wound up in the same box. And together I like the picture we make.

I put the painting down and turn to kiss him.

"Thank you," I tell him again. "Thank you."

#

I can't decide if it's the way he touches me that has me drowning in sensation. Or maybe it's his words.

"Do you like it when I kiss you here?"

"Does this feel good?"

Definitely the words. And the touching. All of the things. "Don't stop."

"God, yes. Tell me if this is okay."

Every taste of his tongue, every stroke of his fingers is followed by more questions. And more questions. Each new exploration raises goose bumps on my skin and the temperature in my blood.

His words aren't out-and-out filthy. I've heard plenty of filthy. Lecherous drunks telling me I've got a great ass and they'd just bet they can show me a good time, and so on.

Ethan isn't being crass. He's asking me what feels good, and the way he's doing it drives me wild.

One finger brushes over the front of my shirt, peaking an already hard nipple. When I draw a sharpened breath, he asks me, "These seem sensitive. Do you like it when I touch them?"

The intense heat between my legs says yes, indeed. Me? I'm too shocked to respond until Ethan asks again.

"Do you, LeeAnne? Does it feel good when I touch you here? I want to take your shirt off."

Yes. Please, God, a thousand times yes. Take off my shirt. Take everything.

But all that comes out is a pained whimper, a combination of frustration and fear. I want him. I do. And I'm selfish and needy enough to take him even if I'm worried about what's in store for us. Because what happened between us before seemed like such a lightning strike. What are the chances it could happen again?

I'm as greedy for these sensations he's pulling out of me as I am afraid they could all suddenly slip away.

"Oh my God. Right there. Right where you're pressing, that feels good." Is that me talking? That breathy, begging gasp hardly sounds like anyone I recognize, but it's only me and Ethan in the room.

Kay, there, LeeAnne. Is that how you're supposed to react when a guy puts his hand between your legs?

I don't even know.

My entire love life has consisted of making sure the person I was with was pleased. I've never gotten what the big fuss was about sex, although after what was almost an out-of-body experience in the back of Joe's Bar, I'm beginning to.

When Ethan put his mouth between my legs until I couldn't stand it anymore…is that the way it's meant to feel with a guy? Because if it is, I need to make up for lost time.

With a burst of frustrated breath, I push at Ethan's hard chest. With power I didn't think I had, I upset his balance and send him flat on his back in the middle of the bed.

"Everything okay?" He huffs a laugh, looking stunned but also sort of amused.

God, I like it so much that he's amused. I *love* that he's amused. "Figured it was my turn to get your clothes off. Is that okay?"

"Honey, you can do whatever you want." As if to show he means it, he spreads his arms and legs wider.

"Oh yeah? So if I said I wanted to tie you to the bed and paint your fingernails, that would be okay?" It's a tease, and I'm laughing, but my heart speeds up as well. These aren't jokes I'd have ever made in the past, and once they're out of my mouth, I'm worried I should've kept it shut.

But Ethan's eyes sparkle as he casually shrugs. "I don't have anything to tie me up with. Or any nail polish for that matter. One of my roommates might have some. If this is, like, a major fantasy for you, we could work something out."

What's funny is, I believe him. Even though I've seen Ethan serious and angry and even full of jokes, I can't say I've seen him ever be anything other than honest.

To be truthful I actually kind of wonder about how that would go, but I don't want to interrupt what we're doing. "Just curious."

He reaches up to stroke my cheek. God, I can hardly stand how gentle, how reverent his touch is. "I'd love for you to come here and touch me."

"Where would you like me to touch you?" I lean forward, curious about everything. Is his tattoo all healed? Does he like to have his nipples played with?

Last time we were together, he gave and I took. Such a rare and mind-blowing experience, I couldn't help but soak it in. Now, I'm above him and I'm aware that he's giving me the power to do anything to him I want, even if that thing is tie him up while I run to the drug store for some of my favorite Razz Ma Tazz nail polish.

It's heady, this power. Part of me wants to sit back and do nothing but breathe it in. Except I realize Ethan's gotten me down to nothing but my underwear, and he's...

"You still have an awful lot of clothes on."

He chuckles. "So you want me to take them off?"

"Yeah. And I want you to do it slowly."

"Like a striptease?" God help me, I was joking around but he actually seems to like that idea.

"Well..." Dammit, I wish I knew how to make decisions faster. For so long, the decisions were easy. I simply did what I knew was least likely to cause trouble. Give me a buffet of choices where no answer is wrong, and I'm paralyzed.

So I say the first thing that comes to mind. "Yes. Like a striptease."

"Little dance and everything? Want me to get up in the middle of the room?" He wiggles his hips and then rises up onto his elbows like he really plans to do it.

I stop him with a hand to his really nicely toned stomach. "That seems like going overboard, don't you think?"

With a slow grin, he slides his glasses from his face and folds them neatly on his bedside table, placing them on top of a stack of books. "You're the boss."

You're the boss.

I'm the boss.

I'm the boss.

I like that way too much. A smile spreads across my face. "Good. Now let's get that shirt off."

"Yes, ma'am." He reaches for the hem of his T-shirt, and something in my stomach cheers in anticipation.

It's scary how much I like the sound of those words.

I expect him to pull it over his head and toss it to the floor, and that would be fine. Not like I'm going to hold him to my silly striptease mandate.

But he does it. No, he doesn't get up, but he gives me a little show all the same. Lying there on the bed, he wiggles and squirms as he inches his shirt up slowly, one…excruciating…bit…at a time. First his navel, then his six-pack. It's subtle, that cluster of abdominal muscles, and they might not even have pinged my radar if I'd spotted him shirtless on a beach somewhere. Some of Dante's old boxer friends at the gym, you could swear they're smuggling a crate of cannon balls.

But I've had a front row seat to Ethan's strength. When he barreled into Charles's friend so hard that he lifted him off the ground. When he picked me up and placed me on the prep counter at Joe's.

Those muscles are an optical illusion. And now they're twitching under my touch.

"Gorgeous," I murmur, running my fingers over his skin as he lifts his shirt higher. The way his muscles bunch and flex against my palm is so subtle, and somehow I can't get enough. Finally the shirt is off. It's on the floor. For some reason, my throat is dry and my chest is burning with the effort of my breathing. All the heat and moisture is between my legs, and it almost embarrasses me.

There's a primal need drumming inside me, eclipsing my fear. Drowning the what-ifs. I want him, and I can see the evidence that he wants me back trying to push its way out of his pants.

When he goes to push them down, I swat at his hands. "Let me."

Enough of the teasing.

15. IT'S PINK

Ethan

I've spent a lot of nights thinking about LeeAnne's hands. In all sorts of ways. She's got fucking gorgeous ones, with long fingers and a scar on her left pinkie and a constellation of moles over her right thumb. I've drawn them. I've dreamt about them. I've pictured them on my dick.

Hey, I'm a guy. It's what we do.

Still though, for a while there I was holding some stupid-ass torch for Shana and LeeAnne had a wedding ring on. Well, those things aren't true anymore, and holy mother of the Moon Goddess, she's got her hand on my dick.

Fantasy never does live up to the reality.

With her warm skin and firm grip, my hips don't wanna stay on the bed. My pants are working their way down my hips so I'm half-in and half-out, sort of bound and at her mercy while she looks at me with a world of mischief in her eyes.

"That's hella hot."

She blinks like I've surprised her. "What is?"

"You. That." I jerk my chin. "The way you're grinning at me all evil-like while you stroke my cock so slowly I'm liable to go insane long before I get off."

I guess I'm kind of a masochist that way.

For some reason, LeeAnne looks like I've worried her. "Am I doing this okay? Should I stop?"

Guess I'm not the only one who worries about performing well in bed. That's a massive fucking relief.

"Hey. No way. Come here." I try to reach for her but my legs are still tangled in my sweats. "Shit. I was trying to say what you were doing felt good."

"No, it's me. I'm not good at…" She gestures in the approximate direction of my still hopeful erection. "Sex makes me nervous. I know half of Evergreen Grove thinks I'm some kind of slut, but I don't have all that much…"

"Hey. Hey. First of all, my roommate, Alonzo, calls me a slut all the time and I'm pretty sure he means it as a compliment. Calls himself one for that matter. So I think it's only a bad word if you let it be. Second, I don't care what anybody says except you and me right now." I push my pants the rest of the way off and pull her against me. I try to angle so my stupid hard-on isn't pushing at her side, but the little bastard is trying to get at her in the worst way.

"So tell me what you want right now. Because as much as I'm dying to be with you, we can get dressed and I can take you home, or we can both finish dinner and watch videos on my laptop 'til we're drooling on my pillows. Tell me what you want, LeeAnne. Because all I want is for us both to feel good and I don't need us to get busy for that to happen."

That's actually pretty true. What I decided about not wanting to wait around for a girl like some shlub, that's also true. I realized the trouble with Shana was that I let her use me in the hopes that one day she'd call me hers. But if a girl really was mine? Then getting what she wants would be what I want. Cool, yeah?

LeeAnne hasn't officially agreed to be mine, but I've got her here with me. I feel her in my heart, and I can tell I'm affecting her just as much.

She brushes some moisture from her eyes. "The thing is, I want to. I've just never actually enjoyed sex much. Until you, I never even…"

"Got off?" I remember from the night at Joe's bar. Dude, you wanna blow up a guy's ego? Tell him he's the first man to successfully ring his woman's bell.

Holy *shit.*

Her face turns redder than Alonzo's tower of Solo cups. "Yes. That. Not unless,.."

Unless what, I don't know, because she doesn't finish. I get it. Talking about sex is weird. And strange. But if we're gonna do it, we should be able to discuss it.

"Are you able to do it by yourself? With your hand or with a toy?"

Even redder. Her hands go over her face. "Yes. I tagged along with AJ to one of those adult stores once during their grand opening. The lady there gave me a door prize. It was this tiny thing that looked like a tube of lipstick."

"Toys. Awesome. I can work with that."

Her eyes go big and round. "What do you mean?"

"Oh, you'll see." I reach over to the bedside table, fumbling around to make sure everything I need is in reach.

It may be cool as shit that I was able to get her off that one time, but I was using my fingers and my mouth. Tonight I'd really like to make love, and I don't know if that's gonna come out the same (Come out. Ha.). So I have a little something I'm pretty sure I can use to be certain.

She crawls over to me. "Ethan, seriously. What are you—"

I pull her in for a kiss, grazing my thumb over her nipple. "Making sure I can blow your mind properly. You like it when I do that, right?"

A high, whimpery noise escapes the back of her throat. "I... Yes."

"What else do you like? Tell me where you want me to touch you."

"Would you kiss them? My nipples? That felt good."

Fuck yes I would. "You want me to kiss them? Lick them? Bite them?"

Her hard, breathy, "yes" almost makes me shoot right then and there.

My hands shake some as I nuzzle and kiss the softness of her sensitive flesh, nipping lightly before I coast down, down, and down some more over the valley of her stomach and the joyful location between her legs.

I tease for a moment, kissing more and sucking again, but I can't hold back a smile at the music of her whispers and her sighs and her moans.

"Ethan. That feels good. That feels...really good."

Something happens when she says my name. Some surge of male pride or whatthefuckever, but the insistent, heavy throb between my legs pounds like a thing on steroids. I want so fucking badly to be inside her.

"LeeAnne. Let me make love to you. Please."

She nods. Barely. A crimson stain riding high on her cheeks and an adorable little lip bite as I circle my thumb over her clit, trying to keep her spun up. Her eyes are scrunched tight though, and I want to see her eyes when she agrees to let me inside her.

"LeeAnne. Look at me. Please."

She does. Those beautiful green eyes zero in on mine.

You know that cliché about your heart skipping a beat? Mine just went out for a smoke break.

"LeeAnne... I want you... I need to know we want the same thing."

I'm reaching into the drawer for the condom. If she told me to stop now, it would be god-awful painful, but I want to know for sure. The way she seems to be surprised when I let her take the wheel, I think maybe she hasn't been asked what she wants too many times. As lame as it feels to be more or less a twenty-year-old virgin, I'd rather wait than be with a girl who's not into me.

She takes the condom from me, and the freeze is like liquid nitrogen filling up my chest. Is this her way of saying no?

Then I hear the foil ripping. "Let me help you put it on," she whispers.

"Yes." Holy fuck, this girl is sexy.

So I do. She does. Then holy shit, I'm under her. Feeling thighs squeeze my hips. Her heat surrounding me. The slick slide of her as she rises and falls on top of me. The absolute rightness of her weight on me, the tangle of our legs, and the sway and bounce of her breasts. Most of all, the heat in her eyes as they stare right into mine.

I thrust up to meet her, until I realize all too soon it's about to be over. I can't stand how good it feels. "I can't take this. I'm going to come so fast you'll never want to see me again."

She laughs and puts her hands over mine, adjusting her position so she's sliding along my body. Her face close to my face. "So come. It's okay."

"No. I want you to feel good, too."

She presses her cheek to mine. "I told you, I've never had one this way. It's okay though. This is already the best sex I've ever had."

She squeezes her legs or something, her muscles clenching around my dick. It's all I can do not to go over right then, but I need to do something first. "No way. I'm gonna make this happen."

"Ethan, don't try. It's okay."

"Bet you I can."

She stops and sits up on top of me. "Did you seriously just make a bet with me in the middle of…of…"

I reach over to pull out my secret weapon. It's pink, it's silicone, and it runs on AA batteries. I roll my hips underneath her, thrusting in and out. As I do, I press the vibrator to the place where our bodies meet and turn it on.

"Aaah! Ethan. Oh my God. Where did you get—"

She shakes and trembles too much to finish her sentence. Good. I don't mind telling her about the toy, but right now I'd rather give us both a happy ending.

With one hand, I grasp her hip and thrust faster, harder, since even though she's on top she seems to have gotten off rhythm. For some reason.

With the other hand, I hold the vibrator.

And I keep holding it.

And holding it.

Jesus Christ, I've never wanted to come so bad in my life.

"Oh, God. Oh God, Ethan, I'm go— Oh God!"

I keep the vibrator in its place as she screams her lungs out, as my orgasm blasts out of me in violent bursts, and even as she slumps on top of me.

I keep it there until she shudders and says, "Okay, that's too much. Turn it off."

And I do, smiling, because I've made her feel good.

"I totally won that bet," I whisper into her hair.

I think she tries to argue, but she's too worn out to move.

I did though. I totally won the orgasm bet.

#

LeeAnne

"Okay, so where'd you get the pink vibrator?" It's been driving me crazy to know ever since he used *it* to drive me crazy.

Ethan's low laugh shows not a hint of embarrassment about having a pink sex toy in his drawer. "It was a gag gift from the Anime Club's holiday exchange. Sure came in handy today."

I don't know how to answer when my face is on fire.

We're eating cold leftovers on Ethan's bed. I've got a sheet wrapped around me as I twirl cold noodles with my fork. Still, the way Ethan appraises me with every bite of his beef and broccoli, every precise snap of his chopsticks, I get this rush of heat and shivers over my skin, like he's seeing right through anything I could put over my body.

He clears his throat. "So can I ask about the scar?"

The shivers change, though, when he asks about the scar. From pleasure to just plain cold. "What scar?"

I know what one he means. I don't want to answer him though, and my usual lie feels like not enough. The way Ethan studies me, wearing nothing but his glasses and a pillow so he won't drop saucy food in his lap, he uncovers far too much without asking anything at all.

"The one that looks like tiny train tracks across your pinkie."

Yeah, the doctor did an awful job with the stitches.

"Oh. Right. Childhood accident, that's all."

Sure enough, he squints and pushes his glasses up his nose, leaning forward for a better look.

"What kind of accident? Looks like it must have hurt." He reaches to stroke the sensitive skin with *his* finger, and without thought, I snatch it away.

"Sorry. It's…it feels funny when people touch it."

"Got it." His Adam's apple bobs slowly. "Sorry."

Somehow, that pisses me off. Not at him. Not exactly. More at, I don't know. The scar? Life? My father and Charles. At the reasons I've been afraid to speak out loud.

All the reasons I've felt like I didn't deserve to be looked at the way Ethan's looking at me now.

That look I guess is what makes me blurt out, "My father slammed my hand in a car door."

And ew. Yeah. There's the wince.

Ethan whispers, "Musta hurt like hell."

I look down at my hand and shrug lightly. "I'm sure it did. I was only five or six at the time, so I don't really remember the pain. I remember blood. Me screaming. My father shouting. My mother coming outside to tell everybody what to do. She was always kind of the eye in the center of the hurricane."

He takes the food container from my hand. When his fingers slip into mine, I wrap my hand around his, and this time I don't even think twice when he pulls me to the bed and against his body.

"When did you lose her?" he asks quietly, but his voice is as strong as his arms.

"Nine." My throat is so sore right now. I clear it, but it doesn't seem to help. "I was nine when she died."

"That sucks a lot."

I nod against his arm. "Yeah. My father... He didn't know what to do with a daughter. That day my hand got caught in the door, it was because I wanted to go somewhere with him in the car. I tried to reach through while his door was open to unlock the backseat. He slammed it shut before I could."

"Fuck."

"In his defense," I say to calm the anger on Ethan's face, "he didn't see my hand there."

"Still, that was... He fucked up."

"I shouldn't have tried to put my hand through the door." My stomach twists over my father's anger that day. I remember it so clearly, mostly because I don't think I ever saw him happy with me again. After Mom died things only got worse.

"No." Ethan is calm in his edict, but firm. The anger is there in his tone, quietly simmering. But he doesn't push it out through his body or use it to make his voice boom.

"No, what?"

"I mean, no. No, you don't go blaming yourself for that fuck-up. You're right, your hand shouldn't have been there. But you know whose job it was to make sure your hand wasn't in the door?"

"I…guess." I know exactly what he's going to say, but I don't think it occurred to me to put the responsibility on my father before. Which I guess is crazy.

"LeeAnne." He flops onto his back with a frustrated sigh. I think he's pulling away until he drags me along, letting me rest my face on his chest. "I was a scrawny kid, okay? I had a real hard time getting up into this van my dad drove so I developed an awful habit of grabbing hold of the doorjamb to hoist myself up and get myself down. Super dangerous if anyone had decided to throw the sliding door shut while I had my fingers there. You know what my dad did every single time? He gave me a lecture about how my hands didn't belong there, and then he made me move them. Every. Fucking. Time. I may have some issues with him right now, but my dad looked out for that shit. Kids are expected to make dumb mistakes and a parent's job is to make sure all their pieces stay attached, if humanly possible. You weren't to blame for that accident. At all."

He's right. Still, hearing someone say it out loud hurts for reasons I don't know how to convey, and when I open my mouth to respond, all that comes out is a painful, embarrassing sob.

"Hey. Hey, I'm sorry, okay? I just wanted you to know it wasn't your fault. Everything's all right."

But it isn't. Why do I feel like everything's upside down?

Ethan peppers my forehead with kisses. My cheek. My lips. The sheet around me slides down, and his skin is warm against mine. My breasts rub his chest, and while it isn't the heated, frenzied feelings from before, I do get a warm glow from the now-familiar press of his body. The fur of his legs brushes mine, and it simply feels right to curl one over his hip. To bring him closer.

"You know, in high school I lost my best friend," he whispers. "Not 'died' lost, but… Dude had a crush on me, which I didn't mind. Except hanging out together got us both picked on a ton. Me, I took it hard when people shunned me, so I tried to be nice to these fucktard bullies. Get them to like us, which was totally stupid. They used everything I did and said against me and Lucas both, and his family ended up moving to San Francisco after these guys got him alone and beat him up. Humiliated the shit out of him. Never saw my best friend again. Couldn't find him on social media. Now, I can tell myself all day it was those dickheads who used me to get to Lucas who deserve the blame, but down in my gut, it'll always feel like if I'd done more my friend wouldn't have felt betrayed and disappeared. So I get why you blame yourself, I just also know why you shouldn't."

I slide a hand along Ethan's back, trying to offer support. "You try to rewrite history. With your friend. Like you were saying about me and how I blame myself for what happened to Charles."

He takes a deep breath, nodding against my shoulder. "Exactly. For all that I've been telling you not to blame yourself for shit you can't change, I'm sucking at it right now. I found out my mom's been diagnosed with ALS and all I can think is maybe I fucked up by not being a better kid, you know. Shoulda visited more and stuff."

I place a kiss on his shoulder. "But you know how often you visit someone has nothing to do with their medical condition."

"Their mood though, it could affect—"

"No." Another kiss on the shoulder. I love this shoulder. "No. I'm going to say what you'd say to me. No, it's not possible and you can't possibly take that on yourself."

He leans down to brush his lips over mine. "You're pretty awesome, you know?"

"You too."

He's like an easy chair and a soft blanket. He's comfort, and the hope and affection I've always secretly longed for, and I'm not sure why I ever thought I could simply walk away. My gut tells me I should grab hold of a piece of this good feeling while I can, because God knows how long it will last.

As if the universe heard me, someone bangs on the door.

"Hey, yo, Ethan. It's Alonzo. So I was, uh, entertaining a gentleman caller in the bathroom when some short blond chick shows up and says she needs to talk to you. I told her you had company but she was like crying with full on Alice Cooper raccoon face, you know? Figured you might want to see what was up."

"Fuck." Ethan pushes back the covers. "That sounds like Shana. I'd asked her to stop by and pick up some things, but I meant at a reasonable hour. I'll tell her to go. Sorry."

"It's okay. I'll be here when you get back."

He kisses me and promises he'll be right back. Then he jumps into his discarded sweats and runs out the door.

This is his ex. Who probably realized she was stupid and wants him back. Who's in college and has the same interests and more money and everything. I pull the sheets up and listen to the churning noise in my stomach and the voices below, hoping I've made the right decision.

#

Ethan

I kicked Shana out around fifteen minutes after she showed. Turns out she couldn't reach my dad and was worried. He'd been having chest pains and wouldn't see a doctor. Thought I should know.

I didn't know which was more fucked. The fact that a twenty-one-year-old college student was afraid she'd driven her college professor boyfriend to a heart attack or the ways that might have happened. *God, don't even think about the ways.*

Worse yet was the fact that I sort of had to ask LeeAnne to leave. Well, I called AJ to tell him I was bringing her home (they put up a fence around the family center and un-listed guests aren't allowed in, especially at night).

I didn't want to cut the night short, but since I couldn't know how long I'd be out searching and Alonzo seemed to be in rare form, it seemed like the right call. How much would she still like me if my roommates banged on the door again in the night, begging her to come play quarters? Or God forbid someone pissed on *her* shoes?

So I dropped off LeeAnne and went out driving around to try and find my missing dad.

"I assume you looked at his house." I'm on the phone with Shana, who's gone to check his office and his campus studio.

"Of course. I went there before I came to see you. He's not answering his cell though, and I know sometimes he turns it to silent when he's working but I don't think—"

"All right." I don't mean to sound so sharp when I cut her off, but her anxiety is feeding mine, and I need us both to stop freaking out. "Hold up. Let's take a breath and break this down."

This is what I do. When that piece of glass gets so big I feel like it might cut me in half—and believe me, it feels that way now—I have to make it smaller. Break down the problem, find a piece I can manage. Take it one step at a time. Or, alternately, I hide in bed and suck my thumb. Can't do that when my dad's potentially dying in the woods because his college girlfriend overtaxed his heart.

As I approach the neighborhood where his house is, I see the turn-off for a dirt access road, a path that's supposed to be the county right-of-way for another neighborhood that was never developed. We'd gone up there in Dad's truck when I was younger, to shoot targets and to hunt deer.

Can I say real quick how much I hate hunting deer? Call me a hypocrite all you want, but I will never warm up to shooting Bambi just because I enjoy a good burger. I know, overpopulation, yaddah, and all, but *still*. I haven't hunted with my dad in a long while is the point.

Anyway. It's crazy late, but I could see him going up to squeeze a few rounds off if he's in a bad mood. *Okay. Start here.*

"Hey. I have an idea of where to look. You go ahead and check on campus, okay?"

"Okay. I will. Th—Th— Thanks, Ethan." Shana's voice wobbles in my ear, and when it does, I manage to let loose the tight clench I've had on my anger towards her.

I don't actually like staying mad. When someone fucks me over, though, I like to remember so I never get screwed the same way again. Maybe if I'd been more careful, Lucas would still be around.

But Shana, I get that she didn't mean to hurt me. More than that, I get that she's stuck in a shitty spot even if she doesn't. My dad, the chances are good he'll screw around on her again in the next few years, even though right now she's having the panic attack of her life about whether or not he's okay. And that sucks for her. It sucks big.

It sucks even more that I'm hoping that's the outcome, because if I get to the top of this hill and my dad's not standing in front of his truck with his gun? Not sure what to do next.

"Thanks for letting me know, Shana. I'm gonna go now, but I'll call you back when I find him."

"If…if you don't…"

"I will, Shana."

"Okay. And Ethan?"

"Still here." My front driver's side wheel clunks sharply as I hit a pothole I couldn't see.

"I'm so sorry about everything. Really."

"We're square, Shana. Honest. I'm gonna go now though, because it's hard to see out here."

"All right. I'll talk to you soon."

This should be the part where I put my phone down and pay attention in the foggy darkness, but I don't. I call LeeAnne.

The call rolls to voicemail. She's probably gone to bed already.

"Hey, I really wish I hadn't had all that drama show up tonight. I'm sorry about Shana. She's, uh…Well, I told you about all that. I'm still out trying to make sure my dad's okay. I also wanted to make sure to tell you I had a great time tonight. I always have a lot of fun hanging out with you."

I clear my throat and lick my lips. In the darkness of my car, this confession feels good. "Hey, so I hope I've made this clear. I like you, LeeAnne. An awful lot. Just to recap: I'm sorry I had to leave, but I'll make it up to you. Any way you want. Even with restraints and nail polish. Swear. Uh, okay. Bye."

I'm in the middle of hanging up when my wheel hits another hole with an explosive crash. This time the car won't go forward.

"Fuck!" I bang on the steering wheel. It's only minimally satisfying, so I bang some more. And some more, until my palms are sore and I've honked the horn a few times.

Finally, I give up and grab a flashlight so I can check the damage. "Goddamn double fuck."

My front end is wedged tight. This is why my dad takes his truck when he comes up here. My little CRX isn't made for this shit.

So I'm a good few miles from my house (even if I could get there, none of my roommates are sober). My car is stuck, I still don't know where my dad is, and it's extra breezy out here tonight.

I grit my teeth and call Michelle. She might give me crap for calling so late, but she's the one person I can think of who will know how to help. The one person whose number I have.

"If you're in a jail cell for drunk and disorderly, your ass can stay there until morning."

Dammit. It's Dante who answers the phone. He doesn't sound happy about being woken up.

"Uh…sorry. Not drunk. Is… Did I call the wrong number?"

"Michelle has a makeup test in the morning. She's been cramming all night and she only went to bed an hour ago. Whatever it is you want, she's going to be too nice to tell you to fuck off, and I'm not. So unless you can't breathe or you're on fire, fuck—"

"Wait. Listen, sorry. My car is stuck on a back road and I need a tow. I know Cassie's boyfriend works for an auto shop. I just wanted to get his number."

Dante mutters quietly into the phone before rattling off the number. "Now fuck off."

"Thanks, Dante."

"Yo, Ethan."

"I know. Don't call back. Unless I want my ass kicked."

Dante chuckles. "Nah, man. You can't reach Jake, call my cell. I'll come pick you up."

I'm shivering from the late-night cold, but I manage to smile. Dante can be a scary guy, but he's honestly a really decent person. Most around here are.

"Thanks, Dante."

"Not necessary. Michelle would be disappointed if you froze out there. Now go get your shit taken care of."

I manage to reach a groggy Jake, who agrees to come and get me but says it's going to take a while. He has to go to the auto shop first and pick up the tow truck. So I leave the car running with my headlights on so I can see, and trek farther on up the path. Maybe my dad's up here someplace.

I stumble into him, quite literally, as I'm about to give up. Actually, I trip over what I think might be a homeless person in a sleeping bag. When the person rises up into the darkness and says, "Ow. Ethan?" I presume my initial assessment was wrong.

"Dad? Seriously?"

He stands and turns on a battery-powered lantern. "What on earth are you doing up here?"

I look around for something to pummel. "Is that a serious question? I just had Shana breaking down my door in the middle of the night, freaking out because she couldn't reach you, and you're asking *me* what *I'm* doing? Who the fuck sleeps up here on the ground by themselves?"

Dad rubs his eyes and reaches into the pocket of a khaki camping vest for his wire-rimmed glasses. "I come up here all the time. It's peaceful. Lots of fuel for the muse out under the stars."

Thing is, I know he likes to get out in the woods now and then. I'd kind of forgotten, on account of everything else getting so fucked up lately.

I look him up and down, anger rising as my fear falls to the ground. He's fine and I'm grateful, but now the fucked-up-ness of this situation is thumping me on the head. How many times has he been up here alone? How long has he been having chest pains without my knowing? Mom said she might only have a few years left, and what if I lost them both?

I growl and give him a hard shove. "Are you fucking stupid?"

"Ethan!"

"It's a valid question. Shana told me your chest has been hurting. You come up here by yourself, no word to anybody, and you think that's smart? What the fuck are you thinking?"

"Ethan." Now he's growling. "I know you've had your issues with me, but I'm still your father and you've got no right to speak to me that way."

"You're not my father. You're the guy who got stuck with a baby after Mom took me in."

"You damn well know that isn't true."

I try to shove again, but there isn't as much heat behind it. I think of LeeAnne, and her dad, and wonder if maybe this is why she and I found each other. We may have both felt unwanted at times, but *we want each other*. I just have to make her believe it's okay. That I can be good for her, even though I'm some nerdy college kid.

Dad grabs my hands and I realize I'm shaking. "Ethan, listen to me. I've had some heartburn, okay? Probably too much of that onion chutney I love from the Indian place near campus. Nothing worth worrying over. It's fine. I'm fine. Hey…"

He gives me a giant bear hug, like he used to when I was a kid. I didn't realize until then how much I needed one. "Listen to me. It shook up my world when your mother…when you came into our lives. But that doesn't mean I didn't want you. Or that I don't love you. You're my son, Ethan. Always will be. Simple truth."

"Dad… Mom's sick," I mumble into his chest. "ALS. She's…they say it's terminal."

My dad's reaction, his sharp inhale and the tears on his face, are a surprise. My parents haven't been together for over a decade. I guess you don't always know how a person's going to react to something.

Dad tightens his arms, hugging harder. I do the same. "Hey. It's okay, kid. It's all going to be okay."

16. CHEAP-ASS WHISKEY

Ethan

So things are cool with my dad. Cooler, anyway. Can't say I didn't have my moment of thinking I'd somehow jinxed him way back when I'd asked him if he was dying in Shana's apartment, and then maybe he actually was lying toes-up in the woods somewhere. Man. Big panic. Fucking huge.

Honestly, this time I don't want to stay mad. I've got LeeAnne, and whatever happens with him and Shana is between them. I've got enough on my mind.

LeeAnne left the painting I gave her last time. I texted a message that said I'd bring it over, along with a joke about what the shirt said to the pants (*'Sup, britches!)* which got an actual cry-laugh emoji in response. A little over the top maybe, but... Ah, who are we kidding? I'm a laugh-riot.

There was some convoluted shit where I had to get permission to visit. When I'd dropped her off a couple of nights ago, AJ had met us outside. To actually visit her inside the gates of the shelter, I need prior approval. Which I totally get for security and all, but it leaves me feeling sort of like I'm back in high school.

Excuse me, sir, can LeeAnne come out and play?

I'm heading out my front door, kicking at the recycling bins nobody *ever* remembers to carry to the curb, when I get rammed by an oncoming train.

At least that's what it feels like must have happened, when my head hits a windowsill and the stars explode behind my eyes.

"Jesus. What the fuc—"

My head flies back again, aided by the blunt fist that strikes up under my chin. Another crack on the sill. "Dammmit. Whoever you are, I don't have any cash, okay?"

My vision's blurred. I can't see who's coming at me, but the dancing shadows under the porch light suggest the ass-hole's standing up, retreating, either because I said I have no cash or so he can come at me again.

Forward movement. Damn. I was hoping he'd go. I really *don't* have any cash. "Fine. If that's how we're playing things." I stick my leg out as he gets close, hooking his foot with mine and bringing him down with a jarring thud.

Or her. I guess it's stupid to assume it's a guy attacking me, but the low, muttered curses and grunts from the form crawling toward me suggest a male. A big one. As in, pretty damn big.

Sour, alcohol-soaked breath pants in my face. "You're going to see *her*, aren't you?"

"No. Not sure who you mean, but I was on my way to see a friend. A guy friend. Not that it's any business of yours." So the lie sucks. Whatever. Whoever the fuck this guy is doesn't need to know where I'm going. I'm rocking my head to and fro against the dusty vinyl siding. Part denial, partly trying to clear the stars in my eyes.

My hands remain pressed to the stone porch as I try to get a sense of my ability to stand, even though my glasses have slipped sideways. Stopping to adjust your specs is one of those moves that comes off looking weak, or at least I feel too much like it does to be comfortable fixing them now. I'd take them off, but I want to be able to see this fucker's face since he's seen fit to come here and accuse me of…well, I'm still not sure what it is he's accusing me of.

"Look, man, I don't know what business you think you've got here, but I can tell you've been giving some cheap-ass whiskey the business already tonight. Why don't you go sleep that shit off, and maybe you can come back and leave me a nice note when you remember what it is I've done to piss you off?"

He doesn't answer, just paces in front of me and breathes like an angry dragon. Briefly I wonder if maybe he's got the wrong person entirely. Three other people live in this house, after all. Four, if you count Tyler, who's still camping out in the basement.

Some of the fuzz clears. I want to say the dude looks familiar, but I can't place him. That guy who came at me in front of the gym one morning maybe?

Evergreen Grove is a small town. Pender Tech is a small campus. Between the two, I could know him from about anywhere. Guy's got kind of a severe look though, muscular, with that sort of haircut favored by law enforcement guys. I've definitely seen him somewhere.

"LeeAnne. I saw you with her in town. She came here. I followed you guys." He's gesturing, using large hands that move with a slow and angry purpose. "You. Came here. With my wife."

Oh. Fuck. That's not creepy. Oh, Wait. "You're…" She's not married. She said *was*. Was. *Was*. "No way."

She hasn't worn her ring in months.

Dammit, I'm trying to remember what she said about this guy, but I can't think. My head's fucking killing me.

In my stunned distraction, I don't see him rushing me until it's too late. Meaty hands grab my shirt, lifting me to standing and shoving me into the wall all over again. "Jesus, dude! I know you're pissed, but do you really want to put me in a coma? Because everything you do from here on out is only gonna get added to the police report."

"What I want is to find my wife!"

"Yeah, is she really your wife though? Because I didn't see a ring on her fing— Oof."

This time it's not my head but my lungs that take a beating when he drops me swiftly, face down on the ground. But his leg is right next to my face, so I grab hold with both arms. Then I have to roll away to stop him from landing on top of me.

"Jesus, would you quit doing that?"

That's almost funny. "Dude." I spit out the moisture pooling in my mouth. Turns out to be blood. "You're the one who came here and attacked me. Made wild accusations."

"So you're not fucking my wife?" His accusation borders on comical, but neither of us are laughing.

"She isn't your wife!" I shout my answer even though the ringing in my head is making me unsure. Did she explicitly say she was divorced? Wait! Yes, she did. I remember. It's not the sort of thing people our age usually have conversations about.

She did say it. She specifically called this guy her ex. I want to give myself a high-five for that moment of mental clarity.

With a growl of rage, the guy pulls himself up and so do I. I'm squared off and ready to face him, but having gone a few rounds with the wall already, I'm dizzy and bruised. My ears are ringing. My movements…yeah. Kinda sluggish.

I'm about to take a run at him all the same, when somebody vaults over the railing of our deck and grabs him from behind.

Dude turns around, but not quickly enough. It's Tyler I see, clinging to the guy's back like a barnacle. One of Tyler's arms is hooked under the other guy's chin who's slowly turning red from the face down as he drops to his knees.

I'm almost gratified—until a pained plea slips out of his mouth. "Please. You don't understand. I need her."

Damn. For a second I actually feel a little bit bad. Whatever's going on with this guy, it sucks. He's confused, and I don't wish it on anyone.

Then again, he wacked my skull against the wall so I don't feel that fucking bad.

As he lands with a *thump* on an ancient porch swing, the chain holding the swing up gives way and the whole thing comes down. Tyler jumps back to stay clear of the mess.

"Shit," he mutters. "Alonzo's gonna be pissed I busted that swing. He likes to smoke out here when the weather's warm. Watch the fireflies."

"If he says anything, blame me. I'll pay for the damage." I rub my hand across my throbbing head. "Hey, thanks for your help and everything, but...please tell me he's not dead."

"Damn, son, what the hell do you take me for? Of course he's not dead." Tyler kicks at LeeAnne's supposed ex, who makes a small moan but doesn't move. "See? Just napping. Probably better call someone though, before he comes to all pissed off."

I lean back against one of the support posts on the porch, nodding my head in agreement. I'm dizzy though, and Tyler's getting garbled. "Sure. Whatever you say."

"Ethan, you hanging in there, man?" Tyler's eyes get big for some reason. Maybe I'm bleeding again? All I know is he looks like he's reaching for me, which is so weird, because he also looks like he's getting farther away.

#

LeeAnne

One of the few things that keeps me sane lately is finding a song that speaks my feelings better than I can and playing it on repeat until I've purged whatever it is I can't express. Or until I can't stand that song anymore.

Sounds kind of crazy, maybe, but it works. On the nights like tonight, when I can't think and I can't sleep and the dark feels like it just might swallow me whole, listening to Wicked Crush sing "Wrecked" when I'm feeling exactly that way keeps me from believing I am completely and utterly alone.

You cried diamonds and you wished me well
My silent tongue betrayed me
I drove so far, so very fast
But missing you left me wrecked and wasted
Sent me straight to hell

It's so obviously a breakup song. A breakup that shouldn't have happened, because someone didn't speak up about their feelings when they should have. Listening to it always gives me that sad drop in my stomach.

I'm lying in my slightly lumpy double bed, missing Ethan. The television sitting above the dresser is on, but muted, so I feel less alone. The bathroom light is lit so I won't be in the dark. It shouldn't be the end of the world, but he said he'd be over and then didn't show. He hasn't answered his phone, so I don't know if something is wrong with him or with *us*.

Or what I should do either way.

I try to focus on wondering why the world needs a hands-free toothpaste dispenser—have we all gotten too lazy to squeeze the tube these days?—but it's hard to keep my mind off of what might be going on. His last text gave me no indication that he wasn't coming.

I knock lightly on the wall to see if Joy is awake. I don't want to bother her daughter, but neither Joy or I are heavy sleepers. A moment later my phone lights up with a call from her.

"Hey, you. Didn't wake you, did I?"

"Oh, yeah. I was in the middle of a hot dream where Tom Hardy and I retire to the countryside to raise alpacas. Sadly, Tom dropped the bomb on me that he's actually gay for Tom Hiddleston, and they wanted me to be their baby momma and knit booties from their alpaca yarn."

I like Joy. She's a perpetually frazzled single mother, but manages to maintain her sense of humor. Reminds me of another certain someone. "So you said…?"

"What *could* I say? I packed my knitting needles and asked when we could board our private jet. So what's up? You sound like you've had a rougher day than I had."

"Eh. I have no job at the moment and I'm getting tired of being in this room. Charles is back in town so I haven't wanted to go anywhere, except—" Except Ethan's, but I'm not sure where he is right now.

"Except where?"

"Except the grocery store. Munchies, you know?" Joy's got a history of bad relationships. So do I. Saying I'm hung up on a guy who's currently standing me up feels... I don't know. Embarrassing.

"Hey, no fair getting high over there without me," she whispers.

I laugh. "Yeah, right. I haven't actually smoked that stuff since high school. I wouldn't know what to do with it now." Where to find it for that matter.

"Me neither. So what's really wrong?"

"Like I said. Just at loose ends. I'm lying on the bed listening to the Wicked Crush on repeat. They have the best songs to get sentimental over."

Joy sighs. "Eh. I can't listen to their music, but that's just me. Maybe you should try, like, some happy songs? Something upbeat?"

I roll onto my stomach and prop my face on my palm, staring at the empty spot on my wall where I'd planned to put that painting. The one Ethan made me, if only I'd remembered to bring it along after the night his ex invaded.

"Honestly, I'm not sure I could handle happy music right now."

"Been there. Well listen, I love a good wallow as much as the next girl, but you truly sound like you need a comedy marathon maybe? Stuff blowing up? Really obscure foreign films, where we turn off the subtitles and make up our own dialogue and shadow puppets, perhaps?"

Someone knocks quietly on my door. "Hey, LeeAnne? Sweetie? It's AJ."

"Joy, hang on."

"Yeah, I heard him."

"Hey, is everything o...kay?"

AJ looks grim when I open the door. He's a colorful guy, AJ. Colorful clothing, colorful personality. Right now, he's standing before me in a rumpled pair of jeans and a hoodie with his lips pressed into a grim line.

"Hey, hon. Sorry to disturb you, but I got a call from a friend over at the sheriff's office. Your ex was taken into custody for aggravated assault this evening. Ethan's over at St. John's Hospital, last I heard. I think the police might be around tomorrow to ask if you've heard anything. Wanted to give you a heads-up."

The phone falls out of my hand.

Of all the things I'd worried could be a problem if Ethan and I got together. It didn't even occur to me that Charles might come after him. I should have considered the possibility, but he said he'd stay away. For all of his faults, Charles wasn't a liar.

Unless he got too drunk to control himself. Then it was a different animal entirely. *He* was a different animal.

"I should go see him."

"Charles?"

"Ethan."

AJ scratches at the back of his neck. "Sure, hon. You want a ride?"

Oh. Shoot. My phone. "Sorry," I say when I pick it up from the floor. "You still there?"

"I'm here," Joy mumbles. "Everything okay?"

"I'm okay. Ex troubles. Gotta go take care of something."

"I heard. Be careful."

I grab my purse and AJ's arm. "Let's go."

17. ACE HIGH

Ethan

"Hit me."

Tyler passes me two cards. "Man, you may as well fold. We both know you suck at this game."

Somehow Tyler flirted his way into getting us a deck of cards from I guess the nurse's station to pass the time.

I scowl and throw my cards down on my lap. I'm not folding because he needled me into it, so much as I am tired of thinking right now. "I'm not really good at anything that requires hard-core left-brained thinking. Math...figuring out winning poker hands. Forget counting cards or any of that mess."

"Man, you don't need that shit. When I play cards, I don't figure out the cards. I figure out my opponent. Same as in a fight. Read people. Get to know their patterns and their tells so you can use them to kick their ass. Like you. You been betting on ace-high all night long. You raise, I know all I gotta do is beat your ace."

"I've been playing with a damn head injury all night. You have me at a major disadvantage." It's so fucking bright in here. And blurry. I throw my arm over my eyes, grateful Tyler doesn't seem to mind how surly I'm being.

"Yeah, that's why I only kicked your ass a little instead of really whupping you up and down the block. Figure I'll save that for whenever you got your strength back."

I use my free hand to give him the finger.

"Man, I feel like we've grown close through this experience, but nonetheless I must decline."

In spite of my throbbing head and pissy attitude, I find myself fighting a smile. "Wish they'd let me go the fuck home."

"Someone has to bring your discharge papers. Pretty sure the police have asked all their questions by now though. Hey, the nurse said she also had Connect Four behind the desk. Want me to get that one instead?"

I manage an irritated grumble. "How do you do it? In the time we've been here, you've even had the doctors and the X-ray techs eating out of your hand."

His laugh is so counter to the grumpy asshole I met down in my basement, but it's something I need right now. Feeling like I have a friend makes this all suck slightly less.

"Well, now. When we were little kids, my granny used to say a smile opens more doors than anything. Guess I give good smile."

"Yeah, I bet that's why all those nurses were ready to swoon into your waiting arms. Your smile."

"Don't hate because you smile like you're in pain. Just gotta relax is all."

Ha. "I don't think I've relaxed since the seventh grade."

Tyler makes a noise of surprise. "No fucking wonder you're so uptight."

"Or maybe it's the head injury."

"Can't blame all your problems on one thing."

"Yeah. So what's your deal? I saw you tonight. Took that guy down in a hot minute."

"Uh-huh." He glances uncomfortably toward the door. "Hey, lookie there. Your girl's here. I'm gonna head on out there and find out who on the floor has a secret stash of chocolate."

"How do you know someone has a secret stash of chocolate?"

He taps his nose. "One of my foster moms was a nurse. Someone's always got sugary snacks. I feel a cheat day coming on."

He leaves me with LeeAnne and an uncomfortable silence settles in the room. Once I stop talking, I'm even more aware of the way my entire body hurts. The bruises and the cuts, the way they pulse with pain, and the mild nausea that makes me feel like I'm drifting on the ocean.

Oh maybe that's just being here with her, and not having a fucking clue why she has that look on her face. She looks like someone died, or maybe that's only because my vision's fucked at the moment.

"I'm so sorry," she says at last. "About Charles. I had no idea he'd come after you."

"Hey, don't. I don't blame you. Not for a second." I try to reach out to her, but she's too far away, hovering in the doorway as if she's afraid to step closer.

"But you should. You *should* blame me. It was because of me that he came after you. He stopped by the bar one day, asking me to take him back, but I guess I never thought he'd actually go after someone I was…involved with."

"LeeAnne, you couldn't have known. Sheriff's office is going to keep an eye out, and if it happens again, I'll be prepared. It's all good."

"No. It's not good at all. You shouldn't have to look over your shoulder all the time. It's an awful way to live, believe me. I should have realized… He's got issues, Ethan. Me leaving was hard enough for him to handle. I couldn't stand it if he came after you again and hurt you even worse. Your dad's out there. He says you have a concussion—"

"Mild one. Should be better in a few days, they said." My dad's here? Why hasn't he come in?

"Ethan, I think the safest thing would be for us to take a bit of a break. For a little while at least. It's better if Charles doesn't think we're together anymore." She words it like maybe there's some chance. Maybe we can sort of keep it on the DL until her ex cools off or whatever, but the way she's got tears running down her face tells me this is way more serious.

"Okay, Mister Kinney, I've got your discharge papers here. Now, you'll probably continue to feel headachy for a few days. I want you to avoid any strenuous mental or physical activity for…"

The rest of the doctor's instructions fade into muffled nothing as I stare at LeeAnne, begging her to not give up before we've had a chance to really get started. We have something worth fighting for. I know we do.

"LeeAnne, don't do this." Hell, do I wish I could march across the room and force her to listen to reason. I'm tempted to try, even though the last time I did I almost fell down, and even though the fucking doctor is in my face.

The doc asks who will be keeping an eye on me for the next twenty-four hours, and my dad pokes his head in to say I can crash in my old room for a few days.

I look back to where LeeAnne was standing, hoping maybe it's an opportunity for us. Maybe she'll take pity on me and hang out with me to make sure I don't go into a coma or whatever.

Except when I look over, she's already slipped out the door.

#

I'm pretty sure I've been sleeping for days.

I went through being restless and pissed off, but I was in too much pain to do anything. My dad stood by like a sentry, making sure I followed doctor's orders and confiscating my phone so I couldn't try to read, text, or do anything else that might compromise my recovery.

I did try calling LeeAnne once, on the house phone. No answer, not that I was shocked.

Now I'm just…I don't know. In limbo. Nothing makes sense so I'd rather not think. I called my mom and she's hanging in there, but I'm worried about the future. I could swear I'm arguing with myself, alternately freaking out about how this will affect my grades, my ability to paint, and being able to drive to see my mom. Then it's as if an another version of me comes back and says there's no point and I should have negative fucks to give about anything at all so go the fuck back to sleep.

I'd like to quit. I'd like to stay here in my oversized ninja PJ pants pretty much until every problem I don't know how to solve goes away. I know that's not an actual solution. It's what I want right now, that's all. My old bed reminds me of when life felt simpler. When my dad was only my dad and not the guy who was sticking it to college girls.

When I didn't know my mom had five more years to live, possibly. Five years before my baby sister, who I've always thought of as a pain, gets sent to England and I see her maybe never again. Before I lost LeeAnne.

Everyone goes away, don't they?

"Wow, you look fucking terrible."

I groan and roll onto my side to see Dante and Michelle standing in the doorway. Well, Dante, big mother that he is, pretty much fills the entire thing. Michelle stands in front of him, clutching a large painting and looking at me with a mix of annoyance and concern.

"Gee. Thanks. Hey, guys." I wince and then pull a pillow over my face. Mostly I'm feeling better, but bright light still bugs me, and Dante's head is right up by the hall light. "Uh, come in and close the door, will ya?"

"Good to see you finally conscious." This from Michelle. She was kind enough to come by a few days ago, but I was even busier feeling sorry for myself then than I am now. I pretended to be asleep until she went away. Some friend I am, huh?

"Yeah, I guess I feel slightly more human."

"Aw, come on. Quit being a pussy." Dante pushes my legs over and sits next to me on the bed. "You're fine. I've had my bell rung a couple times in the ring, so don't go fucking around. They said you had a mild concussion. Mild. So either we need to drive your ass back to the hospital for another scan, or this ain't about your head."

He's tugging the pillow off my face. I fight to pull it back. "It's about lots of things. I don't know what to do with myself right now, that's all. I'll deal. I'll figure it out."

Michelle touches my arm lightly, as if she's afraid she'll scare me farther under the covers. "Ethan, I mean this with love—you sound depressed. I know you don't like drugs, but they do help people. They've helped me. Maybe if you—"

"I'm not against drugs, Michelle." I'm honestly not. People need to do whatever they need to do to get better. Period. "I tried. All kinds. One made me puke, one made me jittery, one made me a raging asshole, and let's not get started on the boner problems.

"What I decided was that drugs weren't helpful if the side effects hurt worse than the thing they're supposed to help. Problem is, I'm stuck right now. Usually I keep my shit together by working out or painting. Maybe writing stupid-ass emo poetry. Can't do any of that when you get your head rammed into the wall, so I've been left with lots of time to lie here and think about how everything is fucked and how I don't have one clue how to go about fixing it."

Dante pushes at my leg. "Look, man. I've been where you are. You start by starting, okay? Shit feels out of control? You find the one thing you can manage. Even if it's fucking tiny. Even if it's putting one foot in front of the other to go take a piss. You start there. Then you figure out the next thing. It's like following a breadcrumb trail. Eventually you'll find your way out of the woods."

Something about Dante's suggestion brings a rush of awareness to the pressure in my abdomen. It's so ridiculous, I have to laugh. "Shit, man. Now I've gotta piss."

Dante smacks me on the arm. "You can thank me later."

"Oh, and Ethan, I'm leaving this here for you. Professor Sloan asked me to return it." Michelle's crossing the room. I don't watch because I don't feel like straining my eyes, but her voice trails over to where my dresser stands at the foot of the bed, and I can make out the gentle thud of her placing something heavy on top of it. The canvas.

"Yeah, okay. Thanks."

"She also said she hopes you'll be submitting pieces for the end-of-year show."

She what? "That show is for seniors."

Michelle's face appears over my bed. She's grinning as if she knows a secret, which she probably does. After all, I've been checked out for a while now. "You're in her senior-level class. I'm guessing that makes you qualified. Plus, officially the deadline already passed but she still asked. So if you're feeling well enough to get your butt up and grab some work out of that massive pile I know you keep, you should really go and make that happen."

More worry slices through me. "I don't know… Most of that shit is stuff I've painted late at night when I couldn't sleep. It's not the kind of stuff you'd hang in a gallery. I'd need to paint something new, which I'm not ready to do yet. I still get a headache if I try."

"Sweetheart." Michelle's holding my hand, which you'd think might piss off her boyfriend, but she's talking to me like a kid, not like a girl would talk to a guy she's into. "I get it. I was so scared submitting my portfolio to the dean of the art department, and that was just showing it to one person. I've never had my work in a gallery but I'm betting it's a lot like standing up on a stage in your underwear and waiting to see what everyone has to say about you."

"Uh… Is this supposed to make me feel better?"

Dante clears his throat. "Right. So I think what my girl's getting at is, do you paint so it'll all just sit in the corner of that rank-ass room you're renting, or do you think there's some chance you might make money on it someday?"

"I tried submitting to galleries. Nobody was interested. I actually sort of think I might try to teach." Not like my dad. Kids. I like doing that.

"So how the hell you gonna teach other people to do art without ever showing anybody your own?"

I don't have a great answer for that one, so I close my mouth and stay quiet. Dante must take my lack of response for a victory because he pokes my leg and says, "That's what I'm talking about, dumbass."

"All right. You've made your point. Now, seriously. Get out of here. I gotta piss."

Dante gets up from the bed. Michelle holds her ground. "I'm not going anywhere until you promise me you're going to go and submit a piece for that gallery show.

"Okay. Fine."

"Promise, Ethan."

"I promise, Michelle."

"Good." She kisses me on the cheek and turns to go.

"Hey, wait." I noticed something on Michelle's hand when she was holding mine. I grab it again for a closer look. "Let me see this rock on your finger. When did this happen? Can't believe you weren't going to say anything."

She glances away, smiling at Dante. "While we were out of town, but the ring was being sized. We, uh, didn't want to make a big deal about it when you were having a rough time."

Dante's arm comes around Michelle's shoulders. "*She* didn't want to make a big deal. Me, I'm taking an ad out in the paper."

I reach up to give Michelle a hug. "Hey. Congrats. Seriously."

Honestly, I *am* happy for them. Doesn't mean I'm not also wallowing a little in my own crap.

When I'm alone, I look at the dresser to see the piece Michelle has placed there. It's one I painted forever ago. Well, maybe it only feels like forever now.

When I needed to turn something in a few weeks ago and didn't have the time or energy to work on a new painting, I pulled it out of the pile. I like it though, and I have a feeling I know why Sloan asked Michelle to bring it to me. Actually, I think it's pretty perfect.

18. DAISY

LeeAnne

I'm packing. Slowly. So slowly, if someone watched me on a video, they'd probably think my movements were some sort of special effect.

I pick up my beads and strings from the table, one tiny item at a time, and place them in the tackle box I'd found to keep them all separated. I wind the leather cord in a tight coil and tell myself I'm crying because I don't want to leave the town I grew up in, not that it has anything to do with leaving the town where Ethan is. With realizing I could feel beautiful when I made love to someone and then having to walk away.

Not that we ever said *love*. I sure didn't, even though I realize now how stupid I've been to miss what was right in front of me.

I'm not even sure when it happened, but it was there. I *am* sure that Ethan became the person I trusted. The way his arms felt around me scared me, but now the idea of leaving him behind leaves me hollow.

"Hey." AJ touches me on the shoulder, making me jump. "It's not too late to change your mind, you know."

I shake my head so fast my hair slaps me in the face. "It's already done. You helped me find that place. New job and everything."

"So if we have to, we can call them and say you aren't able to come. I explained your situation. They'd understand. Don't want you to feel trapped, sweetie, that's all."

Trapped. Sometimes I think that's what I've been my entire life. It wasn't until I met Ethan that Evergreen Grove felt like a place I belonged, and even then I had to worry about Charles and his issues.

I'm working my lip between my teeth and letting AJ's words sink in when an old friend pokes her head around the corner.

Courtney and I were buddies once. Back when I lived in Charles's house, back when Charles and I were a Charles and I. We haven't talked in forever. She's married to Randy, the guy who had it out with Ethan that night. That night feels so long ago.

She's holding a pan of something when she walks up. So very much the sort of thing Courtney would do. Never arrive anywhere empty handed. Stand by your man. "Hey there. I brought brownies. Never a day when chocolate won't make for a good pick-me-up, right?"

Without even meaning to, my hands go to my hips. My all-too-ample ones that Ethan seemed to love so much. "What are you doing here?"

I blurt the question out so rudely, and yet I can't help myself. Courtney was one of the friends who went frosty on me when I left Charles. When, as much as I wanted to help him, I finally put my own well-being before his.

She turns to AJ. "Your, uh, boyfriend? He let me in at the gate. I'm sorry to intrude, but it felt like someone needed to apologize for my husband's horrible behavior, and I thought perhaps he might not be allowed in here. So I came to do it on his behalf." She turns back to me. "I've got him going back to meetings. Him and Charles, they're attending together. I'm so sorry about what he said to you. It was uncalled for."

Many barbed replies perch on my tongue. Things my hurt feelings want to fling out in retaliation, but no longer seem fair in the face of Courtney's apology. They fall to the ground, useless, like my ability to speak. "What meetings?"

AJ steps in and helps me out. "Like AA?"

She nods. "He's gone before. It didn't stick, but he tried. That cute young man dropped the charges against Charles, and well, someone from the Labs for Vets program contacted him about getting a service dog which has been huge. Charles doesn't even recall putting his name on the waiting list, but you know his memory can have holes. It's been the best thing that could have happened. He has to be sober and in therapy. Boy, he just fell in love with that dog. You'd hardly recognize him. He's like a new person."

My hands fly to my face. I'm stunned and embarrassed to find hot cheeks and stinging eyes, and I can't quite figure the reason. "A dog? Someone got him a dog?"

She nods excitedly, almost tipping the brownies. "It's a whole— Oops."

AJ steps in to grab the pan. "Here, let me take these."

"Aren't you the sweetest?" Courtney bats her eyes at AJ and I wonder if she doesn't remember he's gay. Many women have fallen prey to that killer smile. She comes to herself and blinks again, rapidly this time, like she's coming out of a fog. With a throat clear, she says, "Right. So. It's a whole program. They include counseling and then of course training on how to work with the dog, and Charles says Daisy—that's the pup's name, Daisy—is supposed to wake him whenever he's having a nightmare. Among other things, you know. Then she'll lay down with 'im to help so he can get back to sleep. The dog's trained to know somehow, I guess. So no more rough nights, no more drinking to get back to sleep. It's pretty amazing. Randy about tripped over himself to get on the waitlist when he found out."

"Wow, that's...amazing. Good for him."

"Isn't it fantastic? Look, he sent us a picture. Such a cutie." She pulls up a picture of a floppy-eared lab on her phone. The brown and black striped puppy stares soulfully with giant, liquidy eyes.

"She really does look sweet."

"That is absolutely adorable." AJ scoots farther into my room, nudging the pan of brownies into a space between boxes. "Say, why don't you have some of these with us?"

"Oh. I couldn't. I should get back. But thank you. I really only wanted to let you know what was going on with Charles, you know? I know he's had some trouble, but he's working on it, sweetie. I honestly think he's going to make it stick this time."

She steps out, turning back when she hits the parking lot beyond my door. "I know things have been rough, but I sure wish you'd stay. I wasn't the best of friends to you, but I'm hoping you can forgive me one of these days. I've sure missed you, girlie."

A stiff wind blows by and I pull my sweater around me to try to ward off the chill. "Yeah. Same here." I'm not sure which part of what she said I'm agreeing to, but it's nice to talk to an old friend. And truthfully I'm glad she stopped by to let me know what was going on with Charles. In a roundabout way, she also let me know what was going on with Ethan.

Something feels weird inside me as I watch her walk off. Hope and excitement mix with worry. A little confusion. "Something seems wrong. That all sounded…"

"A little too easy?" AJ's words are muffled by a mouthful of brownie. Damn men and their ability to eat without it ever sticking to their asses.

"Yeah. I guess so. After everything, Charles attacking Ethan and all of that, suddenly he gets this dog and everything's super fantastic?"

"Weeeell…" He leaves me waiting while he grabs another brownie. "Oh my God, you really gotta get in on this. It's like, better than sex."

"Seriously?" Finally, I succumb to the rich scent of buttery, chocolatey goodness, and grab a bite from the pan. "All right, delicious. Now, what were you saying?"

He waves a hand. "I don't know much about these therapy dog programs, but I've heard good things. Supposedly, they really are a big help. So maybe, if it's like you said and he really only has trouble when he's drinking, and he only drinks when he's truly struggling with flashbacks or whatever, maybe it won't be easy, but maybe it *will* be simple.

"Like, this dog will be there to perform the role you tried to fill for Charles when he came back from overseas, but undoubtedly will be better equipped for it. Dogs don't have opinions or ask questions and they follow commands really well. They love unconditionally. You didn't marry Charles for love, you married him for security. He might have work to do still, but I don't think you have to keep feeling like you're obligated to carry any of that load."

"I don't know..." But maybe AJ's right.

"And you know, I'll say something that my aunt said to me once, when I first met Hayden and everything felt like it was a little too good to be true. Then I'm gonna steal one more brownie and get out of here."

"Please. Take all you want. And what did she say?"

"Sometimes good happens."

It's so simple, I don't actually have any kind of response. "Sometimes..."

"Sometimes. Good. Happens. That's all. Life isn't necessarily destined to be one long shit-show and then you die. I, uh, added that last part. But seriously. Think about it."

"I will. Thanks, AJ."

He grabs a paper towel off the roll I'd been using for cleaning, and uses it to wrap up a few more brownies before easing out of the room. "And maybe you'll think about unpacking these boxes, too? I like having you here."

I give him a smile. "Maybe."

"Let me know."

#

I realized something after I'd eaten my third brownie. Actually, I realized a few things.

Number one, I need to get a place with a real oven because, size of my ass be damned, I miss having a kitchen for cooking and baking. Number two, when I do that, I've got to call Courtney and find out her recipe for these brownies. The time has long passed for healing old wounds, hasn't it?

And number three—something looked rather familiar about that dog Courtney showed us a picture of.

Now, I'm really not a dog person, so until today I wouldn't have professed to know the difference between one and another. I guess tiny ones versus giant ones notwithstanding. But I remember when Ethan took me for his tour around campus. He took me on a walk with a lab puppy named Humphry. I remember meeting Ethan's surly friend, who said Humphry was a runty reject from a training program for service dogs. That puppy had the same floppy ears, the same black and brown stripes, as Charles's new dog, Daisy.

I suppose it could be a coincidence, but I find myself wondering if these dogs could be from the same litter. I also find myself slipping a couple of brownies and a gift I'd made for Ethan into the pocket of my coat for the bus ride across town.

Ethan is loading paintings or something into the back seat of his car when I walk up to his house. He's only wearing a pair of sweat shorts and a hoodie. Some protective instinct wants me to tell him he shouldn't be lifting heavy things after an injury. He shouldn't be out in the cold so underdressed. So many things I want to say, I don't know where to start.

"You're gonna freeze your ass off walking around in this weather," he says when I approach. Funny part is, he's leaning into his car when he says it, so I don't know how he sees me, but he does.

"He says while wearing shorts and a sweatshirt in forty-degree weather." I try to put a smile on my face, but I'm having trouble, what with the angry cats fighting in my belly. They sense my fear, and I bet so does he.

"I've got the engine running. Only came over to pick up some pieces for an end-of-year art show."

"You're going to be in an art show? That's great. I'm really happy for you."

The red on his cheeks only shows brighter when he goes to push his glasses up his nose. "I got a lucky break, I guess. The professor I have for this one class likes my stuff. Or maybe it's because she likes my dad. Either way, I guess it's a good opportunity."

"Have you asked her?"

He rolls his eyes. "Kinda been out of commission."

"Yeah. I'm really sorry, but, listen, you should ask. Aren't you always saying it's better to be honest? You'll feel better if you know. I bet it isn't about your dad, though. I've seen your work and it's so good."

His lips press into a line. "That why you left the sunrise I painted you?"

I press my hand against the pain in my chest. "I didn't mean to leave the painting and I didn't mean to hurt you. I was trying to protect us both."

He turns away, hands jammed into his pockets. "Yeah. Okay."

"I'd still like to have it. The painting."

He shrugs. "You can't. Your ex busted it up the night he tried to kick my ass."

Oh, Ethan. The loss hurts. He made me something special, something I loved, and now it's gone. "I don't know what to say. I'm so incredibly sorry. I heard… I heard you dropped the charges against him. That was beyond decent of you."

"You weren't supposed to know that, but yeah." He turns back to face me, glancing up at the sky. "I remembered what you said about him. And it's not like he wasn't violent that night, but he was clearly struggling. I've struggled with shit. I've seen big guys taken down by all kinds of ugliness. I don't forgive what he did, but I can understand."

"Is that why you helped him get into that service dog program?"

He frowns. Crosses his arms. Stares at me with a salty expression. "Huh?"

So I take a step closer. My hands ball up and pull inside my sleeves as the tips of my fingers go numb. "Don't lie to me now when you've been all about the honesty. A friend of Charles's came by this morning, gushing about the adorable new dog he got and how he's in this great dogs-for-vets program. I recognized the name of the program. The dog even had similar markings when she showed me a picture. It looked an awful lot like the one your friend let us walk that day you took me over to campus. Yeah?"

"Sounds like a weird coincidence."

I hook my pinkie around his. "Yeah. I guess that could be." His hands are warm, so I take it a step farther and press my front against his side. It doesn't take long to remember how at home I felt here, next to him. Touching him. "Sort of an odd coincidence though. I looked it up online. Brindle, I think it's called."

"So one little whirl around the internet and you're some kind of expert on dog breeds?"

"I know I really want a puggle. And? I know *you* awfully well. I'm betting Charles's new dog came from the same litter as the one in your friend's kennel. Why didn't you tell me you got him into that program?"

He shrugs and kicks at a rock in the driveway, but I can tell I've got him by the way he avoids my eyes. "I wasn't trying to win any points, LeeAnne. I want you to be happy. You were afraid of him, but you were afraid to hurt him. I wanted to make things good for you. That's all I've wanted since the beginning."

This guy. I press my nose to his cheek. "You know, that's even sweeter than the brownies I have stashed in my pocket."

I feel his smile nudge against mine. "You've got brownies in your pocket and you're only telling me now?"

"Save the best news for last."

He huffs a laugh and then reaches around my waist, pulling me closer. I like it when he pulls me closer. When he takes hold of me like he absolutely needs a piece of me in his hands. Funny how I never liked that before.

"No way is that the best. You being here, that's the best." His mouth claims mine. Sweet and warm in the frosty air. "I thought I lost you, honey."

"Honestly, I just didn't know what else to do. When I found out about Charles and Daisy, I was on the verge of leaving."

"Daisy?"

"His dog."

Ethan laughs. "I like that name. Wish I had a dog named Daisy."

"Jealous?"

"Not really. I'd take you over a dog any day."

"You are super romantic." He is though, in his own way, and I need to kiss him again. Harder and deeper, so he knows I'm here for more than a simple thank you about Charles and his dog.

His pocket is buzzing, but he ignores the sound.

"Do you need to get that?"

"Nah. Probably my dad wondering when I'm coming back. He's had quite the mother hen thing happening since I cracked my skull. Honestly though, I'm feeling way better."

"Oh my God." I look at him, and then his car. "Should you be driving?"

He kisses my forehead. "I really am doing better. Alonzo's driving me though. Told him he could borrow my baby while I crashed with my dad, so long as he didn't have sex in there."

"What makes you think he'd do that?"

"You gotta know Alonzo. I'm coming to realize he'll pretty much do anything, anywhere."

I laugh, but mostly I'm listening to him. The deep rumble of his voice, and the way he sounds so much lighter than the last time we spoke. "Hey." I cup my cheek with his hand. "I'm sorry for running. It was a mistake. Do you forgive me? Are we okay?"

His loud, slow swallow worries me, but then he leans his arm on the roof of the car and presses his face against the side of my neck. "As far as I was concerned, we were always okay. You're the one who walked away."

"I'm sorry."

"Don't do it again."

"I won't. Promise."

His phone buzzes again, insistent and urgent, followed by the bing-bing of too many text messages to be a simple "Hey, what's up?" kind of sentiment.

"Sounds like someone really needs you," I whisper.

"Well, I really need *you*, and everyone else can fuck off," he growls.

Someone's buzzing again, and finally he groans and pulls the phone out of his pocket. "It's my mom. Shit. Yeah, Mom? Sorry, I was kind of in the middle of— What? No, of course not. I haven't seen her since... Uh, hang on, Mom."

I follow the direction of Ethan's gaze. There's a girl—too young to be in college, or even high school—plodding up the block with a backpack.

"Fuck. Yeah, Mom. Turns out I do know where she is. I've got her. No worries. You worry about you, okay? I'll call you back."

We meet her at the foot of the driveway. "What are you doing here, Rain? Mom's been calling. You scared the crap out of her."

"You're not supposed to say crap."

"Well *you're* not supposed to hop on the bus to come here without telling an adult. I gave you my new address so we could send each other post cards, not so you could pull a jail-break. What on earth are you even doing here?"

"At Mom's last time, you said if I needed anything I should come to you. So I came. Mom wants to send me to live with stuffy old Aunt Linda in England when she dies, and I don't want to. So I decided to come live with *you*."

Oh no.

I have absolutely no idea what to say or do here. Ethan and I just stepped foot on the edge of solid ground. I just promised him I wouldn't walk away again, and now here comes his sister.

So I say the only thing I can think of.

"Hey, sweetie, would you like a brownie?"

19. SPICY GOODNESS

Ethan

We're at my dad's place. I couldn't fit all of us in my car, and frankly, I wasn't sure what to do with my sister. The place where I'm renting right now is not fit for a kid, not with one of my roommates stoned and watching wrestling on the living room sofa 24/7.

Honestly, as much I've been pissed recently at my father, times like right now remind me that he's actually a pretty okay dad.

He came over, he got Rain, and he didn't give her shit or ask any questions. My sister was given a blanket, hot cocoa, and a spot on the couch while he called my mom to let her know everything was okay. In spite of the fact that it's the middle of the day, Rainbow drank her chocolate and went right to sleep.

I'm betting her attempt to be a pint-sized badass, taking a bus all the way from the cape and everything, was pretty stressful for a kid as quiet and serious as her. In a weird way, I'm proud. Even though what she did was kind of crazy and stupid, I'm not sure I woulda had those kinda balls at her age.

"So is everything going to be okay?" LeeAnne's beside me in the kitchen, making some hot cocoa of her own.

I like the way she doctors it up with a massive swirl of whipped cream and a sprinkle of cinnamon and nutmeg. I reach for the mug, drooling. "So what do I have to do to get you to let me taste some of that spicy goodness?"

"Spicy goodness?" Damn, I love her laugh. "Suppose you ask nicely, and I'll make you some of your own."

I put my chin on top of my balled fist, smiling sweetly. "Honey, I would be ever so grateful if you could make me a mug of that spicy goodness."

She sticks out her tongue. "Okay. But for the record, you're a little strange."

"I think you like me strange. Now stick that tongue out again and I'll show you what else I am."

More musical laughter floats my way. Honestly, right now, I'm as close to happy as I remember being in forever. It's pretty fucking great.

She slides another mug over. "Here. Next time, you don't need to butter me up so much, you know? Just flashing your dimples at me will do."

"You want me to drop my pants? Geez, woman. I mean, I know I rocked your world with that pink vibrator, but come on."

"Not those dimples." She shushes me and looks around frantically, no doubt afraid my dad is about to come back into the room.

"Relax, honey. He's still on the phone. I can tell."

"Oh, well, I guess you know everything." Again, she sticks her tongue out. Again, I want to take hold of it and do wicked things.

"So little it's pathetic. But Dad likes to pace on the back porch while he talks on the phone. I think he has the illusion that it gives him a private place to talk, but it doesn't at all. If I listen closely, I can hear him from here, and even better if I go into his office."

"Oh? So you're a snoopy little bastard."

"Kinda." I shrug my shoulders. "You never eaves-dropped on your parents as a kid?"

The answer presses my chest inward. "There wasn't much to listen to. My parents didn't talk much. My mom had a heart condition, so shouting wasn't her thing. My dad shouted a lot when he wasn't pleased, so I learned to be quiet. When things were good, they were both quiet."

His arms come around me at the counter. "You de-served better, honey."

"I'm getting over it."

"You don't have to, you know? Not all things are easy to get over. Some important people in my life have disappeared. I like to think I've moved beyond it but I can't say it never left a mark. It makes me wonder if I'll ever have the kind of love in my life that my parents had."

"Your parents divorced, didn't they?"

"They did. But they loved each other. I think if my dad hadn't been kind of a manwhore, they might still love each other. You can hear it if you listen. He's still on the phone with my mom out there."

I motion for her to follow me into the next room, a smallish area lined in white tile that I think was maybe supposed to be a mudroom once upon a time. My dad installed a desk, put in floor-to-ceiling shelves for all his books and screened off the adjoining back porch for an art studio. It's nice, but it meant we didn't have barbecues like most families growing up. No room.

Through the door that passes from the mudroom to the back porch, I can hear my father speaking in low, soothing tones. Sometimes laughing. In years past, I'd have pushed my ear against the door, but now I only catch snippets as LeeAnne and I creep around my father's piles of books and paper.

"...nothing to worry about... Promise I'll call... Of course. Absolutely...have her home tomorrow. Your own...what matters now."

"He sounds worried about her."

"I think he is. I don't entirely get it, but I guess just because you can't live with someone doesn't mean you hate them. When I told him she was sick, he took it as hard as I did almost, which seemed crazy."

"Oh my God. Ethan, wow."

"Right? Can't imagine how Rain's feeling right now."

Her eyes take on shadows as she looks down at a dish full of dried rosebuds. Of course. Her own mom was sick around Rain's age. "What's this?"

"More signs that my dad's a sentimental bastard. Dried flowers my dad gave to my mom an eternity ago. He's got tons around here. All over. From different things. That corsage, I remember, is from a dinner they went to when he won some award. Some..." I pull out a book on anatomy, where I know there's a pink rosebud pressed between acid paper. "This one's super old. It's the rose he gave her when he proposed. And this..." I grab an unabridged dictionary from the bottom shelf, stuffed with one red and one yellow spray of baby roses. "From their first anniversary."

"That's..."

"Sweet? Romantic? Weird and creepy?"

"Maybe all of the above?"

I laugh. "Yeah. It's funny. My dad was always the sentimental one. He said he saved a piece of every major moment in their lives."

LeeAnne spins in the center of the bookshelf-lined room. "I don't know, Ethan, I'm sort of leaning toward romantic. Are there more?"

"Tons." I point to the shelves across from me. "You can tell which books have flowers because there's usually a gap in the pages where they couldn't a hundred percent close all the way."

She pulls out an encyclopedia of flowers. "Do you know what this one is from?"

I squint at the peachy bud. "I want to say that's from when they got me? I don't know for sure. That flower seems familiar, but the book isn't. Dad gets new books all the time though."

Really, he should've gotten a bigger office. This little room we're in is going to overflow with either books or all the bills on his desk he's forgotten to pay. My dad's not super organized.

LeeAnne is flipping pages. "These flowers are gorgeous. All close-up and vivid like that Georgia O'Keeffe person who painted— Oh."

A piece of paper falls from the book as she turns pages. Lined and creased and covered with a loopy scrawl I don't recognize, the page clearly isn't something someone wrote recently, but it also doesn't look ridiculously old.

"What is this?" She picks it up. "A love letter or something?"

"No, it's not their handwriting. I haven't seen this before," I murmur as I grab hold of it. "Some kind of letter, but I don't think it's from one of them."

I recognize the name at the bottom before I'm able to make sense of the rest.

Nadine.

"My mother."

"It's a letter from your mom?"

"My mother. My biological mother."

LeeAnne's over my shoulder. Looking. I almost nudge her away, tell her not to look. I don't even know if I want to look.

I've never seen anything that belonged to my mother before, except for a really horribly knitted baby blanket she'd made me before I was born. This is huge. If I'm going to share this with anybody, it's going to be with LeeAnne.

I'm cold though, as my eyes scan the page. The more I read, the colder I get. I realize that what I'm feeling is an awful lot like dread:

Margarete:
I'm so sorry. I want to start off by saying that. How sorry I am. And how good you are. How much I love you.

You've been a better friend than anything I could've asked for.
Better, maybe, than anything I deserved.

LeeAnne makes a noise of sympathy behind me. I grip
the page tighter.

Something is broken inside of me, and I don't know
how to fight anymore. I thought...I thought maybe after Ethan
came, I'd be able to be better. I'd have a reason to do better. I
tried, but I'm so scared of the things I see. I'm scared of what I
could do to my baby boy. The voices... I have to get away from
them. Most of all, I have to protect Ethan. If I don't, who will?
But how does a person escape their own mind?
You'll take good care of him. I know you will.
I always wanted a sister. Thank you for being mine.
Love,
Nadine

"Shit."
I realize there's silence out on the back porch. My dad's
done talking on the phone. I should put the letter away. Move.
Do something. I can't.
"Ethan." This time, when LeeAnne grips my shoulder,
I do brush her off. I can't handle it right now, hearing the pity
in her voice.
My dad opens the door. "Ethan..."
I'm getting tired of hearing my own name.
With the letter in my fist, I turn to glare at my dad.
"You told me she was sick. She was sick and she died when I
was a baby. What the hell is this?"

#

LeeAnne
I've never seen Ethan this kind of furious. Veins pro-
trude on his neck and his eyes bulge so far they look like
they're coming through the lenses of his glasses. The tension in

his lips has turned them white, but the rest of his face is red. A deep, deep crease splits his eyebrows and his forehead.

This isn't the Ethan I know.

Silly and off-the-wall. Soul-searching and willing to say anything out loud. That's the Ethan I know. This guy, he's enraged the way Charles used to get after too many bottles of beer, and I don't like the looks of things at all.

"Dad." He holds up the letter in his hand again. The one he says was written by his biological mother.

He hasn't said much about the fact that he was adopted. I know he wishes he'd known more about her.

Maybe now he wishes he didn't. I wish *I* didn't. Especially since it sounds an awful lot like...

"She killed herself. Didn't she? You told me she was sick, but that's not true. This letter sounds an awful lot like a suicide note."

Ethan's dad removes his glasses and cleans them with the hem of his shirt. Thoughtfully. Slowly. Sort of like he's stalling for time. "It wasn't a lie. Your mother was unwell. Physically as well as emotionally. She had a serious mental illness and she struggled a great deal after you were born. When you were about six months old, she succumbed to her illness. Your mom and I were dating so we got married to make it easier to take care of you. Everything you know is true, we just...glossed over some details."

"Fuck!" He heaves the book across the room with a great spinning throw. The one that had contained the letter and the flower—now lying on the floor.

Heart thudding, I step to the side to pick up the book, but I'm surprisingly calm under the circumstances. Charles would have flown off the handle in a situation such as this. Really lost his temper. That entire bookshelf, from the ceiling to the floor, would have come down. Me with it, probably.

I'm not worried about Ethan doing that. Although, as I look at him now, I'm a little worried about the fact that he isn't flipping out more. His chest heaves and his hands shake in anger. The realness of it builds around him so thick, I believe I could reach out and touch it. But he doesn't move or speak. And I'm beginning to worry about his silence.

He stalks across the room to his father.

"Ethan." As he passes, I try to grab his arm. I get his attention. Hold him back. But he shakes me off and continues on.

"You fucking lied to me. All you've ever done is lie!"

Ethan's dad puts his glasses back on. Funny, you'd never know they weren't related if you didn't *know*. They actually kind of look alike. "We didn't want to burden you with unnecessary information."

"How exactly is it that you think having a mental illness so severe my mother killed herself is 'unnecessary information'?"

Mr. Kinney wrinkles his brow and doesn't answer.

I glance through the kitchen into the living room to see if Ethan's sister is still sleeping. She is, but fitfully. And I've had enough experience with angry outbursts to know that when Ethan's calm surface shatters, the explosion will be far-reaching and loud.

In the interest of breaking the tension, I clear my throat. "Hey." I reach out to wrap my fingers around Ethan's, pulling gently at his hand. "Your sister is still asleep. Why don't you and I take a walk around the block? Get some air?"

He gives his father a glare before turning. "Yeah."

Once we're outside though, he seems more tense than ever. I thread my fingers through his, swinging our arms back and forth a little to try to rid him of the far-off, haunted stare.

"Hey, what's going on in there?" Once upon a time, I would've been too nervous to ask that question.

But I'm still nervous about Ethan's answer. He's so calm. Way too calm. And he stays calm when he says, "I don't think I can handle this right now."

"Nobody's expecting you to. It's a lot to take in. But we'll work it out."

I realize I've said the wrong thing when Ethan shrugs out of my grip. When he ignores the way the wind has picked up and steps away.

"You don't understand."

Uh-oh. "So help me understand."

"My mother. She was fucked in the head. I've always been...shit. I've always had problems but I always figured I could handle them, you know? Stay in shape. Eat right. So I hear some voices in my head while I paint, but all artists have quirks. Except what if this is only the beginning, huh? That's scary stuff in that letter. About seeing things. Hearing things. That's not your average garden-variety case of the blues, honey, that's some dark shit right there. No amount of avoiding artificial colors and preservatives in my diet is gonna help me if I start hallucinating and try to kill you in your sleep."

Oh my god. Is that really what he thinks? "You said if, Ethan. *If.* You get depressed and anxious sometimes. So do I. That's not the same thing at all."

I swear my heart almost breaks when he leans down to kiss me. "It hurts so fucking much that my mother gave me away, but I get it. I'd die if I did something to hurt you."

But he wouldn't. I know he wouldn't. Even now, at his angriest, he doesn't lay a hand on me. "Have you considered it, Ethan? Hurting me?"

His jaw hardens. "No, but I'm betting that ex of yours didn't think he was gonna do it the first time he did, either. It's not right to take that risk."

"Shouldn't that be my decision?"

"Is that really what you want, LeeAnne? Nothing but one guy after another who's only going to treat you like shit? You told me yourself it's time to learn from your past mistakes."

"Ethan, you're different. I'm different. We're together, and we can decide to handle this as a team."

I'm pulling on his arm. Desperate. Begging him to listen, and I can tell he isn't. I hate him a little for sitting there and telling me all I'm doing is repeating a pattern. Part of me, though, part of me sees the truth in what he's saying.

After all, he's standing here telling me he's only going to hurt me, and here I am begging—begging—for him to let me stay.

Why?

My hands drop. Slowly, I straighten my spine. "A few hours ago, you were asking me to promise I wouldn't walk away from you. And I did promise."

I suppose it should have occurred to me that Ethan didn't promise any such thing in return.

"You did. I know."

"So what is it you're asking me for now?"

He sits down on the front step to his father's house. I do as well, instantly hating the cold that seeps into me from the frozen concrete. Watching him remove his glasses and rub his hands endlessly over his face only serves to increase my tension, but I wait all the same. If there's one thing I've learned to do in my life, it's wait.

"Shit. I'm scared, okay? My mom's doctors said she might only have a few more years. My sister…she got on a bus and came down here because she doesn't want to go to live with my aunt, and I don't want her to go. We may not be close, but she's still family. Now I find this letter. I knew a guy back in junior year who heard voices, you know. Sixteen-year-old kid fucking stealing sleeping pills and cold medicine so he could get to sleep at night. He took too many one night and put himself in the hospital. I don't want to put either one of us through that shit."

I wrap my hand around Ethan's arm, gripping the solidness of him. *Hold on. We said we'd be in this together.*

"I understand why you're worried. But I think it's too soon to know anything, and I want to help."

He doesn't answer.

"Ethan, you're not going to hurt me."

He looks with bottomless eyes. "Do you really want to take that risk?"

The awful truth is, I don't know what to say. Yes. Yes, I do want to take that risk. But Ethan's right, the prospect is scary. I don't entirely understand what we might be dealing with here, and I'm also afraid.

When it takes me too long to answer, he says, "LeeAnne, you deserve better than another guy who can't treat you right. You deserve better than a guy who's coming apart at the seams, which right now is kinda how I feel. So I get it, you know, if you don't want to stick around and watch that happen."

I draw a deep breath to try and think. "Hey, remember that painting you made me?"

A dry laugh. "The one that got smashed?"

"That one." I scoot close to him. "It may have been destroyed but I remember it clearly. I made a point of looking long and hard because it was so pretty. You wanted to remind me that the sun always comes up, so I'm going to remind you right now. You're scared. I'm going to be honest, I'm scared as well. But we don't even know if you'll inherit what your mother had, let alone what else will happen. I say we find out what we need to worry about before we start with the screaming and the running and the blaring alarms."

He's running his hand over and over through his hair, but I see a nod and an extremely slight smile. "Okay. Yeah. Good point."

"Thank you. So, I'm not good at this like you are, but more research first, mass-hysteria later? It's a date?"

He chuckles. "You're serious? You still want to be together?"

"I don't know. Do you intend to keep living in that frat house?"

"It's only until the end of the semester."

"Then I'll get back to you." I'm kidding. I wouldn't dump him over his living arrangements, but boy that place is a mess. And loud. Better than the awkwardness of sleeping over at his dad's, I guess.

I reach into my coat pocket and pull out a box I brought for him. "Also, I brought you this. You had your sunrise. I brought you the key to my heart. It's a little on the nose, but I'm way overdue with your birthday and Valentine's gift. Now seemed like a good time to give it to you."

He pulls out the necklace I made him. It's simple, a piece of leather cord with an old skeleton key as the pendant. When I found the key in a dusty back corner of the hardware store, I knew it was for him.

"Wow. Thanks. This is really great." He puts the box down. "Will you totally hate me if I need a minute to sit with all this new info?"

"You're welcome." I give him a quick kiss and then get up to leave. "And take whatever time you need with this. Talk to your parents. Process the information. Hang out with your sister. Let me know when you're ready, and I'll be here. I *want* to be, all right?"

"Yeah. You're right." When he reaches for me to kiss me one more time, I let out a deep breath. Maybe this all really is going to be okay. "Hey, LeeAnne. Really. Thank you."

I head for the bus stop with a wave, trying to hide my nerves. I don't know how he's going to react to this new information he got about his biological mother, but I'm nervous.

Not about him. But about whether or not he's going to be ready to let me in.

20. Listen to Your Mom
Ethan

I'm running late for the after-school program at Grove Elementary. Again. In my defense, I had reasons. Stopping to talk to Professor Sloan this afternoon took longer than expected.

I was able to do a light workout at the gym this morning, and it helped tremendously. Even if I was worn out after fifteen minutes. Like Dante said, just doing something small helped me feel like I wasn't sliding backwards.

Michelle came with me and I explained to her what all's been going on. She looked at me like I was a wounded kitten when I told her about my biological mother, and pointed out that even if I did inherit something like schizophrenia, not everyone who's schizophrenic is suicidal.

Logically, I know that's true. Like I also knew when Grove Elementary announced a lice outbreak last year it didn't make sense that my entire body immediately felt like it had creepy-crawlies, either, but that didn't stop me from scratching like a hyper-caffeinated monkey.

In spite of my worries though, I can tell the piece of glass is smaller than its been in days. Duller. I'll take whatever bit of progress I can grab on my first day back to volunteering.

"Good luck, kid. See you in an hour!"

"Bye, Dad."

Yeah. I'm still having headaches so my dad drove me to school. It's awesome.

I try not to dwell cuz when I get into class, my buddy Max is bringing more of his sketches for me today and deserves my attention.

"Hey, Mister Kinney, look what I drew."

Max pulls out a folded sheet of legal paper, showing a caped superhero fighting a giant tiger.

I'll say it again. The kid's got talent. So much that it kind of drives me crazy his teachers aren't making a bigger deal over this.

"That's pretty awesome, Max. Tell me about it."

"It's a nightmare."

I nearly choke on my tongue. "A what now?"

"A nightmare. I have 'em a lot." He leans in. "And sometimes I wet the bed. So my therapist told me to draw a picture. Or write a poem. But poems are for babies and girls."

"Hey, man. I write poems."

Poor kid's face turns a hot magenta. "Sorry, Mister Ethan."

"S'okay. So did drawing this picture help with your nightmare?"

He shrugs in a way that seems far too mature for an eleven-year-old. "Sort of. See, in the picture the nightmare is a tiger, because they're big and kind of scary, and I'm killing it. The nightmare. I wouldn't kill a real tiger, because Mom said that's wrong. But pretend is okay."

"Yeah, buddy. Good to know the difference."

Max nods, his face so serious that I want to know what's going on in that brain of his. I want to help him slay his pretend tigers. Except how can I slay his pretend tiger when I can't slay my own?

Mrs. T comes by with a paper plate and squirts a massive blob of tempera paint on there. "Put the pictures away, Max, it's time for us to get started on our project."

Max makes a face and slides the image into his notebook.

"Hey, Max. What else have you drawn lately? Just show me super quick," I add when he scrunches his face with uncertainty. "Before the teacher comes back around." I know. Technically, I'm one of their teachers. But I'm also kind of not, so I can be a little more like their buddy. That's kind of cool, too.

So he slides out about half a dozen more drawings. Of robots fighting monsters. Of a bunch of ninjas doing battle. Of some kind of guy in a spaceship fighting another guy in a spaceship.

The kid's got a future in drawing comics if he wants one, no question. It's amazing at such a young age. His lines are crisp and bold. His style is unique. "Man, I never had this kind of skill at your age, buddy. Hel—uh, heck. I don't draw stuff like this as well as you do, even now."

"But you said you study art."

"I do. We've all got different skills. Some people are good at portraits. Some folks like flowers or landscapes. Or the kind of stuff you do. You read a lot of comics, buddy?"

His nod is full of the kind of effusive enthusiasm I haven't had about my work in years. The kind I need to get back. "I like *Monster Truck Robots* the best."

"What's this?" I pull another page out, showing a simple house with flowers and a fence, but the pointillism and shading uses expert technique.

"That's for my mom. Because I love her. She's not into robots."

Mom. Love. Max spells it all out so simply, but it opens a deep well inside me. Hopes and fears I've been avoiding come gushing out in a massive swell, and I have push down the lump in my throat.

This right here in front of me is love. A kid who has so much amazing talent, and he makes a point of saving it for the woman who takes care of him.

Mrs. T is talking up at the front of the room. "Friends, I've got your prompt on the board. It's time to grab your papers and start painting." She gives me a knowing glare.

I push the papers together in a neat stack and hand them back to Max. "Hey, I know your mom is going to love this picture. And listen, I want you to promise me something, okay?"

He busies himself with putting his papers into his note-book, his notebook into his bag, and taking up his brush. I'm about to ask him if he even heard me when he splats some blue paint on his paper and asks, "Promise what? I can't promise to steal or lie. Mom says it's wrong."

"Yeah, buddy. You should always listen to your mom. I don't want you to steal or lie. I want you to promise you'll stick with this drawing stuff, okay? No matter what anyone tells you. You're a good artist. If you want to do it, you should."

He looks uncomfortable but nods and proceeds to splat more paint on the paper. "Kay. Hey, did you hear the one about the religious horse, Mr. K?"

Nice try, kid. "I wanna hear it. First, tell me what you're painting there." It looks like nothing but blue blobs and green swirls. Clearly the kid doesn't paint as well as he draws.

"It's a battle. These blue guys are trying to kill the green guys."

"You do an awful lot of battle scenes."

"Sometimes I wish I was big and strong. Sometimes though, it's not about how big or small you are, but how you use your brain. And sometimes admitting you're not strong is the toughest thing of all. That's what Mrs. O says."

"Who's Mrs. O?"

"My occupational therapist. I don't hold my pencil the right way."

"Do you mind that? Doing all sorts of therapy?"

He shrugs. "They let me play Legos while I talk. It's pretty okay."

It's pretty okay. Huh.

Ever since high school, I've been worried about being strong enough. I tried to push LeeAnne away because I thought it was the strongest thing for both of us.

Maybe this kid is right. And maybe so is this Mrs. O person of his.

Maybe it's time for me to start using my fucking brain.

#

LeeAnne

I'm at the park with Joy and her daughter. It's a gorgeous, sunny day in spite of the chill. I love the sunshine, and I'm so tired of being cooped up in my little room. It's the first time since my day out with Ethan that I've really felt I can breathe, and I'm torn between gratitude and melancholy.

I miss him. I do. Even though I said I'd wait to hear from him, I can't seem to let go of how wrong being apart feels.

So I guess for now, sitting on a bench and watching Joy's little girl kick her new ball up and down the shiny, frosted grass, is as good a way to go as any.

Rubbing my chilled hands together, I lean over to Joy. "You did tell her it's cold out here, right?"

"I did. That's why she has a hat and mittens on. Where are your mittens?" She gives me a grin.

"Yeah, my gloves got lost. Buying new ones hasn't been high on my to-do list," I grumble and puff hot air into the space between my fingers.

"I'll have to knit you a pair. Or…" She reaches into the "mommy bag" sitting on her lap. "I suppose if you're feeling impatient, you could go and get yourself some with your mega wads of cash."

"My what?"

Her hand withdraws from the bag holding a check for… "Holy cow, you're kidding!"

"Nope." Joy makes a popping sound with her lips. "Handmade stuff commands a high price. Incidentally, if you're willing to do custom pieces, I've received some requests."

My heart goes into a panicked, uneven rhythm. "I don't know how I'd make custom pieces. I mostly make stuff with whatever I find."

She purses her lips and them makes another popping noise. "Let's think it over. In the meantime, I know it might not be as good as what you made slinging drinks, but if you can make more, I can sell those too. Or I'll show you how to set up your own shop."

I stare at the check. Two hundred and forty dollars in my hand for a bunch of jewelry I made late at night while I was watching TV. "And I didn't have to get my ass groped or beer spilled on me to get it."

"Huh?"

"Nothing. Just…I think I like this better than bartend-ing."

Joy shifts her attention to keep an eye on her daughter. "Well, like I said. They were well received. I even bundled a few. You know, my scarves with your necklaces. Like a pack-age. Those were a big hit. So, you know. If you wanna stay in business together, that'd be awesome. Might be a little harder if you're leaving town, but we could find a way to make it work."

I stand, suddenly full of energy I can't contain. I've got half a mind to run over to Joy's daughter and start kicking the ball with her, or running circles around her like a crazy person.

"Here." I push up my sleeve to pull off a piece of leather cord where I'd strung a few metal beads, and the star thing I found on that playground Ethan took me to. I'd been saving the bracelet for sentimental reasons, but I have another piece from our day on campus that's more important.

"This one's nice." Joy nods. "You sure you want me to take it?"

"Take it. I'll make more."

The bracelet disappears into the cavernous depths of Joy's purse. "I think this is the start of a beautiful business rela-tionship."

"You know, I'd really like that." I watch Joy's little girl for a while—so carefree, running around by herself with a ball.

I rub the paper of the check Joy handed me between my thumb and forefinger. "You know, Joy, I'm kinda pissed?"

"At me?"

"Oh God, of course not. At myself. And Ethan. And my dad. Charles. Mostly myself." I shake my head. "For taking so long to learn when to listen to others and when I need to tell everyone to shut up so I can listen to myself." I lean back on the bench with a sigh. "Ethan got all nervous about being good enough for me. I decided that's not up to him and I'm not going to keep waiting around for him."

New epiphany. Wish I'd had it sooner.

"Well," Joy says slowly. "Do you think there was possibly any truth to what Ethan said?"

I think for a minute. Not that I have to think long, because I've been chewing on this nonstop. "I think it's possible. It's equally possible that he's overwhelmed because too much is going wrong and he can't see what's right. Ethan isn't anything like Charles. Or even like Jake. I'm having trouble seeing the point in walking away from the first guy ever to treat me well because he's afraid he might hurt me at some unknown time in the future."

Her hand lands on my arm. I can see her worry in her eyes and feel it in her gentle touch.

I watch her daughter, running with the ball she's so excited about. It's a nice one, I realize. The tough, shiny kind they have in school gym class. It looks expensive.

"Where'd she get the ball?"

Joy frowns slightly. "My boss."

"Is that a problem?"

Joy nods. "It's a gift. That's all."

I hear the concern in her voice. What if the gift comes with strings? What if small gifts lead to bigger attachments? It's hard to trust that someone is simply doing good for the sake of being kind.

"Ethan would never hurt me," I murmur. "I believe that. But I promise you, I'll call AJ at the first sign of trouble. The first throw or hit or accidental push. I promise."

I'm saying it more for Joy than I am for myself. I don't know what happened to her before she and her kid came to Evergreen Grove, but I don't want to see either of us fall into familiar but unhealthy patterns.

"I promise, too," she whispers.

"Good."

21. MEATBALLS ON TOOTHPICKS

Ethan

Turns out the end-of-year gallery show isn't in a gallery at all. It's also not quite at the end of the year, but for this class, my showing replaces my final grade, so I'm done with at least one thing for the next few weeks.

That's the cool thing about being an art student, I guess. Longer studio classes, but fewer finals.

So the student gallery is actually the upstairs portion of the Pender Tech student center. The same student center where I brought LeeAnne to bowl and act like a goofball for a day, and I can't lie and pretend it's not making my insides all squirmy to be here and remember the fun I had with her.

It makes me think of what else we did that day, that night, and how much I miss being next to her in my bed. In my life.

I left a message inviting her here. I also sent an invite along via AJ, who said he'd see she gets it, but he seemed seriously distracted. The good news, I guess, is that the place is full of hand-wringing artists tonight.

Up on the second floor, all the balcony doors have been opened. They've classed up the joint, not only by hanging artwork, but by having students from the hospitality and tourism management department dress up in douchey uniforms to pass around meatballs on toothpicks and glasses of champagne.

I'm one of the only students showing work who isn't a senior, so I figure nobody will notice if I grab one of the champagne flutes to steady my hopping nerves.

Hey, at least I don't look like I'm about to puke over the balcony like Todd Ruskman. Art kids are a nervous bunch.

It's good to see I'm not alone though, as I look around and sip my really cheap adult beverage. Man. We're all wigging out over what? Our professors are going to come and look at our artwork and give it a grade. That's the same thing they do every semester. Except this time, it happens to be attractively displayed on lit backdrops. And this is an area students can walk through, so some of them may stop to look at it. Some might be assholes.

Some might even like it.

I wonder which option is worse.

This is the question I'm still pondering when a sweet voice whispers in my ear, "Are you sure you should be drinking?"

LeeAnne's whisper makes me rub my chest. I could pretend it's about the tattoo, but that's long healed over.

It's about her. LeeAnne's here. I turn to face her, discarding the champagne on a windowsill. "You came."

"You did invite me."

"Yeah, I also went MIA for a bit there so I was worried… Anyway, I'm so glad you're here." So fucking glad. Her smile makes my stomach clench.

I reach out to grab hold of her hand. "This is cool, right? We're still a couple and everything?"

Her fingers squeeze around mine. "Ethan, I told you I wasn't going anywhere. You needed to have time to work things out with your family. I really hope we can agree to lean on each other next time something big happens."

"Honey, if you stay with me, I'll agree to anything you want."

Her lips brush my ear. "Anything? Are we going to revisit the bondage-and-nail-polish scenario, then?"

God, I'm getting hard. So inappropriately hard. I shouldn't have had that champagne.

My nails dig into my palm as I try to calm my ass down enough to have a rational conversation. "You seem...different."

"Yeah? Well I've come to some important conclusions."

She stops a waiter who's got some kind of puff pastry thing on a platter and grabs like five of them before she lets him go. It's totally not the kind of thing you're supposed to do in polite company, but I'm the only one watching her aside from the waiter, and I don't care. The waiter is some hospitality student who only seems irritated that he doesn't get to keep circulating.

"Ohmygod, this is so good. You wanna try one?" She holds out an appetizer.

"I wanna hear your conclusions, dammit." My hands are starting to tingle from clenching so hard.

"I'm getting there. See, one of my conclusions was that I'm allowed to make decisions, too. I'm not used to deciding what I want for myself, and it's time that I start."

"Sure. Absolutely. That makes sense."

She nods, sipping my discarded champagne as if this is a normal thing. "It does, doesn't it? And you're the one who told me I deserved the best. That I deserved whatever I wanted. So I don't know what it's like to have a normal, healthy, adult relationship, but you and I should start."

"God, I hope so. You know, not to freak you out or whatever, but I noticed Michelle with a ring on her finger and I was actually sort of jealous. We're supposed to be too young to get married, but all I could think was you've already done it and I wish I'd been the guy."

Her eyes soften. "Ethan, I didn't have a clue back then. We've got issues. Both of us. But maybe if we take what we've learned from our collective screw-ups, we'll have something between us that can really last. Nobody's made me feel the way you do. I can't tell you what that means."

I want to put my arms around her right now. I want to hold her and kiss every inch of her apple-scented skin.

"You know, you blow me away by how amazing you are."

She rests her chin on my shoulder. "You too, you know. You gave me the kick I needed to get up and start thinking for myself. So I decided what I wanted is to be sure I keep you."

Same here. "I want to show you something."

I pull her to the gallery area, where my images are being displayed. "These go back a long way. From before, you know. That night at Joe's."

She puts her hand to her lips, scanning the images. I get a charge of electricity in my veins, seeing her face as she discovers each one. The mosaic piece containing a poem about the first time I ate at Joe's and she convinced me to try the calamari. The painting that looks like a mural on a dirty brick wall, showing an angel whispering in my ear, except the angel is my curvy-hipped, pouty-lipped, freckled, LeeAnne.

"Oh my God. These are all about me?"

I rub the back of my neck, tense with worry. "I was going for romantic and not creepy, but you're standing there with your mouth open, so I'm worried now I may have crossed a line."

"They're great, it's just...I had no idea."

"That I love you? Yeah, I've done a shitty job of saying so. I'm gonna do better." I grab her hand. "The best, because like you reminded me, that's what you deserve."

I love it when she bites her lip.

"It's not enough. I know. I have more."

"More than this?"

I pull a card out of my back pocket. The one I've been carrying around. Saving for just in case.

"Who is Murphy Edmond, LCSW?"

"The counselor-therapist-type person Student Services referred me to. He's really cool, and as long as I stay enrolled, my dad's insurance covers it, and..."

My neck gets hotter and tighter. I don't know why saying this is so hard.

"Look, I wanted to be strong for you. All this shit in your past...and you do deserve better. You deserve better from me, too. It took someone reminding me that sometimes to be strong you need to get help, so I went and got some. I thought you'd wanna know. Also, he felt it'd be a good idea for you to come by and for us to do a session or two together. If you're willing. We can schedule it around whatever's convenient for you."

"In all this talk about us and the future, Ethan, you should know I still have baggage. I can't have kids, should we ever get to that point. My dad and I don't speak much, but he's unwell and—"

"Hey, hey. One thing at a time. Like I said, I love you. And I can't even say now that I want to have kids, you know? I get a nice dose of them working at the school. Maybe that's enough."

She reaches for the card I'm holding, but her hand closes around my fingers, taking my hand in hers. "I love you, too, Ethan. Of course I'll go. Whatever you need. I told you that day at your father's house, I'm ready for us to do this together."

I resist the urge to pull at my tightening tie. "You went through all that shit with your ex. I didn't want to make you do it again."

"Charles wouldn't get help when I was with him. And we weren't partners. Charles yelled and I did what I could to keep him happy. I'm not taking orders from anyone anymore, Ethan. Not even you."

It shouldn't, but that gets me thinking dirty things again. "Does that mean you want to keep telling me what to do in bed?"

She smiles a rare, devilish smile. One I haven't seen since our night in my bed. "Especially then."

"I'm good with that."

I put my arms around her and she lets me, and I'm kicking myself on the inside for ever being stupid enough to think I might need to let her go.

"I feel like you're my missing piece, you know? Like I've always been this thing that was trying to fit but didn't, all round-peg-in-a-square-hole-ish, and you're the place where I click."

I need her to stay. Always.

She gives me that smile I spent so long working for. "What are you saying?"

"You're the one thing that keeps my mind from racing and the ache inside from feeling like it'll tear me apart. I don't know how I forgot."

"You won't forget again. I won't let you."

A few feet away, my art professor leans down to examine one of my pieces. She looks at me, then LeeAnne, and walks away with a smile. Not sure what that says about my grade, but that's okay.

"I won't forget again," I murmur into LeeAnne's hair.

"See that you don't, or I'll have to find some handcuffs and some nail polish."

I love that a little too much. "Okay, honey. I think it's time that I take you home."

#

Ethan

"Happy birthday to Raiiinbooow..." My dad elbows me in the back. "Sing, kid. It'll make your mom happy."

I can't sing worth a damn. Ordinarily I don't mind, but Rainbow's got friends over and our house is full of giggling preteen girls. My nightmare come to life, but I didn't want to embarrass my sister, so I decided to stand in the back and move my lips.

Except my dad knows the phrase that gets me to play. *It'll make your mom happy.*

So my glass-shattering screech joins the rest of the gang. LeeAnne looks up from where she's cutting the cake. Nobody else seems to notice, since the teenyboppers are all caught up in the ice cream cake. Or maybe the fact that it's got a handsome fireman holding a kitten on it, and the cake says, "Hey, Karen, I heard your kitty was stuck…"

My dad was in charge of the cake. There was a screwup at the bakery. He thought not fixing it was funnier. That's my dad.

LeeAnne works her way over to me and slides an arm around my waist. "That was some top-notch singing, my man. Next up, you need to try out for that *America's Next Singer!* show I'm always hearing about."

"Always hearing about, my behind. I know damn well you stream it online when I'm up late painting. I can hear you singing along."

Her flushed cheeks tell me everything I need to know, but she's not admitting to anything and that's okay. LeeAnne and I have agreed to total honesty, but I don't push her on the little things, and she knows I know the truth anyway. It works for us.

"So I grabbed you a piece of the fireman before he was all gone."

"Aww, you're the best. I bet he's delicious." I lean over to kiss her warm lips before getting a forkful of cake, moaning at the deliciousness. "Aww, man. The fireman is cookies and cream. That seems extra naughty somehow."

"You're really awful, you know that?"

"I'm a guy. With an awesome girlfriend. Who promised to take me back to our place later and order me around. You can't blame me for being excited."

"Don't get too excited. I was planning to make you do the laundry. Alonzo left wet stuff in the machine again."

"Uh-huh. But after that, the naked time happens?"

LeeAnne laughs and slaps me on the arm. "So. Your sister seems mortified by the cake, but her friends seem to think it's hysterical."

I roll my eyes. Proof I've been in a room full of girls for too long. "Yeah. They think she's got a cool 'dad.' I just hope he doesn't try to date one of them."

"Well first, I don't think even *your* dad likes them that young, and second..." She points across the room to where my mom is pulled up to the table in her wheelchair.

My dad hands her a piece of cake, taking time to feed her a bite. He doesn't do it because he has to, although she does have more trouble with her motor skills lately. Seems like they're in the schmoopy stages of re-dating, or whatever it's called.

I get the weirdy-jeebies when he moves in to wipe off the bit of frosting he got on her nose, and then kisses her on the cheek. "Ugh. My parents are kissing."

"You poor thing." But her fingers trail along my chin, and she doesn't actually sound all that sympathetic. Moreover, I find it hard to mind. "I think it's sweet."

"It is. Bittersweet, I guess. I wish it hadn't taken my mom getting sick for my dad to tell her he still loves her."

Shana and I haven't talked since the ugliness of my dad dumping her. Actually, I hear she's not talking to much of anyone. I get the feeling she really cared about my dad and I honestly worry for her, but it's hard to be sorry when I see my parents so happy.

"It takes what it takes." LeeAnne sighs. "I tried a zillion times to encourage Charles to get help, and usually that ended in him storming away. Or throwing something. Your friend gets him into that therapy dog program and he's a changed man."

Huh. Yeah. "I guess that explains how some folks like animals better than people."

"You know what I like?"

"Hmmm?"

The backs of her fingers trail over my neck.

"Please say it's me. Who are we kidding? Of course it's me."

"I like cake." She laughs and steals the plate from my hand.

"Hey!"

"What? I didn't get to taste the fireman. Why should you get all the fun?"

I fake a pout. "I thought you were going to say me. You do still like me, don't you?"

"No."

I whip my head around. "That's it. Give me back my fireman."

"Mmm. Cookies and cream." I can't be mad when she kisses me. Not even fake mad. She tastes like vanilla ice cream and chocolate.

"You took my fireman cake," I murmur.

"You love me."

"You're right. I do. And you know damn well anything that's mine is yours." It so is. I know there was a time she was afraid to ask for what she wanted, to speak her opinion. With me, she's in charge. Totally.

Am I whipped? Fuck no.

I speak my mind when I want something. So does she. Sometimes, we even fight a little. I think at first it made us both nervous. Neither of us wanted to get the other one pissed. Now we know it's okay, so long as neither of us gives up and calls it quits.

Her cold tongue traces my ear. My libido doesn't mind the chill. At all. "So do you think anybody will notice if we leave?"

I look around. In the kitchen, my dad is chatting with my mom at the table. Their loving gazes would be gag-worthy if my mom didn't look so fucking happy. And right now, she deserves every moment of happy she can come by.

Rain is tearing open her presents. It's a veritable cornucopia of teen pop star memorabilia. Everyone is pointing and talking and explaining why the thing they got is better than the thing someone else got.

"Yeah, I don't think anyone will notice if we leave."

She takes my hand. "Let's go then. I talked to Alonzo, and he told me everyone was headed out to something called a field party this afternoon. He also told me where I could find a pair of handcuffs. And some other things."

I'm officially into this plan. "Whatever makes you happy, baby."

"Mmm. You make me happy. Right now, so do handcuffs and nail polish. Maybe that vibrator of yours."

Damn. When my girl talks about kinky stuff, her face turns the same color as her Razz Ma Tazz polish. She might be fucking with me. She might not. Either way, I'm game. "Sounds like a piece of heaven."

I stop and turn to her on the way out. "Hey, can we get Chinese after?"

She smiles and drags me out to the car. "Maybe."

"Awesome. Hey, so what do you call a labradoodle mixed with a porcupine?"

She cuts me a look at the bottom of my dad's front stairs. "What?"

I shake my head. "It's too dirty. I can't say it out loud."

LeeAnne rolls her eyes. "What am I going to do with you?"

I toss her the keys to my CRX when we reach the driveway. "Honey, I can't wait to find out."

Thank you for reading LeeAnne and Ethan's story! To keep up with the Evergreen Grove series and my other books, please sign up for my newsletter at tiny.cc/StaabNews or find me on Facebook (Elisabeth Staab Romance) and Twitter (@ElisabethStaab).

Also by Elisabeth Staab

The Evergreen Grove Series (At the Stars, Acts of Creation, By the Rules, Piece by Piece)

The Chronicles of Yavn (King of Darkness, Prince of Power, Hunter by Night)

The Lone Wolf Series (Wild Nights with a Lone Wolf, Wicked Days with a Lone Wolf, Blood Moon Over a Lone Wolf)

About Elisabeth

Elisabeth Staab loves passionate stories and happy endings. Her books have been called "sexually charged," "action-packed," and "gloriously snarky." When not writing romance about vampires and werewolves and CEOs (oh, my!), she enjoys date night with her husband, reading Harry Potter with her kids, and marathoning her favorite books or TV series. Find out more at ElisabethStaab.com.

Acknowledgements

I always have to thank my readers first, because without you I'd writing on my walls with crayon and muttering to myself.

HUGE thank you to Kelli Collins for editing the crap out of this book. Thanks also to Jena at Practical Proofing and Shelly at Small Edits for helping me to polish out the rough spots. Hugs to Angela Quarles as always for formatting, and massive love to Elizabeth Babski for pulling out all the stops for Ethan's cover.

To my awesome author buddy Joan Swan a.k.a. Skye Jordan, thank you for providing your home and your insight to help with the final push to finish this book. Without you, LeeAnne and Ethan may never have gotten their happy ending.

To the authors who've mentored me and the bloggers who've boosted me, I can't thank you enough for your time and support. Lori Wilde, Elisabeth Naughton, Damon Suede, and Marie Force, I wouldn't be where I am without your advice, and that's a good thing.

For Ethan's corny jokes, HUGE thanks go to Jillian Stein, Carol Buswell, P, and that red-headed guy I used to drink with sometimes. Also, thanks to The Staab Mob for their ongoing support, and to Heather for picking LeeAnne's nail polish color. I envision Ethan and LeeAnne having *lots* of fun with it in the future with Razz Ma Tazz polish.

To Tom, I wouldn't, *couldn't*, do any of it without you. Thank you for being my rock, even when we're two rocks banging against one another (Wait, did that sound dirty?).

56436464R00147

Made in the USA
Lexington, KY
22 October 2016